Praise for Natalie J. Damschroder and Carina Press

"*Fight or Flight* is one high-octane adrenaline-filled thriller that doesn't quit until the very last page. I honestly don't know when I've been this excited while reading a book."
—*Joyfully Reviewed*

"Damschroder definitely knows how to write one sexy, saucy, exhilarating tale."
—*RT Book Reviews* on *Acceptable Risks*

"[T]he forbidden romance was absolutely delicious."
—*The Romanceaholic* on *Acceptable Risks*

"A helluva suspense novel... first class entertainment."
—*RomanceBooksForum.com* on *Fight or Flight*

**Also available from Natalie J. Damschroder
and Carina Press**

*Behind the Scenes
Acceptable Risks*

FIGHT

➤ OR ➤

FLIGHT

NATALIE J.
DAMSCHRODER

**CARINA
PRESS™**

Recycling programs for this product may not exist in your area.

ISBN-13: 978-0-373-00219-1

FIGHT OR FLIGHT

Copyright © 2011 by Natalie J. Damschroder

www.CarinaPress.com

Printed in U.S.A.

Dear Reader,

One day, I was puttering around the kitchen when I heard a high-pitched noise, like some kind of gas being squeezed through a too-small escape point. I frantically searched for the source, only to laugh at myself when I realized it was the eggs I was hard-boiling on the stove. From that unlikely prompt, *Fight or Flight* was born. What kind of heroine would panic at such a sound? What could have made her so paranoid? The obvious answer was a mother who'd struggled for her daughter's entire life to keep her safe from an unknown enemy. I had a fantastic time writing Regan's journey from panic to trust, and (shh, don't tell anyone), even more fun writing her daughter, Kelsey's, point of view. I hope you have as much fun reading them. Thank you!

Natalie J. Damschroder

For my mother, Terie, for the genetic affinity
for words and the years of incredible,
unwavering support. I miss you.

FIGHT
OR
FLIGHT

ONE

REGAN MILLER FOLLOWED her daughter Kelsey up the dormitory stairwell, their footsteps thudding on the cement. Clangs, shouts and squeals echoed around them, the acoustics making it difficult to tell where the sounds originated. Regan gripped the handrail to keep herself from putting a hand on her daughter's back to urge her upward.

When they reached the third floor, Kelsey flashed a grin over her shoulder. "This is it."

Regan managed to smile back, but noted that someone had propped open the stairwell door with a folded piece of paper. She toed the paper out and let the door close, then nudged it with her fingertips. It drifted open again. Great. The latch didn't work.

"Don't use the stairs when you're by yourself, Kelsey."

"I know, Mom."

Regan could almost hear the eye roll. At least she'd kept the sarcasm out of her voice. "What's your room number again?"

"Three ten." Kelsey stopped halfway down the hall, distant from both elevator and stairwells. Some of Regan's tension eased.

The door to room 310 was locked, and Kelsey gleefully used her key to open it. Regan suppressed a sigh. Until the full-tuition scholarship had come through, she hadn't been willing to consider letting Kelsey go away to college. Even afterward she'd been reluctant, since the scholarship had an anonymous backer. But Kelsey had pitched a fit over her mother's insane caution—only the third time she'd ever rebelled—and Regan had finally let her win one. Watching her joy now, Regan was glad.

The suite's center room held four built-in desks. Twin beds showed through the small gaps in the slightly open sliding wooden doors on either side of the room. Regan went straight ahead to the large window that looked out over the grounds behind the building rather than the parking lot. Kelsey wouldn't be able to see who was coming in the main entrance, but she'd be less vulnerable on this side.

"There's a tree out here, Kels." She glanced behind her. Her daughter had gone into the left bedroom. "It's close to the window." She slid it open, grimacing against the late-August heat, and flipped up one of the hooks holding the screen in place. "You can shove this out and climb out onto the limb, and then—"

"Mom, let it rest, will you?" Kelsey came up behind her and gently pushed the window closed. "You've trained me to recognize all this stuff, but when have we ever needed to use it?"

Regan hesitated, then stroked her hand down Kelsey's long brown hair. "You're right. We haven't." Not that Kelsey could remember, which made Regan both damned grateful and more afraid every day. "I just—"

"I know what you just. You don't have to explain."

Regan could see she meant it and swallowed the guilt. She never had explained, not fully. She hadn't wanted to frighten her daughter with the story of her attempted kidnapping. Kelsey deserved to know about it, and how it connected to her father's death before she was born, but Regan didn't know how to tell her. Why would an eighteen-year-old care about a five-minute event that occurred so long ago? How could she understand why Regan had let a few words dictate every decision she'd made for her daughter's entire life?

Anyway, now wasn't the time. Kelsey had never known a different way to live and had come to accept her mother's idiosyncrasies—or mental illness, as she often called it. Regan had always struggled between keeping her daughter safe and making her life as normal as possible. Today's milestone illustrated her success at both, but made her think maybe it was time to come clean. Soon. It had waited eighteen years, it could wait a few more weeks. Give her time to figure out *how* to explain, and brace herself for all the questions she had no answers for.

"Besides, I already checked out both bedrooms," Kelsey said. "That one," she pointed to the left, "has a closer branch. And the bathroom is a deathtrap or a shelter, depending on whether we're talking fire or hurricane."

"Oh, baby." Regan pulled her into a tight hug. "I love you."

Kelsey's response was muffled, but Regan heard her. Her heart welled with joy and fear. Her arms tightened until Kelsey squeaked, but she hung on, trying to memorize her daughter's scent, the feel of her hair against her cheek. Trying to hold it together when all her cells seemed primed to explode.

"Hey, y'all!"

They broke apart and turned to the pixie who'd burst into the room. Her short hair spiked and swirled from her scalp, and even the tallest spike only came to Kelsey's shoulder. She was dainty from the tear-drop earrings on her mini earlobes to the size five feet dancing toward Regan and Kelsey.

"I'm Van. Short for Savannah, of course, but that's such a prissy name I never use it. Kelsey, right? When we got the letter saying who our roommates would be, I glommed on to you right away." She eyed Kelsey up and down. "Yep, we're gonna be friends, I can just tell."

Kelsey's eyes sparkled in amusement when she looked at her mother, and Regan winked. Van was right. Her bubbly charisma would complement Kelsey's serenity. But Regan sensed aural exhaustion barreling toward them. How could anyone with such a strong southern accent talk so fast?

Van turned her attention to Regan. "And you must be Kelsey's sister. Let me guess, I'm good at this." She pressed a finger to her lips and narrowed her eyes. "You're probably twenty-five, twenty-six. Yeah, you got the look of a woman who's been in the world a while."

Regan laughed. "Van, you may be southern, but you've definitely kissed the blarney stone."

Van looked between them, puzzled. "What? You're twenty-eight? I'm usually within two years."

"She's my mother. She's thirty-seven."

"No *way!*" Her mouth dropped open. "You gotta tell me what you use on your face. You don't look near thirty!"

"Thank you, Van." Regan held out her hand, still chuckling. "Regan Miller."

"Pleased to meet ya. Wow." She shook her head. "So anyway, I took this room." She pointed to the left. "I haven't met the others yet. Wanna share? I know I like you and you'll be a considerate roommate. But it won't hurt my feelings if you say no, 'cause I know my mouth keeps runnin' like that battery bunny, you know, in the commercials? I even annoy myself."

"I'd love to room with you," Kelsey said. "Mom, let's go start unloading my stuff. Will you let me use the elevator?"

"Of course I will." They started out of the room, and Regan gave Kelsey a little shove. "It's the least I can do, since you'll be carrying all the heavy stuff."

"As if."

They spent the next two hours unloading Kelsey's belongings from the back of the Highlander and getting it put away in the dorm room. At noon, Regan took Kelsey and Van to lunch. Van's parents had dropped her off the night before, since they had a longer drive home to Georgia than Regan did to nearby Columbus. Regan asked Van, once they'd been served their wraps at the little bistro downtown, how she'd ended up in a small college in Ohio.

"My dad's from Ohio, actually. My mother is a proper southern belle and refused to move. They met at a conference—they're both Realtors with a capital R—and did the long-distance thing for about a year until Momma got pregnant with me. You know, it's nice to be able to say that without worrying about bein' judged. Not that I care." She took a large bite of her wrap and chewed furiously before continuing. "It's not like I did something wrong, and anyway, everyone has something they could be ashamed of if they really wanted to be. But since you were a teenage mom, you, like, automatically won't judge me, right?"

"Right." Being a teen mom had become the least of Regan's problems, but she imagined it had been a bigger deal for Van's mother. "So, Ohio?" she prodded.

Van flashed a grin. "My dad grew up in Delaware, you know, outside Columbus? And he went to Ohio Wesleyan and really *really* wanted me to go there. Momma of course said a nice southern university would be best, but dad convinced her my personality's not quite nice southern, you know? I didn't get into OWU, it was probably my essay, who knows how people will take personal politics, right? So this was the next best thing. Excuse me, I gotta tinkle." She got up and trotted toward the restrooms, and the silence was almost oppressive.

"Sure you can handle her?"

Kelsey shrugged and licked mayonnaise off her thumb. "She's cool. I can tune her out and she won't care. And I won't have to talk much."

Regan pulled out a notebook. "So, your room's mostly settled. You have registration this afternoon, and we can take a tour of the campus from the admissions building."

"You don't have to stay, Mom. I mean, not overnight," she hastened to clarify, obviously seeing the flicker of hurt Regan hadn't been able to control. "I want you to take the tour and everything. But there's no sense paying for a hotel room. Tomorrow I can buy my books and scope out my classrooms and stuff, and you'll be bored."

Of course she wouldn't, but Regan understood. She'd expected it, even. "Okay, then. I'll leave after dinner. It's only a two-hour drive, and there will be less traffic at night. Easier—"

"To spot a tail. I know." There was the eye roll. "Thanks, Mom."

Regan inhaled deeply against the burn of tears in her throat. "You're welcome."

SHE WASN'T THE only parent leaving after dinner. The parking lot was full of tearful goodbyes and teenage exasperation. The kids' excitement was intoxicating, though, and Regan could barely speak past the ball of emotion in her chest. She'd had a lot of practice combating her fears and was pretty sure Kelsey hadn't been aware of the panic threatening to overtake her. Threatening to make her shove the teenager back in the SUV and roar out of there. But she had nothing to distract herself from those fears all the way home.

Kelsey's school, Whetstone University, was about two hours south of their home on the outskirts of Columbus. Not far at all for routine weekend driving, but too long when your thoughts were full of the past and dread of the future.

Regan had avoided thinking about Kelsey's father today, but really, when most of the parents were in couple units, it was hard to block out how alone she was. She wondered what today would have been like if Scott had lived.

Inevitably, memories flooded her mind. The dark, empty road ahead required little concentration, and it hurt too much to hold back thoughts of the past. There was no one to hide them from now, so she relaxed and let them flow.

She and Scott met when they were both seventeen and enrolled in an elite boarding school in California. Scott's parents were high-ranking Air Force officers, and he was the third Harrison to go through the Blaydes Academy. He was brilliant, taking courses three years above his age level and starring as the school's quarterback.

On the other hand, Regan's poor, uneducated, miserable parents had died in a home invasion when she was twelve. The police and social workers Regan had encountered after the crime had been callous and cold, on top of the trauma of hearing her parents killed while she hid in the basement. "Mistrust of authority" had probably been part of every psychological assessment she'd ever had, and still drove many of her decisions. She disrupted an orphanage for a few years, then out of desperation one of the social workers did some research, found the Academy and pushed Regan into applying. She'd gone from being a freak to being one of the crowd, and thrived for the first time in her life.

Working on a science project together, she and Scott fell instantly and powerfully in love. Most people didn't think teenagers could fall so hard and so honestly, but they had. Unfortunately, no matter how real their love, they had still been young. She'd gotten pregnant in the middle of their senior year, and suddenly any self-confidence and hope she'd gained at the academy disappeared. Everything frightened her. Being a mother. Having to drop out of school. What Scott's parents would say, and especially that they'd take him away from her. He insisted they wouldn't, they couldn't, but he'd gone home to tell them alone, and her fear had built every minute he was away.

Even the worst scenarios she'd conjured hadn't come close to what actually happened.

Lights flashed in the rearview mirror and Regan blinked, astonished to find tears blurring her vision. She glanced at the speedometer, but she was cruising at the speed limit. She looked back in the rearview mirror. The red and blue lights were flashing from the dash. It was an unmarked car, and this was a deserted highway in a rural area.

Her breathing suddenly quick and sharp, she kept her speed but turned on her hazard lights, then retrieved her cell phone from the console between the seats. She held it up and flipped it open, making a big show of it, and pressed the buttons for the police. Behind her, the siren chirped once.

"State police."

"I'm going the speed limit on a deserted highway being followed by an unmarked police car, and before I pull over I want to be sure it's really the police." She related her location and vehicle information, maintaining her speed while the dispatcher put her on hold. A few moments later, the woman came back on.

"Trooper Driscoll is stopping you for a non-working tail light, ma'am. It's safe to pull over. You may remain on the line if it will make you more comfortable."

"Thank you." Regan maneuvered to the shoulder and waited for the trooper, her shoulders burning with tension.

"He's still in the car," she told the dispatcher.

"Standard procedure, ma'am. He's running your information."

Regan bent to get her registration and proof of insurance from the glove compartment. When she straightened, the flashing lights reflected directly into her eyes, making her squint. She adjusted the mirror toward the ceiling. Her head began to throb, and she ran through evasive maneuvers in her mind.

A few minutes later the cop finally stepped out, adjusted his belt, and approached.

"He's nearly to my window," she reported. She rolled the window down an inch as the officer bent.

"Regan Miller?"

"Yes, officer." He'd no doubt got her name off the plate registration, but it was still unnerving.

"May I see your license, registration, and proof of insurance, please?"

She handed them over and studied his uniform, badge, and equipment belt. "What's your unit number, officer?"

He raised his eyebrows but didn't look up from her documents. "Unit seventy-two, ma'am."

She relayed the number to the dispatcher, who confirmed it was correct. Regan thanked the woman and hung up, daring to relax enough for her shoulders and neck to ease up.

"You're a mite cautious." Trooper Driscoll returned her information through the scant two-inch gap at the top of her window. "Any particular reason?"

Any explanation close to the truth would sound stupid or take too long, so she blamed the internet. "You know how it is these days—every time you turn on the computer someone's emailed you another frantic warning. But you can't be too careful, right?"

"Just get that bulb replaced, ma'am. Left rear light." He scribbled on a form and slipped it through her window. "This must be completed and mailed back to us within five days to avoid a fine. Any questions?"

"No, thank you."

"Have a nice night." He touched the brim of his hat and strode back to his car, mercifully flicking off the lights when he climbed in. Regan sighed and pulled out, more than ready to get home. Living life this way took a toll that she never got used to.

She'd barely managed to unknot her shoulders when her phone rang. Panic surged through her like electricity. Kelsey. Something was wrong already. *No, that's foolish mother-worry.* She'd probably just forgotten something and wanted her to send it.

But the name on the screen wasn't Kelsey's. Regan sighed. "Hello, Alan," she answered.

"Hey, babe. How're you doing?"

"It was hard, but not more than I expected. I'm on my way home."

"How about I meet you there? We can find a way to distract you, I'm sure."

Regan knew Alan expected her to sleep with him now that Kelsey was out of the house, but he didn't understand why she'd kept him at bay. He thought she was normal.

Kelsey had asked for a puppy once. Regan said no, and Kelsey had thrown her first real fit. Only six, she'd tried to talk their neighbor into letting her take home one of their dog's new litter. When Regan dragged her home empty-handed, Kelsey went on a hunger strike, forcing Regan to explain that they couldn't take anything into their lives they weren't willing to leave behind if they had to run away. Kelsey somehow understood enough not to ask more. She'd applied the philosophy to everything, a little at a time, until it became second nature, like it already was for her mother.

Not that Regan maintained complete isolation. She gave in to loneliness or flirtation from time to time, but never let anything get to the level of a relationship. Never let anyone into the cocoon she wrapped around her daughter. Once, when Kelsey was about thirteen and they were struggling to fix the broken screen door themselves, she'd grumbled, "How about a guy you *don't* mind leaving behind? Even they have their uses."

Then Kelsey started refereeing soccer, and Regan had met Alan, the ref coordinator. He asked her out, and Kelsey encouraged her to go.

"You deserve to be happy, Mom, and I think I want one of these." She'd gestured at a pair of five-year-old twins tussling on the soccer field.

Regan finally gave in, not because she wanted to get married and give Kelsey siblings, but because it was an element of normalcy that might offset the strangeness of knowing the best routes to lose a pursuer when she left the field after a game. Balancing safety and normality was Regan's biggest challenge.

"I'm sorry, Alan," she said now. "I just want to be alone. You know, walk around aimlessly and look at her things, sniffle over the photo album."

"Sure, hon, I understand." His voice softened, as it always did when she played Suburban Single Mom. She had no intention of walking around aimlessly, staring at the stuff her daughter had deemed too unimportant to take with her. But it was something an empty nester would do, and something Alan would understand. It would keep him away, at least for to-night.

"I'll call you," she told him, and tried to convince herself it was time to break things off. She was starting to enjoy his kisses and gentle caresses, and was afraid if it went further, Alan would become the first thing she didn't want to leave behind.

TWO

Kelsey checked her watch and picked up the pace. Less than two weeks into her first term and she'd already been late to her English class twice. Rookie mistake, scheduling back-to-back classes on opposite sides of the campus, but an excuse her prof didn't accept. Dammit. She was not going to flunk out!

Her cell phone buzzed, sparking an answering buzz of annoyance. The text message would be her mother with one of her daily check-ins, poorly disguised as a cheery message about her garden or something funny their neighbor had said. Kelsey didn't bother to answer.

Cutting across the grass, she swung around the corner of the stone building, legs burning with the effort. She'd skip the super-slow elevator and kill herself on the stairs right inside the door. But she was going to make it.

Wham!

She slammed into something hard and flew backward, landing on her ass and smacking the base of her skull against the corner of a book in her backpack. Stars did a chorus line across her vision, but she could see the hand reaching down for her. With a rush of adrenaline, she instinctively batted it to the inside with her left hand, then grabbed it and yanked with her right. Her attacker crashed to the ground beside her with an *oof.* She jumped to her feet without an ounce of grace, due to her hefty backpack, and whirled on her attacker, lifting her foot, ready to stomp him.

"Wait, wait! I'm sorry!" The guy who'd knocked her over pulled his knees up to shield her target and waved his arms, palms out. "I didn't mean to run you over! It was an accident!"

She froze, her brain catching up to her training. Then she realized who lay at her feet. And prayed for a natural disaster to end her sudden and unrelenting misery.

"God, I'm sorry." She reached to help him up. "I don't—I mean, my mother… Hell." Heat rushed to her face, and she stared at the ground, totally mortified.

"It's okay." The captain of the football team, their best inside linebacker, dusted himself off. "I get it. Most moms want their kids to take self-defense training nowadays. I'm impressed, actually. We've got an opening on the team." He flashed his amazingly sexy grin, and Kelsey got lost for a moment in his bright blue eyes. His shaggy haircut only half hid them. He was gorgeous, and she was an idiot. She didn't even know what to say.

"Hey, it's okay," he assured her. Then he frowned. "Are *you* okay? I didn't hurt you when I knocked you over, did I?"

"Hurt me?" She put her hand to the spot at the top of her neck without thinking.

His frown deepened and he stepped closer, touching her neck and then retreating quickly when she winced. "I'm really sorry."

"No, it's okay, I—" A bell rang inside the building. "Shit, I'm late." She started to run, but he caught her arm.

"Wait! I'm Tom!"

"I know," she yelled back, shaking him off and running faster. No way in hell was she giving him her name. She might be the joke of the week at the frat party that night, but no one had to know it was her.

Still, she couldn't help smiling. Maybe she'd made an idiot of herself, but she *had* taken down the school's record-setting tackler.

"Nice buds."

Regan snapped her phone shut and shoved it guiltily into her pocket. Kelsey had been at school for weeks, and you'd think she'd have adjusted by now. But it didn't matter how many times she told herself to leave Kelsey alone, she couldn't go more than a few hours without checking on her. It was borderline psychotic.

But not something she wanted to explain to the man lounging against the wooden fence between their yards, leering at her. She groaned at his lame attempt at innuendo and shielded her eyes from the sun.

"That was really bad," she told him.

"I know. They're not buds, they're bulbs."

She shook her head and stood. "Why do I put up with you, Tyler Sloane?"

"You don't have a choice." He paced her down the fence as she walked to the end and grabbed another handful of bulbs. "Where'd you get those moves, anyway?"

She frowned and returned to her original spot. "What moves?"

"You stood up all at once. You know, one move. You used to be a dancer or something?"

Regan sighed. Ever since Tyler had moved in next door two years ago, he'd quizzed her like this. She never told him anything—had, in fact, fed him quite a few contradictory lies. He seemed to find the game delightful. She was tired of it.

"Not a dancer? Maybe a ninja."

She snorted. "Leave me alone or this dirt I'm digging might fly a little far afield."

"Yeah, right. You can't get me from there."

She flipped the trowel, and lumps of dirt hit him in the chest.

"Damn."

"Told you."

"All right, I give." His bantering tone disappeared. "Actually, I wanted to ask you a favor."

"You can ask."

"I'll be going out of town soon. Can you pick up my mail and paper and water my plants while I'm gone?"

"You don't get the paper and you don't have any plants." She'd caught him stealing her newspaper enough times, and he just wasn't the kind of guy to nurture houseplants.

"Oh, yeah, right. Mail, then? And just keep an eye on the house?"

"Sure."

He didn't say anything else, and she stopped digging to look up. He stood there, studying her.

"You still seeing that Alan geek?"

"He's not a geek, and yes. Why, you interested?"

"Definitely."

She laughed, but he didn't. She set down the trowel. "Seriously?"

"Of course. Why wouldn't I be?"

"You never were before."

He shook his head, the smile sitting sadly on his mouth. "You weren't paying attention. Anyway, thanks for taking care of the mail. I'll bring you a key before I leave." He tapped a fist on the top rail of the fence and turned to go into the house.

Regan watched him, frowning. She'd always been aware he was a good-looking guy, but hadn't exactly analyzed his parts. Now she saw they weren't too bad. His butt was tight enough, and looked good in the faded jeans he always wore. He had broad shoulders, his muscles falling squarely between lean and bulky. Solid. He wore a T-shirt, as he usually did, but she bet he had a six-pack. And most women probably found his sun-streaked longish hair sexy. Hmm. Funny how she hadn't paid attention to him that way.

Of course, she'd pegged him on day one as a constant flirt, which was why his seriousness now surprised her. He gave everyone nicknames and winked his way through conversations. She never paid much attention to people like him. They'd become sort-of-friends only because of proximity and a tendency to drag their trashcans to the curb at the same time.

She sat, still watching, as his screen door banged closed behind him, and wondered if ignoring him had been a mistake.

Her phone chimed, making her jump and then her heart leap. Kelsey had texted her back. She dropped her trowel and pulled the phone from her pocket, frowning at the words on the screen. *In class. Lay off. I M fine.*

Oh, well. Regan sighed and returned to the bulb planting. She'd known her daughter would only put up with it for so long. She was outside Regan's influence now, as well as outside her protection, and there wasn't anything she could do about that. She wasn't going to be able to completely eliminate her neurosis, but she could at least switch to email.

"FOR A little person, you sure sneeze loudly." Kelsey frowned at her roommate. Van was bundled in flannel pajamas, a chenille bathrobe and a fleece blanket, looking utterly miserable but still trying to keep up with her homework. "You should be in bed."

Van snuffled and burrowed deeper into the blanket. "I hape cobes," she groaned, her stuffed sinuses making her words difficult to understand. "And tests. But I can't believe you haven't gotten it. I...I..." She sneezed again, trying to cover her face with the blanket and not entirely succeeding.

"I have a good immune system, I guess." Kelsey

turned back to her laptop and typed a quick email to her mother, reassuring her that everything was fine. She added a snide reference to something only she'd know about, so her mother would know she hadn't been abducted and her email hijacked. Annoyance that her mother made her do this drove the snideness; guilt at being annoyed kept her from being completely generic. "I never get sick," she added absentmindedly.

"Never?" The velvety voice came from the open doorway. "Sounds like a challenge to me."

Kelsey couldn't stop her goofy grin when she saw Tom. "Hey."

"Hey." He tapped Van on the top of the head as he passed, then bent and gave Kelsey a soft kiss. "I have a cold, too," he whispered. "Wanna go in your room and see if I can give it to you?"

She delighted in the shiver going up her spine. "That sounds like an idea. But I need to study for my physics exam."

"I'll help you." He nipped her cheek, then her earlobe. "You can have a kiss for every question you get right." His lips slid down her neck, and the shiver turned into a shudder.

"Umm. Van, we'll be in the room studying, if that's okay with you."

"Fine." She blew her nose.

Kelsey stood and reached for her book, but Tom grabbed it first. She smiled at him. "Just come in if you need something, or wanna go to bed, or whatever," she told her roommate.

"Don' worry, I'm not shy." She waved them off

and went back to her book. "Don't forget the rain-coat, kids."

"Van!" Kelsey's blush rose from her feet to her scalp all at once. "We're not—" She couldn't look at Tom. They hadn't even *talked* about sex yet. It had only been a few weeks since Tom had tracked her down and asked her out. Anyway, no way would she do it with her roommate right on the other side of the wall.

Tom didn't seem to have the same inhibitions. "Don't worry, Van, we won't do anything you wouldn't do."

Van snorted, which sent her into a coughing fit. "Get outta here."

Kelsey let Tom tug her into her room and slide the door shut. He took the book out of her hand and fell onto the bed, propping himself up on one elbow as he flipped pages. She sat, leaning against his abdomen, and he reached automatically for her hair, twirling a lock of it between his fingers. After a moment he flipped the book closed and looked up at her.

"Sorry, Kels, but I don't think I can concentrate on this right now."

Her breath caught at the look in his eyes. "I… um…have a test."

"I know." He cupped the back of her head and guided her to lie down beside him. "I'll help." He lowered his head. "Later, I promise," he whispered. His mouth touched hers and she melted like she always did. His lips were hot and coaxing, his big hand strok-ing up over her hip, then tightening on her ribcage to pull her closer to him. His hard-on pressed against her left thigh, and her body quickened, making her want to lift up, rub herself against him. Something tensed low in her body, tightened. Her breasts ached.

The kisses went on and on, his tongue dipping in and out of her mouth, his hand now cradling her head, his thumb stroking her jaw. He wasn't pushing her, wasn't getting any more urgent, but the moment came when she had to stop him or continue all the way through.

Hating herself, panting, she pulled her head back and pushed at his shoulder just hard enough to break the kiss. She braced herself for his anger, annoyance, derision. She'd come to expect it whenever she put on the brakes with other guys.

But he didn't respond with any of those things. His eyes were soft beneath their heavy lids, and his mouth curved up in a tender smile.

"Not yet, huh?"

She shook her head, her gaze lowering to the V of his polo shirt. She toyed with the buttons. "Not yet." Her voice was husky. "I'm sorry."

"Don't be." He stroked a hand over her hair. Her heart seemed to fill her chest. "I'm not here just for the sex, Kels."

She snorted. "All guys are here just for the sex."

Tom looked around, mocking jealousy. "Where? I'll beat their heads in."

Laughing, she shook her head again. "You can say it, but I know better. But it's not why I'm holding out," she hurried on, not wanting to argue about basic nature. "It's more complicated."

He gave her the universal look guys get that says "women."

"I know, I know, we make it more complicated when you guys think it's as simple as can be." She sighed. "It's my mom."

He frowned. "You don't want to have sex with me because of your mom? No offense, but you're an adult. I don't think you need her permission."

"That's not it." She abandoned the button and looked up. He must have understood it was a long story, because he settled on his side with a groan, tucking her into his shoulder.

"Go ahead. Tell me."

Since his tone was resigned but not uninterested, she did. "My mom's only thirty-seven," she began, giving him a minute to do the math.

"Well, that says it all." His muscles bunched as he started to turn, but she put a hand on his chest to keep him still.

"There's more. My dad was eighteen, too, when she got pregnant, and he was killed before I was born. He'd gone to tell his parents about my mother, who was an orphan, and something happened. She never knew what. Or at least, she never told me. He died, and she had me, and ever since has been totally paranoid about life. About my life." She told him some of the survival tips her mother had drilled into her.

"What the hell's she afraid of?" He laughed at the

extremes, but sobered quickly at the look on her face. "You don't believe it, do you? That you're in danger?"

Kelsey hated to admit she didn't know what she believed. For a long time, she'd just accepted that was how her mother was. She hadn't known other people didn't see danger and escape routes and odd behavior all over the place. As she got older and realized it wasn't normal, she'd started to resent it, especially with no proof of real danger. When her mother tried to move them again a few years ago, Kelsey ran away. It backfired, because for one, leaving to protest leaving kind of defeated the purpose. And when she went home, fully intending to scream her mother into letting her have her own way, her mother had collapsed, white as a corpse, vibrating with fear. She'd said it was like losing Kelsey's father all over again. He'd died trying to keep Regan and his unborn child safe, and Kelsey's recklessness had dishonored her father's sacrifice.

"She's afraid of losing me, I guess. We have this thing." She couldn't look at him and started playing with the button again. "We never take anything into our lives we can't leave behind." He didn't say anything. This time, when he shifted to loom over her, she let him.

"You don't have to be afraid to let me in, because you won't have to leave me behind. I won't let you." He brushed her hair off her face, his gaze going to her mouth. "I promise, everything will be fine." A bigger, harder, more promising kiss, then he sat up, opened her book, and leaned against the cinderblock wall.

"You have a test tomorrow, don't you?"

REGAN PULLED INTO her driveway earlier than usual,
absurdly excited to have an extra hour at home before
Alan came over. Now that Kelsey was gone, alone
time wasn't as hard to get as it once had been, except
for two things: work and Alan. The fitness center
she managed was doing booming business, and hir-
ing good help had been difficult. And Alan had gotten more entrenched in her routine over the last two
months. She wasn't sure that was a bad thing anymore, but she still enjoyed the time she had to herself.

She parked and walked down to the mailboxes to
get her mail and Tyler's before crossing the yard between their houses and using his key to open the front
door. She dropped his mail on the hall table without looking at it, as she had all week, and started to
walk back out again. Then she hesitated, noticing how
stuffy it was. It was the third week of October, but
they were having a heat wave and the temperature had
been near eighty today. The house felt stagnant and
stale. Tyler was coming home tonight from wherever
he'd been, and he didn't need to return to a muggy
house. She'd just open a few windows, now that the
sun had set and the temperature was dropping.

Dark blue drapes pulled across the picture window dimmed the living room. Regan opened them,
then unlocked and lifted the two small windows on
either side of the larger one. A breeze fluttered the
short sheers in front of them, and she nodded, pleased.

She turned and started to walk across the living
room to the kitchen. Opening the window over the
sink would create a cross-breeze, and that should be

enough. But she hesitated when a computer desk on the far wall caught her attention. She hadn't come past the foyer all week, but simply listened for running water, sniffed for smoke and relocked the door on her way out. Now curiosity fed by chronic suspicion crept over her. Who was this guy, living so close to her and making new overtures? Could he be part of what she'd run from? Maybe whoever had hired the thugs to kidnap Kelsey as a baby had gotten smarter, more subtle. More patient. Shouldn't she know all she could about Tyler Sloane?

Slowly, she crossed the carpeted room to the desk. The surface was empty save for the keyboard and monitor. The hutch on top of the desk held a few note-pads and an electric company mug with two pens, a pencil and a pair of scissors sticking out of it. She riffled through a small stack of bills on the left-hand shelf, but there was nothing unusual there. The phone bill was still sealed.

She carefully slid open the top drawer. A small case of disks, three loose CD-Rs—the kind you got free with a new computer—a ruler and a sticky pad. The bottom drawer, file sized, was locked.

Interesting. Was he in the habit of locking things even though he lived alone, or was there something he didn't want her to see if she went snooping?

In any event, there was nothing to find here. She continued into the kitchen and shoved open the window. The drawers and cabinets revealed a typical selection of mismatched utensils and plates and microwaveable food. The only odd thing was that he didn't have a junk drawer.

There was an empty dining room and a half bath looking disturbingly clean for a bachelor male. Maybe he'd cleaned it in case she used it while he was away. She hesitated between the bottom of the stairs and the front door. Up or out? She had no reason to go up except nosiness. And that was hardly sufficient.

But with the exception of the locked drawer, the house felt staged to her. Like a model home, or one prepared to sell. Or a fake one. This house told her nothing about the guy who lived here. She had a duty to herself and her daughter to do everything possible to protect them. Right?

"Right, Regan," she muttered as she started up the stairs. "This is a bit much, even for you." For two years, he hadn't given her reason to suspect him. And if he was hiding something, he wouldn't have given her access to his house.

But she couldn't help herself.

The first room was his bedroom, and as soon as she set foot in it, she realized it wasn't suspicion drawing her up here. His scent surrounded her, even after a week of his being gone, and she hadn't even been aware that she knew what he smelled like. Heat, and mown grass, and something smelling like nothing else except Tyler Sloane. She inhaled, then gasped in horror at her body's response. A surge of desire, an urge to prowl…

Hell, no.

She abandoned her self-guided tour and ran down

the stairs, grabbing her keys and her own mail off the hall table as she wrenched open the door and pulled it closed behind her.

Thank God he was coming home tonight.

That thought could be interpreted in more ways than one, and she slammed the brakes on the list her brain started to make.

As if to admonish her further, Alan pulled into her driveway behind her truck. She crossed the grass to him, smiling, but the smile faded when she saw the look on his face.

"What's wrong?" she asked when he emerged from the sedan. He didn't answer but glowered at the house behind her, and she understood. She wasn't about to indulge his jealousy, especially given the feelings she'd just dealt with. She didn't give him a chance to respond.

"I just have a few things in the truck to bring in, and we can figure something out for dinner," she said.

Alan's face cleared and he bent to kiss her. "I'll help." Ever efficient, he opened the back of the Highlander and collected her gym bag, a box of fliers she needed to fold for the fitness center, her lunch box and two bags of dry groceries she'd bought at lunch. Nothing remained for her to carry.

"You busy?" he asked, eyeing the fliers.

"No, they don't have to be done tonight."

"Good." He gave her a significant look she ignored, leading him around to the back door.

"I'll put these away." Alan deposited most of her things on the kitchen island and lifted the bag of toiletries bound for her bathroom. "I know where they go."

Regan only said thanks. Since Kelsey left, Alan had been trying to pamper her by doing these little things. Arguing with him about her capability would just make her look stubborn and overly independent and reinforce his opinion that she needed someone to take care of her. For some reason, the harder a woman worked, the more everyone else believed she needed help.

The phone rang and she snatched it up. Alan was here, so it had to be Kelsey.

"Hello?"

"Hey, Mom! Guess what!" Her voice was breathless and high-pitched. Regan's heart slammed against her chest. There was only one thing that would make her daughter—any teenage girl—that excited.

"What?"

"I totally aced my English lit midterm!"

Regan slumped against the counter. Thank God. As soon as Kelsey let a man into her life, her mother's influence would decrease by half. The longer it took to happen, the longer she could hold on to the illusion she could keep Kelsey safe.

"That's wonderful, hon!" As Kelsey went on about British poets and bullshit essays, Regan opened the refrigerator and grimaced. There wasn't much to make for dinner, even with the groceries she'd picked up. Not really caring, she pulled out a carton of eggs. Egg salad sandwiches sounded good enough to her.

"And Mom, I swear, you're going to kill me for saying this, but I think I'm in love with him."

"What?" Regan realized she'd stopped listening for a crucial moment. "I'm sorry, I got distracted. Please tell me I didn't hear what I think I heard. Who is this guy?"

"The football player. Come on, Mom, we've talked about him. The guy I crashed into a few weeks ago?"

Regan remembered. She'd quizzed Kelsey for fifteen minutes about why he'd hit her, what he'd said, who else had been around, until her daughter had practically hung up on her in disgust. She'd made a few mentions in her emails about a guy she'd gone out with a few times, but Regan hadn't clued in that it was that far along.

"What's his name again?"

"It's Tom Johnson." She went on about his being a linebacker and holding school records and hoping to get drafted into the NFL, but Regan hardly heard her. She had a flash memory of Scott's face, as clear as the last day she'd seen him, and old grief throbbed. She wanted to believe this was a passing thing, Kelsey's first independent fling. But she remembered too well how it felt to fall in love, real love, and she knew Kelsey was there. Knew it was far too late for her to interfere. She just wished she knew if it was a good thing or a bad thing.

She pulled a pan out and filled it with water, set it on the stove, and started setting eggs in it, all the while listening to Kelsey rave about how sweet this kid was, even though she'd flattened him.

"I mean, he did flatten me first, but not many people could knock him down even on the football field, never mind off it."

Regan noticed the latch on the screen door was undone, and she crossed the kitchen to slip the hook into the eye. Alan re-entered the room in time to see her do it. He looked displeased, but she didn't care. She was who she was, and if he couldn't accept that, too bad.

As she listened to her daughter babble on about all the great changes in her life, though, she wondered who it was too bad for. Regan had coworkers and staff, a bantering friendliness with her next-door neighbor, and a daughter starting her own life a hundred miles away. That was all, and why? Because of something that happened a long time ago and, despite her readiness, had never happened again.

They could have found her if they wanted to. She had been afraid to do anything illegal, so her name change had occurred in the courts in Illinois, her first stop after leaving California. She'd moved several times while Kelsey was very young, but once she hit school age Regan was less willing to disrupt her life unless she had to. They'd settled here, in this small town in Ohio, where she worked a legitimate job and paid her taxes and utilities and rent. Constantly alert, she'd been prepared to run at the first sign someone had found them, even after Kelsey's second freakout. They never had.

"I'm happy for you, sweetheart," she said softly when her daughter paused for a breath.

"You are?"

"Of course I am. I know I don't talk about your father much, Kels, but I do remember. I want you to feel that way."

"I do. And Mom, don't worry. We're gonna practice safe sex, *double* protection, and everything. I know I'm not his first, we've talked about it, and we're both going to get tested for AIDS just in case, because we want to start our life together pure and honest."

Regan squeezed her eyes shut as Kelsey rambled on. Could any mother hear about her daughter having sex, even safe sex, and talking about AIDS, even in a responsible manner, without this pain in the chest? She was proud of her, so proud, and yet it hurt more than anything ever had.

"I think Van is having an influence on you."

That stopped Kelsey, and she laughed. "I'm rambling, huh? It's not like me."

"No, but I'm not complaining. I love to hear what's happening up there."

"Mom, I'm really happy. Thank you."

"For what?"

"For being so brave."

Regan blinked. "I'm not brave, Kels."

"Yes, you are. You've been afraid my whole life. I don't know why, but I know how deep it goes. But you never held me back. And you let me go, when I know it couldn't have been easy for you. I just wanted you to know I understand and I appreciate it."

As she hung up the phone a few minutes later,

Regan wondered what the hell she had done to deserve such an awesome kid. She could have rebelled harder against her mother's protectiveness, could have acted out and done dangerous things. Could have hated Regan for not fully explaining her fears, especially when she'd never seen evidence of the danger. Maybe it really was time for her to—

A squealing, hissing sound penetrated her thoughts. Like gas escaping through a tight valve. She spun, looking for the source. She checked the windows, then hurried to the screen door. She couldn't see anything. She was about to run out to the hall when Alan stepped in front of her.

"What's wrong?" He had been leaning against the counter, patiently waiting for her to finish talking to Kelsey. Now he gripped her upper arms. "What's the matter?"

"That noise. I hear—" She looked toward the stove, flushing. It was the eggs. As the temperature changed in the pot, so did the pressure, making them squeal. "Never mind."

"Honey." He stepped closer and put his hands on her shoulders. "Sweetheart, you need to let go. You are wound far too tight. I don't know what happened to make you like this, but you have to stop. It's too much stress. Can't you believe you're safe? From whatever you're afraid of?"

She looked up at him, finally sensing the truth of his question in her gut. Scott's warning that they were in danger had been true. The attempted kidnapping right after Kelsey was born proved that. But she didn't know for sure what had caused them to be in danger, and the eighteen years without another attempt was pretty good evidence the danger had passed.

Maybe it *was* time for her to let go.

She switched off the burner, took Alan's hand and led him without a word through the tiny house to the bedroom. Ignored the open back door and unset alarm. Sent as clear a message as she could without actually saying the words.

"Oh, baby," Alan breathed as she shut the bedroom door behind him. He took her face in his hands and kissed her reverently. Her brain, her body, resisted for one more moment, then released her.

It wasn't like a storybook. She didn't burst into flames and passion didn't overcome her. She couldn't get lost in his kisses. But he was tender and gave her all the time and attention she needed. She came in a long, slow, sweet rolling orgasm that catapulted Alan into his, and they dozed, cuddling.

She thought about how she hadn't allowed herself this before, this complete package of comfort and pleasure. Why had she let the bad guys steal a large part of her life, just by keeping her afraid? She wondered what it would be like to really let go. What it would hurt. The answer lay in a memory that never faded, but after all this time, maybe it was okay to start letting it. She dropped into a deeper sleep, and it was dark when she jerked awake in response to a dull, squishing *thunk*. When her eyes flew open, they focused instantly on the handle of the giant knife protruding from Alan's chest.

THREE

HER NIGHTMARES HAD never been like this. She'd always been alone, trying to protect Kelsey against the foes she'd defeated before—two men, unarmed but for their strength and evil plan. This was totally different.

Inside she screamed in horror as Alan gasped, his eyes already vacant, his hands trying to clutch the knife. There was nothing she could do for him. There was almost nothing she could do for herself, as a second knife descended toward her.

A few things saved her. Her position—she was lying on her side, presenting a much less obliging target for a kill strike. Her nightmares, which had conditioned her to consider what she would do under any circumstance she could think of. And her knowledge that if anything happened to her, Kelsey was a sitting duck.

The knife grazed the side of her left arm as she rolled to her right and kept going, her momentum taking the attacker by surprise. She had a vague thought that he hadn't been aiming to kill, but she had no time to consider that. They tumbled to the floor together. Regan was on top but she had no weapon, no leverage, and no clothes. There was less for him to grab, but absolutely nothing to protect her.

He swung his knife hand twice, cutting her both times but not doing any serious damage. Someone shouted, an angry "No!", but she didn't know who he was shouting at. She managed to get a foot on her attacker's wrist and push it downward, then pulled herself up to put her weight on that foot and one knee on his chest. A heavy brass elephant sat on the nightstand next to her. Not a very lovely decoration, but it made a good weapon. She held it by the trunk and swung it into the man's head, knocking him out.

She had no time for relief. Already the others were on her. Four of them. They must have learned their lesson last time. Even with everything she'd done in preparation, the odds weren't in her favor.

She grabbed the knife off the floor and swung it in an arc as someone caught her from behind. She used him as a brace, lifting her feet and kicking out. Her bare feet wouldn't do much damage, but she did manage to clip one guy on the jaw, giving her a little space.

He cursed and glared. "Dammit, it wasn't supposed to go like this. He said she'd be alone."

The guy behind her grunted as she wriggled. Despair welled in her chest, pain for Alan for being here when he normally wouldn't be. Her fault.

So don't let it be a waste.

She fought harder. Her guy had her by the arms instead of the neck, which gave her more flexibility. She twisted the knife, biting back a cry when it sliced across the top of her hip, and aimed it backwards. When one of the others swung a fist at her face, she pushed off the floor, then planted a foot on his chest, shoving hard and falling backward onto the man holding her. They landed on the bed, Regan on top. His yell escalated to a scream when he realized what the pain in his abdomen meant.

Regan bounded back to her feet, but now without a weapon and still facing three large men. They were all on her side of the bed, blocking access to the window. But the doorway was clear. They'd hesitated when she gutted their colleague, and seemed to think she was trapped.

She wasn't.

She turned and jumped onto the bed, leaped over Alan's limp body and ran out the door. They pounded behind her, booted feet thundering down the hall.

"Stop her!" bellowed one man. She thought of her goal, the gun in the kitchen, and wondered why no one was shooting at her. Why they'd brought knives and five men, instead of a pistol with a silencer.

She shoved through the swinging door into the kitchen, immediately turned, and slammed the door back the other way, into the person nearest her. There was a crunch—hopefully his nose—a thud, and a bellow. Two down? Scrambling around the center island to the towel drawer, she yanked the drawer out too far and it fell, sending the gun clattering across the ceramic tile. She dove for it, the island giving her a little protection, a few seconds of cover, and hopefully an element of surprise. The gun shifted in her slick grip.

The safety seemed to echo as she clicked it off, straining to hear where her pursuers were. Had they even come into the kitchen? She couldn't wait for them, there wasn't time. Kelsey. She had to warn Kelsey.

Regan stood with a roar, aiming and firing at once, but it was a stupid move. Two of the men had entered, but neither stood where she was aiming. All she did was kill her Audubon bird clock. The guy on her left grabbed her left arm and reached for the gun. The guy on the right grabbed her right arm and did the same. Penned in from either side, she dropped straight down, but not before the guy on the left batted the gun from her hand. It clattered on the tile again as her weight pulled the right-hand attacker to the floor with her.

She screamed at a sudden, sharp, burning pain in her left shoulder. The left-hand guy had held on to her arm and stayed upright, dislocating her shoulder. Her vision went black, her stomach churning. She retched. He let go, and she yelled again when her arm hit the floor, reigniting the pain. She tried to roll away from him, knowing instinctively he was going to kick her. But she had nowhere to go. The guy on the right blocked her way. He didn't seem to be moving.

She was trapped now, boxed in by her cabinets and her enemies. *Let go*, her mind whispered. *Just give up.* But Kelsey's laughter echoed in her head. Kelsey, who'd met a new guy. Who'd thanked her for being brave.

Gasping for air, she forced herself to block out the pain in her arm and rolled back to the left, into the feet of the one who'd dislocated her shoulder. He was only standing on one foot, the other swinging forward to kick her. Instead of her kidney or ribs he hit her hip, and she was closer so the strike wasn't as bad as he'd intended. She kept going and knocked him over. Unlike his buddy, he landed on her and knocked her breathless. Her left arm useless and still excruciating, she tried to drag herself out from under him with her right arm. Odd mewling, panting sounds echoed in her ears, seeming to come from someone else's lungs. Hands grabbed at her hips, slipped away, then found better purchase on her lower legs. She kicked ferociously and contacted rough fabric over very soft tissue. Bull's-eye.

He let go of her for a moment, long enough for her to struggle to her feet. She had to call Kelsey. Her phone. The cell phone was plugged in, in the front hall. She had no time to get there. But the kitchen phone was cordless. She leaned against the counter, trying to catch her breath, knowing she had seconds before he'd be on her again. She staggered toward the door, grabbing the phone off the hook with her right hand, fumbling it. The inside door was still open, and the screen door had been ripped off its hook. She was through, and he still wasn't behind her. She had a few more seconds. He'd started cursing.

She pressed pound-oh-one and tried to run across the back yard. Wrong way. It was all enclosed. Stupid. Why hadn't she realized? She turned left, toward the rail fence between her and Tyler's yards. The screen banged behind her. Kelsey's dorm phone rang once, followed by a decade of silence. Footsteps in the grass. Ragged breathing. She swung a leg over the fence and teetered with no free hands to balance herself. She half fell over the other side, listened to another ring. More silence. Why the hell wasn't she in her room at this late hour? Wood cracking. Kelsey's voice.

"Hello?" Hopeful. Cheery. *Alive*.

"Kelsey, it's Mom. They're here. It's happened. Run. You have to run. Go to the police. Get safe. Go. Now!" The last word cut off as she was tackled from behind. The phone flew out of her hand, the tackle knocking the air out of her again. Her attacker crawled up her body, faster than she could crawl away. A fist hit her bad shoulder. She screamed. He flipped her over and hit her again, on the cheek. Light exploded in her vision, tinged with red. He growled words, things like "collection" and "don't kill" and "blood" and "bitch." The pain blazing up and down her entire left side made it impossible for her to put the words together and make sense of them.

Still, she fought. Tried to kick, to gouge him with her right hand. She scratched his arm, his hand, as he grabbed her hair and lifted her face to his.

"You goddamned bitch. This wasn't supposed to be this hard. Fuck him. You're not worth it." He straddled her and knelt on her bad arm. She screamed again, but the sound was thin, airy, not enough for anyone nearby to hear. He pulled a small switchblade from his pocket and sliced her arm open, pressing something cold and hard under the cut.

He panted harshly as he squeezed her arm. "I'm gonna let you die slow, so you can think about this." He let go of her arm and something clinked and rasped, metal on glass. Regan swung her right arm up, trying to hit him, but he blocked it easily. He lowered his head until his mouth was next to her ear. "We're goin' after little Kelsey next."

"No." It came out a whisper. She struggled to move, her shoulder shrieking, as his hand clamped over her throat. A hundred images flashed through her vision, and then the world faded to black.

KELSEY STARED AT the phone on the wall, the receiver to her ear. "Mom? Mom!" She could hear muffled sounds. Then her mother screamed. "MOM!" A man's murmuring voice, more rustling, another scream, and then…silence.

They're here. It's happened. Run. You have to run. For a minute, Kelsey didn't know what to do. Her mother was hurt, she knew it. And she thought Kelsey was in danger. *It's happened.* Whatever her mom had been afraid of for so long had finally happened.

"Kelsey?"

It was Van, probably wondering why she was staring at the phone while the off-hook sound clanged in her ear. She slammed the receiver onto the cradle. She knew what to do, for God's sake. She'd been training for it practically since she was born.

"Van, can I borrow your cousin's car?" Freshmen weren't allowed to have cars on campus. Her mother had thought about having one for her parked off campus, but if she was caught she could be expelled, so they'd decided against it. Van's cousin was a senior. He rode his motorcycle most of the time and let Van keep his car in her dorm lot.

"Sure, hon. What's goin' on?"

"I don't know. Something. I just…forgot about an assignment. I have to go to the store." She ran into her room and grabbed her backpack, stuffing whatever she could think of into it. Wallet, phone, charger, keys. She grabbed a pair of underwear off the clean laundry piled on her bed, and the pack of new pens next to it. God knew why. She didn't have time to think. Or to deal with the bile rising in her throat. *Hang on, Mom.* A weapon, a weapon. She had no frigging weapons! How could her mother do that to her! Hell with it—she'd use her teeth if she had to.

She dashed into the bathroom. Floss, eye cream, toothbrush, toothpaste, hairbrush, uncapped mascara, cotton swabs, she swept it all into her bag. As an afterthought, she snatched a first aid kit off the shelf and dashed back out. Van stood there, arms folded, hair spikier than usual.

"Yeah, sure, you've gotta go to the store. What's going on? Can I help?"

"No, thank you. It could—I gotta go on my own. Thank you." She hugged her friend impulsively. Tears pricked her eyes, and she wasn't sure how much was because of her mother being hurt, and how much the idea she might never see Van again. "Take care. Bye." She snatched the key Van held out and left.

In the hall, she hesitated. Panicked flight was stupid, could get her killed. She didn't know if those after her were here yet, so she didn't know which way was the safest to go. Shit. Should have gone out the window, like her mother told her the first day. A few students hung out in doorways or lounged on the floor talking on the phone, but she recognized everyone, and they all ignored her. She knocked on the door across the hall. Rachel, a senior, poked her head out.

"Hey, can I look out your window a sec?" Kelsey asked her. "I need to see if my boyfriend's here."

Rachel made an annoyed face, then shrugged. "Go to town."

"Thanks."

She switched off the light, ignoring Rachel's squawk, and moved up to the side of the window. Two women were leaving the building, holding the door open for a guy she couldn't see clearly. Dammit, they weren't supposed to do that. They were supposed to be buzzed in. What if he was after her?

She called out her thanks again, hitting the light switch on her way out. She paused, thinking hard through the daze of shock. He'd probably take the elevator, if he didn't know her mother had warned her. Otherwise, he'd take the steps. But which ones? The ones to her left were closer to the rest of campus, and more people would be around there. The ones to the right were rarely used because there was nothing at that end of the building except the football field. Shit. Would he use the more vacant stairs, or the ones she'd be more likely to take?

The ones to the right were closer to Van's car.

She headed that way, certain no matter what she did she'd make the wrong decision. The door hung open, warped hinges keeping it from closing all the way. She leaned in, listening. Silence. She pushed through and headed down, trying to keep her footsteps light and quiet so she could hear if anyone else entered the stairwell. A voice echoed from above, something about pizza, but she made it to the bottom without seeing anyone.

Just as she reached the door, it opened and a man stepped in, almost bumping into her before he looked up. Her whole body jolted with a burst of adrenaline before she saw his face and those familiar blue eyes.

"Tom!"

He grinned happily. "You almost plowed me over again. I need to wear my helmet." His smile disappeared. "Kels, what is it? What's wrong?"

"My mother. I gotta go. I'm sorry, Tom, I love you, but I gotta go, and I may never see you again." Her voice caught and she angrily brushed away the tears that did more than threaten this time. "She was right," she whispered. "My mother was right. It's real."

"What?" Confusion turned to shock. "No way!" He grabbed her shoulders. "Talk to me, Kels. Tell me what's happening."

"I *can't*. I don't *know*. All I know is someone's after me and my mother's hurt and I have to *go* to her!" She bent, trying to pull away from him.

"Okay, okay. I'll drive you. My car's in the stadium lot, I'll just—"

"No, it's too far. I've got Van's keys. I can drive. Tom, I don't want you hurt!"

His face hardened and her breath caught. He looked like a man. Tall, strong, solid—someone she could count on. In the midst of her fear and uncertainty, it was as much of a turn-on as his kisses were.

"Shut up, Kelsey, and let's go. I'll drive you. I'm not abandoning you, no matter what's going on."

Tears welled up in the wake of a relief so strong it told her just how afraid she'd actually been. She threw her arms around him, held tight, and dragged him out the door.

But when they got to the car, Kelsey wanted to scream with frustration. Van stood there, pacing and staring back and forth from the street to the building.

"There you are!" She ran toward them. "The phone rang, and it was a man asking for you. When I said you'd left, he asked where you were going. I didn't want to tell him, but he started yelling at me."

Kelsey gasped. "You told him?"

"No! I told him to screw himself, hung up, and ran to catch up with you. I grabbed this." She picked up her field hockey stick from where it lay on the trunk of the car. "Don't even think I'm not going with you."

WHEN REGAN WOKE up, she knew instantly where she was and remembered everything that had happened until she blacked out. She didn't know or care how she'd gotten into the hospital or how long she'd been unconscious. She had to get out of there, get to Kelsey.

She was alone in the hospital room but, as she

discovered when she started to climb out of bed, she wore a stupid open-backed gown. With her left arm in a sling, she couldn't tie it. It didn't matter. She had to have been naked when they brought her in, anyway.

An IV stuck out of the back of her right hand. She wanted to rip it out but she had to be smart. Her entire body ached, her shoulder and left cheek most of all—she also had trouble seeing out of her left eye, she realized—and she didn't need any more damage. She closed the clamp on the IV tube and carefully peeled off the tape over the catheter, then slid it out. Blood trickled across her hand, faster than she'd expected. She yanked three tissues from the box on the nightstand and pressed them to the back of her hand, ignoring the ache in her left shoulder.

They must have given her painkillers. The throbbing in her shoulder was dull, and the room swam every time she turned her head. She could feel the tug of bandages taped to her hip, left and right arms, and right leg, but the cuts didn't hurt. She swayed when she stood, but couldn't rest. She had to make sure Kelsey was safe.

She was almost to the door when it opened.

"Oh, no, missy, you get right back into bed. What did you do? My goodness!" The nurse took Regan's elbow and marched her back to the bed, ignoring her protests. "I don't care if the Vatican needs you, you're not going anywhere. Now settle down. The police need to speak with you, and that nice neighbor who came in with you is frantic with worry. I made him go outside because he wouldn't stop pacing in here."

She clucked at the IV catheter on the floor and bent to pick it up. Regan stood again and tried to slip past her, but the nurse was quick.

"You think I'm a newbie? I've had bigger patients than you try to get by me and fail, missy."

"Stop calling me missy!" Her voice was hoarse and her neck hurt when she talked, but she ignored it. She could breathe, and that was enough. "I need to get out of here. My daughter is in danger!"

"Tell it to the cop. You sit, I'll get him." She pointed the Mom Finger at Regan, who had an unexpected surge of amusement. She hadn't been on this end of the Finger in twenty-five years.

"Okay, I'll sit. But get him *now*."

The nurse was true to her word. A minute later the cop—John Boyse, according to his name tag—was ponderously asking her questions about her story.

"Look, I'll tell you everything, but first I want to know my daughter is safe! I called her. I told her to go to the police. *Please*, call campus security, call the town police, do something to assure me she's okay. If you can't, I'm out of here."

"Hey, what's this shouting?" Tyler leaned around the door, surveyed the room, then came straight over to Regan and took her right hand. "What are you riling her up for? You saw her condition when she came in here! I swear—"

Officer Boyse sighed. "Mr. Sloane, I assure you, it was not my intent to rile Ms. Miller. I just need to get the facts."

"I told you how to get the facts," Regan said.

The officer eyed her implacably, then turned. "I'll be right back."

Regan stood.

"Hey." Tyler shoved her with his fingertips against her chest, and she plopped back down. "You're not going anywhere, Regan. Tell me what's going on while we're waiting."

"She needs her IV back in. Mr. Sloane, if you'll please move over."

He did, and the nurse moved in on Regan's right. Regan ignored her.

"You tell me first," she said to Tyler. "How did I get here?"

"I got home late, but your lights were on, so I was coming over to see how things went while I was gone. When I came out the back door, you were lying in my backyard, naked and beaten to a pulp."

She snorted. "Hardly a pulp, and it wouldn't have been so bad if there weren't five of them." A sneaky hint of pride overrode any embarrassment she might have felt at being discovered naked in his backyard.

"Five!" He stared at her. "Who the hell were they?"

"No idea. So…"

"I called nine-one-one for the police and ambulance. They set your shoulder right there, almost made me puke. You've got cuts all over you and you're lucky your cheekbone isn't fractured. Who did this to you?"

His tone was getting demanding. "Ask them." She motioned toward the door. The nurse, who had finished collecting her equipment, tried to grab her right arm. Regan shrugged her off and lifted the tissues. The bleeding had stopped.

"Ask who, the cops? They don't know."

"Didn't they interrogate any of them?"

"Any of who? They didn't catch the guy."

"The ones in my house! Don't tell me they didn't go inside!" She huffed. "I knocked one out on the floor in my bedroom, another was stabbed in the stomach. Alan! Oh my God, Alan." She closed her eyes. "They killed Alan. Another one might have been knocked out in my kitchen. Probably the one with the broken nose and the one who busted my shoulder got away."

"Regan, honey." He crouched in front of her and took her right hand just as the nurse reached for it again. "Alan's dead, yes. But there was no one else in the house. The police told me that much—after they decided I hadn't done this to you."

He let go of her hand and let the nurse take it. Regan pulled away and glared at the woman, who glared back.

"Where is that cop? Why is this taking so long?" She tried to stand again, and both Tyler and the nurse stopped her. "Don't you understand? *Someone is after my daughter.* I can't just sit here waiting to hear if she's dead or alive or missing. Will you stop it!" The nurse backed up at her yell. "I don't need the damned IV, but thank you for your diligence. It would be very helpful if one of you would go find Officer Boyse."

The nurse stalked out, but no one came back in. Tyler stayed at her feet, his thumb stroking over the back of her hand. "Regan, talk to me. What's going on?"

"I can't, Tyler."

"Can't? Why?"

She looked at him. Why? Because the first time she let down her guard, it bit her in the ass. The one person she'd allowed close to her had been murdered. She couldn't let Tyler become a victim.

Or allow herself to turn to him. Her anger was keeping her sane at the moment, and if she leaned on him, even a little, she'd fall apart. So she retreated into old habits. He may not have been part of the attack, but he could have ordered it. She didn't know anything about him, except he never seemed to work. He exercised at her fitness center and mowed his yard twice a week and dragged his garbage cans down his driveway at five-thirty on Wednesday. None of which made him a good guy. She stayed silent.

Finally the cop came in, and he didn't look happy.

"Kelsey?"

"She's not at the police station. They contacted campus security, who called her room. When no one answered they went over there. The dorm room was empty. There were possible signs of a scuffle or someone leaving in a hurry, but unfortunately, those could also be the signs of a messy college student." He flipped open his pad and looked down at it.

"That's it? That's all you have?"

"Patience, Ms. Miller. They tracked down two of her suitemates at the library. They hadn't seen her since lunch. Her other roommate, Savannah Leigh, is unaccounted for as well."

"Oh, God, tell me they didn't do anything to Van." Regan felt sick. It was all her fault. She'd been the one to let Kelsey go away to school.

"We don't know. They questioned people in the area. The girl across the hall said your daughter came in to look out the window and turned the lights off to do it. A few minutes later she was leaving to go out and saw Ms. Leigh running down the hall with a backpack and her field hockey stick."

Regan took a deep breath and finally calmed down, her brain clicking into gear. "Okay, she left. I need to call her." Why hadn't she thought of that first? "I need a phone. I can call her cell phone. She always has it." She leaned for the phone, but Tyler got there first and handed it to her. She dialed and got a fast busy signal. "How the hell do I get a line out?"

Tyler read the instructions off the phone and started dialing. "What's her number?" Biting back a protest, Regan told him. He finished dialing and handed the phone back to her.

It went right to voice mail. "Shit." She waited for the beep. "Kelsey, it's Mom. I need to know you're safe. Call me back. Uh—" Tyler recited his cell phone number and she repeated it, narrowing her eyes at him. He knew she wasn't staying here long, or he'd have given the hospital's room number.

Officer Boyse said, "Now will you please answer my questions?"

"Of course." At his prompt, she dutifully explained

what had happened that night, right up to what the last guy had said to her before she'd blacked out.

"You didn't know any of them? Did they say what they wanted?"

She shook her head. "I'd never seen any of them before. I know they're stupid, because he said he'd leave me to die slowly when he should have known my injuries weren't life threatening. And there were more of them, because at least one of them wasn't in any shape to leave on his own. They needed help getting their own bodies out of there." She remembered the press of cold—glass?—on her cut arm but hesitated to describe it. Why on earth would they want her blood?

"Where did you get the gun, Ms. Sloane?"

"It's mine. It's registered." She'd memorized the number and gave it to him. "Can I have it back?"

"We didn't find it."

"Dammit."

He grilled her relentlessly, the clock on the wall ticking minute after far too many minutes, until she was ready to beat him up just to get out of there. She tried calling Kelsey twice more, with the same result. And Tyler, at her urging, went outside twice—per hospital policy—to check his voice mail. The last time, he came back in just as Boyse closed his pad.

"I got a message. It sounded like Kelsey. She said she's okay, she's with friends, and they're coming here to see you. I couldn't reach her when I tried to call back."

Officer Boyse unclipped his radio. "We'll put out

an APB. Do you have any idea what car they're driving?"

"She didn't say." Tyler looked at Regan.

"Kelsey doesn't have a car. Her boyfriend might have one, though, and I'd bet anything he's one of the friends with her. His name is Tom Johnson."

"Okay, we'll look into it. We'll let you know any information as soon as we get it. Please just rest and recover. Your daughter'll be fine."

"Thank you, Officer." There was no point arguing, protesting or asking them to do anything more. He left, and she stood. "Tyler, I appreciate your help. I don't want to drag you into this, but I need two favors. Can you please get me some scrubs or something to wear, and take me to get my truck?"

"You're going after her. Regan, if she's on her way here…"

"They'll intercept her en route. I'm not lying here waiting patiently for it to happen. I'm going after her. I won't let you stop me," she warned. "I got the best of five guys who tried to kill me. Or something," she amended, remembering the things they'd said. "I can get the best of you."

He smiled briefly. "I doubt it. But you don't need to. I'm coming with you."

"Tyler."

"Look, I'll cut to the chase, Regan. I know a lot more than you think, maybe more than you do. I can't tell you who I work for or what I know. But I can tell you this."

He waited for her to focus her full attention on him. Her blood chilled at the hardness in his eyes.

"You won't get very far against these people without me."

FOUR

"WOULD YOU PLEASE get me something to wear?" Regan repeated softly. She looked steadily at Tyler, who eyed her mistrustfully but left her alone for a minute.

Regan sank onto the bed once he was gone and rested her head on her good hand. She had to think. Her brain was still fuzzy, her reactions slow. It was an effort to talk, and she was in no condition to drive. Tyler was willing to, so she should be grateful.

But he knew things. She had no idea what or why, which meant he couldn't be trusted.

Well, she didn't have to trust him in order to use him.

He returned a few minutes later with a set of navy blue scrubs and a pair of shower shoes.

"Best I can do." He dropped them onto the bed next to her. "I half expected you to be gone."

Regan saw no need to lie to him. "I thought about it." She started to pull the gown forward to take it off. Tyler spun around and she smiled. "You saw me naked already, Tyler."

He just kind of grunted.

"I would have left if I wasn't drugged. I'll let you drive."

"Gee, thanks." He took a deep breath and turned back around. "You're going to need help with that." Regan had managed to get the scrub top over her head and her right arm through, but couldn't handle the left arm. Tyler unhooked the sling at the back of her neck and supported her arm while he pulled the top into place, then reconnected the sling and made sure her arm was properly seated in it. She ground her teeth, hard, to avoid hissing with the pain, but it subsided once her arm was still again.

"Thank you." She lifted her feet as he held the pants and pulled them up to her knees. "I can take it from here, since I'm going commando," she told him. He backed off and looked away again. "What time did Kelsey call?"

"Nearly an hour ago," he said. "She's probably halfway here."

"We need to get moving." She shoved her feet into the rubber flip-flops and headed for the door.

"You need to be discharged," he said.

Regan stopped and stared over her shoulder. "Kelsey is in danger, and you think I want to bother with paperwork? You're a Goody Two-Shoes, Sloane."

He shrugged and held the door as she went through. "I guess."

Regan walked as fast as she could past the nurses' station. The nurses there didn't even look up. The elevator doors opened right away, and Tyler barely got through before she punched the "close" button inside. She stared at the numbers as they ticked down, wishing it didn't feel so much like ticking toward doomsday.

Alan. Oh, Alan. Any strength she had held on to drained as she remembered. For the first time in years, tears rolled down her cheeks. It was her fault he was dead. If she hadn't let down her guard, he wouldn't even have been in the house when they came after her.

"Hey." Tyler's hand landed on her good shoulder, squeezing gently. "You okay?"

She sucked it up, pulled it all inside and shrugged him off. But she didn't answer. How could she?

"Did anyone call Alan's mom?" she asked.

"The police will take care of it."

She nodded. The elevator dinged and the doors opened. She let Tyler go through first, since he knew where his pickup was parked. She remained silent as they walked to the truck and exited the parking garage.

"Do you want to go home first?" Tyler asked. She gave him a look. "No. Okay, then." He aimed for the on ramp for the highway toward Whetstone.

The road was just as dark and deserted as it had been when she drove it last time, in the opposite direction, after leaving Kelsey at school. Where it had been lonely but comforting then, it was sinister now.

"Is your phone on?" she asked.

"I think so." He angled his hip up. "You can check."

Regan slid her hand into the pocket of his khakis. She had to push aside awareness of warm skin and hard muscle on the other side of the thin fabric while she pulled out the phone. It was on, but there was no signal. "Dammit."

He glanced down, then back at the road. "Keep an eye on it. We're probably just in a dead spot."

Regan split her attention between the phone and the sparse oncoming traffic, trying to spot Kelsey and Tom, even though she had no idea what they were driving. How could she not have asked everything possible about her daughter's boyfriend? How could she not have anticipated this?

"Stop beating yourself up, Regan."

Easy for him to say. "Do you have family, Tyler?"

"A brother. Jackson works in DC, travels a lot. We're closer than we should be, for as little as we see each other." He glanced at her. "I have an inkling of what you're going through, Regan. I don't have kids, but I do understand."

He sounded sincere, but she wasn't confident of her ability to read him. "Who are you? And what do you know about these guys?"

He shook his head slowly, not looking at her. "I can't tell you. I'm sorry."

"What *can* you tell me?"

"Not much you don't already know."

"Let's hear it anyway."

His jaw pulsed. "Fine. Your name wasn't always Regan Miller. Before you changed it in Illinois eighteen years ago, it was Chelsea Conrad." He stopped a second. "Why Regan, anyway? It's not a very common name."

She shrugged impatiently. "I was barely nineteen. I thought 'Jane Smith' would be too obvious, and I wanted something I liked." She nudged his arm to continue.

"You went to Blaydes Academy, where you met Scott Harrison, who got you pregnant. When he went to tell his parents, some people they were working with—"

Regan gasped. Tyler stopped talking. "Go on," she urged.

"Some people they were working with found out about your pregnancy. They were going to send someone to get you, and Scott tried to stop them, tried to get away." He glanced at her. "After Kelsey was born—"

"Wait. Who stopped him? Who was coming to get me? Why? Why did they kill him?" She turned in her seat, eager for answers she'd long abandoned hope of getting, but already frustrated at the gaps in his recitation.

"I can't tell you," he repeated.

She scowled. "Can't, or won't?"

"Can't. I don't know."

"How can you know what you just said and not know the rest?"

His jaw flexed again.

"You recite facts like you're reading a mission file," she accused. "Am I your mission?"

He didn't answer.

"Who assigned you?"

No answer.

"Who are these people?"

His jaw unlocked. "I only know they want Kelsey. I don't know who they are or why they want her."

Her soul screamed at the thought. "How do you even know that?"

"I was told."

"How do I know you're telling the truth? Maybe you led them to us. I mean, if you've known all along who I am…"

"I didn't lead them to you." His voice rang with truth, stated with the first hint of emotion he'd displayed since he started talking.

"Where were you all week?" To her knowledge, he'd never left his house for that long before.

"I was called in to report." His jaw had tightened again. He didn't like what had happened, but she wasn't sure why. Maybe he'd been pulled to give her attackers a chance to move in. Maybe it was just bad timing and they hadn't even known he was there. Maybe he'd left because he didn't want any part of what was going to happen. She had no way to be sure. There was no point in asking him, because he'd either not tell her, or lie.

She looked down at the phone. There was a signal. She immediately dialed Kelsey's cell phone, but got her voice mail again.

"Kels, it's Mom. Please, call me again. Tell me where you are. We're coming to get you. We're at…" She stared at the guardrail until a mile marker came up, and read it off. "Don't go home. Don't go to the hospital. I'm not there. If you've passed where I am, go to the police. Officer Boyse is the one handling our case. Please, Kelsey, call me." She hung up and hit the button for voice mail.

"What's your code?"

Tyler didn't hesitate to give it to her—probably trying to win her trust. There was one message, the old one, and Regan's throat closed when she heard her daughter's voice. She sounded apprehensive but determined, and Regan had to swallow an involuntary noise. She wouldn't call it a sob. She couldn't be less strong than her daughter was.

But there were no new messages. She tried not to think of why that might be, and stared down the long road into the darkness.

VAN, DRIVING, CURSED a blue streak as sirens approached behind them. Hoping it was an ambulance, Kelsey looked over her shoulder, holding her breath. But it was a cop car. She remembered her mother telling her she'd been pulled over on the way home after dropping her at school.

"Maybe you have a tail light out," she said.

"Maybe I was doin' eighty." Van pulled over.

Tom, in the back seat with Kelsey, unhooked her seatbelt and slid her across the seat to the center of the car. "Just in case," he told her. He climbed over her to sit behind Van, putting himself between Kelsey and the cop who was walking up alongside the car.

"That's an unmarked car," Kelsey said, studying the vehicle. The flashing lights were in the dash instead of on top, and the dark sedan, which was angled to block their car from oncoming traffic, had no side markings. "Could not be cops."

"There are two of them," Van muttered, rolling down her window with the crank. "One's on your side, Kels."

Tom tightened his grip on her shoulder.

"Please step out of the car, ma'am," said the man at Van's window.

"What seems to be the problem, Officer?" Van asked in as deferential a voice as Kelsey had ever heard from her. She kept both hands on the steering wheel but didn't move to get out of the car.

"Please step out of the vehicle," he repeated. He bent to peer into the back seat. He had a trooper hat on, but Kelsey couldn't see his uniform clearly. "All of you, please."

Van looked back at Kelsey. She shrugged and nodded, not knowing what else to do. Maybe her mom had called the state police, or the local police put out a BOLO or something. Van eased open her door. Tom did the same, blocking Kelsey with his body as she got out behind him. They all remained behind their car doors.

The cop scanned Van up and down, eyed Tom, and moved to the side to examine Kelsey.

"Kelsey Miller?"

Adrenaline flooded her. This guy was either a cop sent by her mother, or one of the bad guys. She knew better than to trust blindly. But she couldn't say no, in case he was a real cop.

"Yes."

"Please come with us. Your mother's been hurt and sent us to get you. She was concerned."

"Where is she?"

"She's safe. Please come with me." He moved to take Kelsey's arm. She tried to step back but the car was in her way. Tom shifted to block the officer, who glared at him.

"You want to be getting back in your car, sir, and going on your way." He looked at Van. "You, too, ma'am."

No way. "They have to come with me," Kelsey said. "Where is my mother?"

"She's in the hospital. She'll be fine. But she's very concerned about you, and she'll be better if she knows you're safe."

"I'll call her." She flipped open her phone and pressed the "on" button, fidgeting as it started powering up. She'd shut it off to save the battery, and hoped it had enough juice for a call.

The officer reached over and took it out of her hand. "She's not reachable at the moment. She's in surgery." He turned the phone off and handed it back. "We need to leave now."

Kelsey didn't want to go. She turned to look at the man behind the vehicle, who'd so far been silent and unmoving. He had the same hat, but his uniform wasn't the same as the first cop's. The colors were off. Alarm bells clanged in her head, but she wasn't sure what to do. If they fought or ran and these were real cops, they could be in trouble.

"What's your unit number?" she asked the silent one, trying to buy time.

"Four six three two, ma'am."

Uh-uh. Unit numbers were two digits. These guys were definitely not state police.

"I'm sorry, I'd rather just go with my friends to the hospital where my mother is," she told them. "Thank you for your time. Which hospital is she in?"

The "cops" looked at each other. "St. Rosa's," said the one in the back.

"Why is she there? Municipal is closer to our house."

"She wasn't at home," the first one said, and now Kelsey knew they were lying. Her caller ID had shown their home number.

She leaned close to Tom and tilted her head to whisper in his ear. "I can't go with them."

That was all he needed. He pulled back the door he was holding and slammed it forward. Despite his short range, it smacked the cop in the torso hard enough to knock him back.

Van had been ready, too. She swung her field hockey stick out of the car and slammed it into the back of the cop's head. He fell sideways, and Tom shoved him down.

Kelsey was aware of this only peripherally. She expected the other guy to go for a gun, and as soon as Tom moved, she jumped out from behind him, heading for the rear of the car. The "cop" was crouching, pulling the gun from its holster, when she jumped onto the trunk and pushed herself across it, aiming at him with both feet. She hit him in the shoulder and neck. He yelled and went down. Kelsey slid down onto him, pressing his face into the macadam. He couldn't bring his gun around to shoot her, but he lifted it a few inches off the ground and aimed behind her. Where Tom was. Kelsey screamed and lunged for his arm, but he fired. Not at Tom, but into the tire.

Tom kicked the gun out of the guy's hand. It slid under the car, which now listed to the rear left. They weren't going anywhere in that.

"Let's go." Tom swung Kelsey's backpack up onto his shoulder and took her elbow, leading her into the strip of woods bordering the highway. Van followed, her field hockey stick tight in her grip, her own backpack already on her back.

"Where are we going?" Van gasped, dodging tree trunks and leaping roots.

"Away," was all Kelsey could say. She had no idea where they were. "Just someplace where we can hide and I can call my mom."

"Man, I hope those weren't real cops." Tom grunted, pushing Kelsey a little ahead of him. "We're in a hell of a lot of trouble if they were."

"They weren't." She was certain of it. "Wait." They all stopped abruptly. She listened, trying to calm her breathing. They could hear the men crashing through the underbrush, clearly headed in their direction. "Let's go that way," she said, pointing left. "Get out of their path. We've got to be quiet, too."

"Yeah, right," Van and Tom both said. They headed the way she'd pointed, and moved a little more slowly with a little less noise. The dried leaves underfoot made it impossible, but if they were lucky, the men behind them made enough noise to cover theirs.

After they'd gone a few hundred yards, she aimed them back toward the far side of the woods. The strip bordering the highway wouldn't be very wide, and sure enough, they soon emerged onto a big empty cornfield, shorn for the season.

"Dammit. We could have hidden in there," Kelsey muttered. Now there was no cover. Also, no farmhouse or barn or any other kind of building that might have a telephone.

Tom squinted as he scanned the darkness. "Let's just follow the tree line." He pointed to the left. "We can move faster, and duck into the woods if we need cover."

Kelsey agreed, having no better idea. They started running again, hugging the edge of the woods. Van took the lead, with Tom behind Kelsey. She knew they were bracketing her on purpose, to protect her. She hated to put them through this, but was so grateful, too. She would never have a chance if they weren't with her.

"You okay?" she asked Van, who was running at an easy lope now.

"Sure. This is nothin' compared to an hour of field hockey."

Kelsey knew Tom ran miles every day, too, for football. She, herself, conditioned every day. She briefly wished soccer was the only reason she was in shape. But all those years of paranoia hadn't been unwarranted. There were people after her. She wished she knew why.

Add it to the list. Where was her mother? How badly was she hurt? Who was after them, and what made her so important that they hadn't given up after eighteen years? The urge to call Tyler's phone again grew so strong her step faltered. Tom bumped into her and caught her shoulders before she fell.

"You okay?"

"Fine."

He held her for a second. Van stopped a short way ahead and leaned on her stick, panting. Kelsey looked around, wishing for better light. She couldn't see if there was any place to hide.

The noise behind them had receded. She couldn't tell where their pursuers were.

"Maybe they've given up," Van offered.

"No. They won't give up." She may not know much about what was happening to her, but she did know that.

"Stop!"

Tyler slammed on the brakes and skidded onto the shoulder. Regan shoved her door open and ran across the road to the center median, stymied by the cement wall and her shoulder. Tyler caught up to her after a few seconds.

"What the hell?"

"Look."

He followed her eager gaze to the cars across the road. One, an old Chevy, was sitting with its doors open and a rear tire flat. The one behind it was a plain dark sedan, but Regan could see there were lights in the dash. They weren't on. And no one was around.

"Help me over." She swung a leg up as Tyler grabbed her waist and hefted her on top of the wall. She sat, aimed, and slid off the other side, landing on her feet and running to the cars.

Both doors on the Chevy's driver's side were open and the keys were still in the ignition. She slid into the front seat and looked around, but it was empty.

"This might not be theirs," Tyler cautioned, leaning into the back seat to look under the rugs. "It's empty back here."

Regan opened the glove compartment and grabbed the only thing in it, a white envelope with a blank face. She fumbled it open. The registration inside was to Donald Leigh.

"It's theirs. The car belongs to Van or one of her relatives. Where are they?" She struggled back out of the car and looked around. There were scuff marks in the gravel. She looked up as a car passed them. They could have been taken in a third vehicle, but it didn't seem likely unless the one behind theirs was disabled.

"I think they went into the woods," she told Tyler, praying it wasn't a mother's foolish hope driving her thoughts, "but please see if that car is working." She motioned with her chin. "If not, they might have been taken in another one."

While Tyler went to the sedan, Regan stepped to the edge of the shoulder, looking into the woods. A trail through the tall grass could have been made by people, and a couple of branches at different spots along the edge of the trees were bent.

"It seems fine," Tyler called to her. He joined her on the roadside. "It's not a cop car."

"Great." She took a deep breath. *She's okay. She's got to be.* "We have to follow them. It looks like they might have taken off and been chased. God, I hope they weren't caught."

"Don't think about that." He helped her down the short slope to the grassy ditch and let go as soon as they were on level ground.

She started trotting, but pain flared through the cut on her hip and her jarred shoulder. The flip-flops weren't helping, either. "I'll never catch up like this."

"Let me scout ahead," Tyler offered. "You follow best you can. I'll pick out their trail so we don't have to backtrack or anything."

"You can track?" It was one of the few things she hadn't learned how to do. She'd never thought she'd be doing the chasing.

"Sure. Military training." He smiled and headed off. She followed as quickly as she could, listening to his progress.

The phone in her hand beeped. The battery was dying. Why hadn't she asked if he had a charger? They could have been charging it as they drove. She looked at it, torn, and finally shut it off. It might be necessary later.

"This way." Tyler's soft call barely carried to her. He did know what he was doing. The bad guys would have to be very close to have heard him. She angled left and caught up to him a moment later.

"Whoever was following them is good," he said. "They veered off their initial path, and it wasn't obvious, but the two guys following them saw it. They have training."

"Same kind of training you have?" she couldn't help asking.

He hesitated. "Maybe."

Just great. He could be leading her into a trap. Not that it mattered, if Kelsey was there. She'd do anything to get to her daughter right now. "Let's keep going."

Tyler took off again. Regan sucked in a deep breath and picked up her pace. Every step took her closer to Kelsey. She had no choice but to push through the pain.

Despite all her training, all her preparation, she'd never had to do this. It was much harder than she'd thought it would be. But dammit, the wherewithal to do it was inside her. She just had to dredge it up.

THERE WAS NOTHING. They'd struggled along the tree line for what felt like forever, but all they found was more trees. They probably hadn't gone as far as it felt like, but exhaustion swept over Kelsey. This wasn't working. She stopped and put her hands on her knees. "We can't just keep running," she panted.

Van collapsed on the ground beside her. "What else we gonna do?" Kelsey knew Van was tired or she would have said a hell of a lot more.

"Circle back," said Tom. They looked up at him. He was leaning against a tree, watching behind them. "Cut back through the woods to the highway, follow the verge back to their car. Maybe we can take it."

"That's brilliant," Kelsey said. "But what if they kept their keys?"

He shrugged. "I don't know what else we can do. Some of these farms out here are huge, and there are a lot of miles between exits. We could run until we die of exposure."

He was exaggerating, but she knew he was right. "If there are no keys we can try to flag someone down. But we have to be careful."

Van struggled to her feet. Her efforts were showing, with her hair flattened and dripping with sweat, and her shirt torn in two places by branches.

"I'm sorry, you guys. I never meant to drag you into something like this." Despair threatened to engulf Kelsey. "If anything happens to you…"

"Shut up." Tom closed his hand over the back of her neck. "Let's go." He pointed into the woods. "There's a deer trail. Run full out, and stay together."

"Okay. You okay?" she asked Van, who nodded and clutched her stick.

They ran, the trail blissfully smooth, though narrow. The strip of woods was thicker here, but Kelsey could see a flicker of passing headlights. They were almost through when Kelsey heard a shout. She cursed as they all staggered to a halt, not sure where the shout came from, which way they should go.

"They saw us," Van gasped.

"Just run." Kelsey pushed them ahead of her on the path and sprinted behind them. Hopefully, their pursuers would just follow, not figure out their plan and angle back through the woods, cutting them off.

Please, God, let them be stupid.

FIVE

KELSEY, TOM AND Van made it to the road but stopped inside the trees. They couldn't see or hear anyone else, but by now their gasping for air sounded like a bull pen. Kelsey's lungs burned in her chest...or maybe that burning was fear.

Tom pulled himself up the short bank to the shoulder. He peered around, then turned to look down on the girls. "I don't see anything up here." He held a hand to pull Van, then Kelsey, up to the roadside.

"Where are the cars?" Kelsey looked for herself when she reached the street. She could barely make out the vehicles down the road. There were no human shapes between them and the car. She started trotting along the gravel shoulder, much slower than she'd started, worn out from running.

"Kelsey!"

The shout made her jump. She didn't consciously recognize the voice, but turned almost automatically. She could make out three figures, two wearing dark clothing, one farther back in a light-colored shirt. Judging by distance, the man in the light shirt was the one who had called her name. The other two were probably the "cops" chasing them.

One of the two in the middle turned back, toward

the other man, but the other one continued running toward her and her friends.

"You know that guy?" Van pulled at her arm.

"I think…" But she didn't have time to think. The fake cop started to hit the man with his billy club, and the other one came closer to them, pulling something from his hip. A gun?

"Go, go, go!" Tom yelled, pushing both Van and Kelsey ahead of him. Adrenaline gave them new speed, and soon they'd passed their disabled car. Van scrambled into the fake cop car, Tom and Kelsey diving for the back seat. Van cursed when she came up empty at the ignition, and started flipping visors and console compartments. Metal jangled, she whooped, and the car started with a roar. She peeled out before Tom closed the door.

Kelsey stared through the side window, trying to see what was happening as they passed. The "cop" who'd been after them was braced as if he had a weapon.

"Duck!" she yelled.

The car swerved as Van obeyed, her foot still to the floor. Something pinged off the roof. They all lifted their heads a little, Kelsey and Tom peering through the rear window.

"I think we're clear," Tom said.

Van sighed and sat up straight. "Good, 'cause I can barely see over the wheel already, never mind when I'm dodging bullets." She glanced over her shoulder and let the car slow a little. The others couldn't follow in the damaged Chevy. "You know that other guy?" she asked again.

"I'm not sure." Kelsey paused to buckle her seatbelt with shaking hands. Tom put his arm around her and squeezed reassuringly as she leaned against his shoulder. "I think it might have been Tyler. Our neighbor. It was his cell phone number my mom gave me." She looked around. "This doesn't look like a cop car." There was no grate between the front and back, and the back doors had handles.

Tom bent to open the backpack he had set at his feet. "We'd better charge your phone."

"Yeah." While Tom pulled the charger free of the mess inside her backpack, Kelsey reached into her pocket. Her empty pocket.

"Shit." The back of her throat stung. She blinked furiously, trying not to let the tears make it to her eyes. It was stupid to cry now, after they'd gotten away. Even stupider to cry in front of Tom.

"What's the matter?" He leaned forward to look at her, and she swiped at her cheeks.

"My phone's gone. I must have dropped it when we were running."

"It's okay, I've got mine," Van said, holding it up. "It's mostly charged."

"Call now. Maybe she'll answer," Tom added soothingly.

"I can't. I don't know the number. I programmed it in the first time and forgot it."

Her friends didn't say anything. They didn't need to. The silence pressed down on Kelsey until she felt immobilized. She didn't have time to give in to it, though. They neared an exit, well lit. Other cars were merging onto the road.

"On or off?" Van asked.

Kelsey wavered, glancing at Tom.

"Traffic is still really light," he said. "Hard to get lost up here."

They're counting on you. "Okay, off. Get away from the highway. We'll call the police at home and find out what's going on." She didn't know what came next. She wanted her mother, needed to know she was all right, but was afraid to go home. They'd be waiting.

She leaned back, exhausted, letting Tom keep lookout behind them.

One step at a time.

REGAN BROKE OUT of the trees onto a cornfield, struggling to see in the meager glow of light reflecting off the clouds. Tyler was dozens of yards away, along the tree line. At least, she thought it was him. He moved like Tyler. But as she started in his direction, she saw two more shadows duck into the woods ahead of him. God, was it Kelsey? Was she running from Tyler? Ignoring the shoulder ache and blazing knife wounds, she kicked off the flip-flops and started running as fast as she could. Which was about as fast as a turbo-charged snail.

Shit. She'd never catch up. She couldn't tell where they'd re-entered the woods, but they had to be heading for the road. She ducked between trees, held her right arm out in front of her to block branches, and prayed not to trip over anything.

She came out of the woods again, this time in a deep ditch. There was no way she'd get up to the road here. She listened. No more shouts. No running footsteps. She had no idea where anyone else was, or who'd been chasing whom.

Panic threatened to overwhelm her until she battled it back with clenched fists and sheer determination. Then she began slogging through muddy water in the bottom of the ditch, looking for a place where the slope was gentle enough for her to climb out. Scant minutes had passed when she heard a shout that might have been Tyler. A moment later a car roared by. She froze, listening. There was a sound like a gunshot, then more shouts. Then silence.

Cursing, she grabbed a root with her right hand and tried to pull herself up the few feet to the verge. Her shoulder screamed, and she felt the cut on her hip split open. Her right foot slipped in the wet dirt, but her left foot held, and she managed to roll onto the grass. A couple of cars flashed by. One braked briefly, then kept going. Regan wondered what they thought they saw.

She started to rise, then caught her breath and flattened herself into the grass. Two men stood arguing by the Chevy. The other car was gone. She was too far away, her view blocked by the center barrier, to see if Tyler's truck was still there.

The men started walking toward her. There was no way they wouldn't see her lying there. There was no time to consider. She inched slowly sideways, watching the men, who walked with their heads down. One appeared to be on a cell phone, though he wasn't yet close enough for her to hear him.

Moving slowly made her heart nearly burst with pent-up adrenaline, but fast movement would definitely be seen. She reached the ditch when they were about fifty feet away and slid feet first into it, bending her knees to keep her head out of sight. She pressed tight to the dirt wall and tried to breathe silently. Her pulse pounded at every pulse point, the throb in her ears almost loud enough to drown out everything else.

Footsteps came nearer, crunching on gravel, and she could hear voices.

"Yes, sir, I understand. I never thought they'd—" A moment of silence. "I wasn't driving, sir. I didn't leave the keys in the car."

"Bastard," another voice muttered. "I should shoot you right now."

The men passed Regan with a few more "yes, sirs" from the guy on the phone and unintelligible grumbling from his partner. She stayed where she was for several minutes, giving them time to get further down the road. Then she walked along the ditch until it rose to near ground level, about ten feet in front of the abandoned Chevy. She walked to the car, wincing with each step as stones cut into her feet.

Tyler's truck wasn't across the road anymore. He'd likely driven to the next exit to turn around. She hoped he hadn't passed her already. But wouldn't he have stopped to look for her?

Not if he thought getting rid of her was a better option. Or if he didn't need her anymore, now that he knew what Kelsey was driving.

She stared at the black screen on his phone, debating whether to turn it on or not. She could call the police and get picked up, maybe update the APB on her daughter. She hadn't gotten a good enough look at the other car, though. Idiot. She looked to her right, the direction Kelsey had to be going in when they took the bad guys' car. Then she looked to her left, the direction Tyler would be coming from. Assuming he was okay and hadn't left her.

Headlights appeared out of a dip in the road, approaching fast. She thought about hiding in the car, just in case, but was too wiped out to move. She watched warily as the vehicle slowed and pulled over. By the time it stopped, she recognized Tyler's truck and managed to limp to the passenger door.

"Thank God you're all right," she and Tyler said at the same time. Regan froze with her hand on the door handle, surprised at the sentiment not from him, but from herself. If he was working against her but wanted her to think otherwise, he'd pretend to care she was okay. But her unguarded reaction to seeing him, a leaf in his hair and a bruise on his cheek but otherwise looking strong and capable, made no sense. She didn't trust him.

Did she?

"Get in."

She yanked the door open and climbed into the cab, which was awkward with her left arm disabled.

She slammed the door and reached for the sling clip, but Tyler stopped her. His hand was warm and rough, and pissed her off because his touch calmed her. As if she were a high-strung horse.

"Don't undo it. You'll make it worse."

She left the sling alone. "Tell me what happened."

Tyler put his hand back on the wheel. "I think Kelsey and her friends got away. There were two people chasing them. Cops." He glanced at her.

"Or not."

"Right. I figure Kelsey wouldn't be on the run if she believed they were real. I shouted a warning and the guys split up, one trying to take me on, the other chasing the kids. The kids made it to the other car and took off."

"How long ago?" She'd heard the car go by, but had lost all sense of real time.

Tyler didn't look happy. "About fifteen minutes ago. We won't catch them. Look out."

Regan saw them at the same time he spoke. The fake cops, trudging along the side of the road. She slid down and back until the doorjamb hid her face but she could still see them. One had the gall to turn and stick out his thumb.

"You want to stop and confront them?" Tyler asked.

"No. Keep going." Tyler might be able to over-power both of them, but not if they were armed, and she was in no shape to help.

A green exit sign flashed past. Two miles. Regan tried to think. Would Kelsey go home, or pull off here? They were driving a stolen car. The road was pretty deserted this late at night—nearly early morning now. She lifted the phone to call her and find out where she was, remembered it was nearly dead, and looked down to see the charger dangling from the lighter socket.

"Thank goodness," she breathed. She plugged the phone in and thumbed it on. It took forever to boot up. The one-mile sign flashed by. "Come on, come on." The main screen flashed on. She hit the buttons to find and dial Kelsey's number and lifted the phone to her ear.

"Hello?"

The voice was deep, too deep to be a college student's. But Regan was so shocked to hear it, she didn't think of that right away. "Is this Tom?"

The hesitation was too long. "Who's this?"

Regan's brain caught up with her mouth. "Who's this?"

"Regan?"

Dammit. She didn't answer.

"This is Tom. We're okay."

"Is Van with you?"

"Yes. She's fine. Where are you?"

"If this is Tom, tell me what Kelsey did to you the day you met."

Another long hesitation, without the "uhs" or "ums" or confused stammering that might result from such an unexpected question.

"She spilled her drink on me."

"Wrong answer, asshole." She punched the off button viciously, wishing she could slam the phone down.

"What's going on?"

"He has her phone." The exit sign came up, and she made a quick decision. "Get off here."

"Who has her phone? Her boyfriend?" He signaled and zoomed down the off ramp.

"Not hardly. Tried to make me believe it, though. He can't have Kelsey with him—you said you saw the kids getting into the car and driving away by themselves. She must have lost her phone."

Tyler braked at the light at the end of the ramp. "Someone else might have caught up with them."

"Don't pull any punches, do you, Sloane?" She craned her neck, looking around. There were half a dozen gas stations and fast food restaurants, places where there would be people and phones and a spot to rest. But they were too visible. She'd taught Kelsey better than that.

"Where next?"

The light turned green, and Regan didn't know how to answer him. She was so tired, so sore, she couldn't think. Everything in her screamed to find her daughter, but going in circles without any clue to guide her would only drain her minimal resources.

"There." She pointed to the red roof of a motel just off the highway.

"Good," Tyler murmured, maneuvering into the right lane. He didn't say anything more, and Regan was glad. It shamed her to stop the search, even temporarily. They were so close.

Except maybe they weren't. Maybe Kelsey hadn't gotten off the highway at all. If she hadn't, their paths were diverging once again.

Regan waited in the car for Tyler at the motel, her mind racing. She'd told him to give a false name and use cash, even though whoever was after her and Kelsey shouldn't know she was with Tyler. If Tyler was working with her pursuers, they already knew where he was. Right now, Regan didn't care. She didn't know where her daughter was, so she was no help to the enemy. At worst, they'd finish the job they'd come to do at her house.

Her door opened and Tyler offered a hand to help her out of the truck.

"Our room is right here, next to the office."

One room? She didn't say it out loud. He was spending his own money to help her. It was presumptuous to expect him to pay for two rooms. Still…

"Next to the office isn't a good idea."

He shrugged. "Not much choice. Anyway, the walls are paper thin. We should be able to hear anyone who asks about us. You go inside and I'll park the truck at the other end. I saw a space down there."

Regan swiveled and slid off the seat, ignoring his hand. "When did you become an expert at on-the-run tactics?"

He just smiled enigmatically and took her good elbow, holding it loosely in case she needed to lean on him. He released her at the door, handed her a key card, and turned back to the truck without waiting to make sure she got inside.

Regan couldn't help smiling at the line he was trying to walk. Hell, maybe he really was just a nice neighbor helping her out and struggling not to be autocratic.

She went inside and immediately called the police at home, using the landline and a prepaid calling card number she'd memorized. The clerk said they had no new information and addressed her rather coldly, as if they didn't believe her story anymore.

"Where are you, Ms. Miller?"

Keys tapped in the background. Were they tracing her call? How long was safe to stay on the line?

"I'd appreciate if you'd continue looking for my daughter," she said. "She's in a new vehicle, a dark sedan. I don't know the make," she added reluctantly. "But she seems to still be with her friends."

"Please hold, Ms. Miller. We have a call coming in from your daughter now."

A click led to electronica music. Regan listened, torn. It could be a ruse, trying to keep her on the line to trace the call. Or it could be legitimate. She held. Word about Kelsey was worth the risk. She closed her eyes and prayed until the door opened and Tyler came in. He raised an eyebrow.

She shook her head. "I'm on hold with the police. They say Kelsey's calling— Yes, I'm here."

"Ms. Miller, your daughter refuses to tell us where she is, only that she's safe at the moment. She gave us a number to give you."

"Hang on." Relief made her fingers clumsy as she grabbed at the pen on the table between the beds. She tore a piece of paper off the little pad so what she wrote wouldn't impress the pages below it. "Okay, go ahead."

The woman rattled off the number. "We're canceling the APB on Kelsey Miller, ma'am. It doesn't seem she's in any danger and the resources of this department—"

"Yeah, whatever, thanks." Regan hung up, not regretting her sarcasm. They'd been no help at all, except as a relay service. She quickly dialed the number Kelsey had provided, using Tyler's phone this time, and held her breath.

"Hey, it's Van. I know, I hate voice mail too, but you know how it goes. Leave a message."

Regan could hardly speak past the swelling in her throat. "Van, it's Regan. Kelsey's mom. The police gave me this number, said you had just called them. Please, please, call me back." She relayed Tyler's phone number again, even though caller ID should capture it. "As soon as you can." She waited foolishly, as if Van would pick up, and slowly folded the phone closed. Since Van's number was now in Tyler's phone, she got up and flushed the paper, then returned to the bed, unable to stand very long.

Tyler seemed to have gotten the gist of the conversation, because he didn't ask. He took the phone out of Regan's hand and set it on the nightstand.

"I'm going to run across the street. There are a bunch of stores over there. Should be an all-night superstore or someplace I can get you some clothes."

Regan tried to look up at him, but her head didn't want to tilt. "Thank you, Tyler. I'll pay you back."

"Don't worry about it. It won't be designer stuff." He walked back to the door. "I know you need a shower, but don't take one until I come back. I want to be here in case you pass out."

"I'm fine."

"No, you're not." Before she could protest any more, he was gone.

She would have defied him, just to do it. But her body sagged sideways onto the bed, and she couldn't get up. Immediately, the sheer nerve she'd been running on refused to bear her weight anymore. Her eyes closed and darkness descended.

It was a short reprieve. Regan jolted to consciousness and whipped her gaze around the room, looking for the disruption that had awakened her. Everything looked the same. The bathroom door was open, the light off. Tyler wasn't back. She hadn't been asleep long. The digital clock said it was just before four in the morning.

The curtains hung undisturbed, and the main door was tightly closed. But her heart pounded, her breathing rushed, readying her to fight or fly. She inhaled slowly, trying to calm herself. Maybe the jolt had only been a reaction to the last several hours.

Then she heard it.

The rumble of voices came through the far wall, the one the room shared with the office. She couldn't distinguish words, but could hear enough to tell there were three people. The night desk clerk and two men, she guessed.

Rising slowly, mindful of her knotted muscles, she crossed to the AC intake vent on the wall and carefully slid the lever to open it. The voices instantly became clearer.

"I'm telling you, I'm not allowed to give out that information." That had to be the clerk, an elderly black woman Regan had seen through the office window when Tyler checked in.

"And I'm telling you, this badge and the extension of the Patriot Act require you to give it."

"Puh-leeze. If those two are terrorists, I'm God's mama."

Regan sighed wearily. She appreciated the woman's resistance, but she'd just confirmed their presence.

"It's not for you to decide if they are or not, ma'am. Now, please tell us what room they're in before we arrest you for obstructing justice."

The woman's response was drowned out by the rumble of a vehicle turning into the parking lot and moving past the window. Regan recognized Tyler's engine and hoped he'd be alert enough to spot the men in the office. The rumble faded as the truck kept moving.

"Hey. There he is."

Shit. Regan hurried to the window, peering through a slit in the curtains just as the two "cops" came out of the office and hurried past. She waited a minute before slipping out the door, leaving it open behind her so it wouldn't make noise closing. The men didn't turn, and there was no sign of Tyler's truck.

Regan turned to the right and hobbled around the end of the building the other way. When she rounded the second corner, Tyler idled next to the walk right in front of her. He spotted her and rolled forward as the fake cops, running now, came around the far end. They shouted. Pointlessly, as Regan was already scrambling into the truck. She slammed the door as Tyler took off.

"I swear, I don't know how they found us," he said, making a squealing right turn onto the divided highway. He raced toward the light ahead.

Regan looked behind them to see if the fake cops had a vehicle, but the road remained empty save for a tractor-trailer turning off the main highway. She didn't say anything. Kelsey's cell phone number was in Tyler's phone memory. He could have called his buddies to tell them the hotel room Regan was in. His rescue could have been an attempt to get her to lower her guard.

The part of her that was weakening didn't believe it. If he'd called them, why show up and rescue her yet again? *He could still be trying to "prove" his loyalty because he needs Kelsey.* That was logical, too, but it was just as likely the men had simply stopped at the first motel they saw.

"Where to now?" Tyler asked, slowing as they approached the next light.

Regan still watched behind them. A car soared out

of the hotel parking lot, bouncing at the dip where entry met road, and headed their way.

"Circle back to the highway," she said. "They're coming."

Tyler floored it and squealed into a U-turn, the truck's heavy hind end resisting the move, as the light turned red. Regan slid all over the slick seat before righting herself and grabbing the seat belt.

"Sorry."

"Get on the ramp going back to where we were," she instructed, shoving the belt into the latch with her right hand. It was becoming easier to compensate for the sling, but she still wished she could get rid of it.

"Don't you think it would be easier to lose them on surface streets?"

"Yes. But do as I said."

He did, and just as they got to the top of the ramp, before it curved right to merge, she said, "Cut left."

Tyler didn't question her this time. The truck plowed over a tall, narrow reflector that *pingping-pinged* against the undercarriage. Then they were jouncing over rough terrain at top speed.

"Down there." Regan pointed to the lower road, then put her hand on the ceiling to keep from hitting her head as they bounced. "Then make the next left, through the shopping center."

Once they were in the parking lot, she chanced a look over her shoulder again. The car that had flown out of the motel parking lot was stuck off the road at the top of the ramp, unmoving. She assumed the little tires had gotten caught in the soft earth, maybe even in the churned-up tracks from Tyler's truck.

"Get out of their line of sight," she told Tyler. "Angle away from the highway and keep driving. I have to think."

Something that was getting harder and harder to do.

SIX

"WHAT KIND OF network do you belong to, anyway?"
Kelsey cursed, pacing and checking the signal on
Van's phone every few steps, knowing full well the
lack of bars wasn't going to change.

Cursing herself, too. She'd screwed up. When they
got off the highway she'd directed them into a quiet
residential area, figuring the fake cops would expect
them to stick with bright lights and retail traffic. But
none of them had checked the gas gauge, and they'd
run out of gas a few miles from the highway.

She'd called the police back home, who at first
claimed they knew nothing but then told her they
had her mother on the other line. She'd started crying and had barely been able to give them Van's number. But before her mother could call her back, the
car had sputtered to a stop in a pocket with no signal
for the phone.

Van managed to get the vehicle to the side of the
road. Tom found a gas can in the trunk and headed off
to fill it—assuming he could find a gas station open at
four in the morning. He'd been gone a while, and the
tension of waiting made Kelsey want to puke. While
Van dozed on the front seat, she'd walked a couple
of blocks in each direction trying to get a signal, to

no avail. They were sitting ducks with no protection and no way, still, to contact her mother.

She desperately wanted her mother.

Not just because terror was digging in and she was frantic to hand over the controls to someone. Not just because that same terror tried to convince her that her mother was dead, or mortally wounded, or abducted. But because her mother was the one with answers.

Since her mother's call, she'd been reacting, thinking ahead, looking forward. Not back. But since Tom had left and all she could do was pace here, worrying, she'd had time to entertain the parade of questions that had been warming up, ready to march through her skull. What the hell was happening, and why?

"You should be resting," Van grumbled through the car's open window. "You're gonna call attention to us."

"No one's up." But Van was right. She had to calm down and be the person her mother had trained her to be. They should be ready, with a plan, as soon as Tom returned with gas.

In the dark stillness an engine approached, sounding as if it was moving slowly. Kelsey froze. "Van."

"What?"

"Get out of the car."

"Why?"

"Someone's coming."

"So get in here and hide."

"They might recognize the car. Come *on*." She yanked open the door and pulled her roommate out by the sleeve.

"All right! Geez. Where are we going?"

Kelsey had cataloged their surroundings while she paced. "There." She pointed to a shed at the rear of a corner property. They raced to it, Kelsey praying it wouldn't be locked. It wasn't, and she exhaled in a gush.

They ducked inside and pulled the door closed. The angle of the door blocked their view, even if they cracked it, and the other side was latched. They didn't have time to undo it without the movement being seen. Kelsey strained to see in the darkness. There was a single small window above her head. She thought she could climb the stack of boxes underneath, if they didn't collapse under her. She tested them and when they held, she gingerly made her way up the stack until she could see through the dirty window. Van braced her leg against the box and her torso against Kelsey, helping her maintain her balance.

"What do you see?" Van whispered.

The car they'd heard rolled slowly by, barely above an idle, and pulled over in front of their stolen car. The streetlight down the block glimmered on the bar on top of the vehicle.

"Shit. It's the cops. The real ones."

"Then let's go! They'll help us!" Van let go of Kelsey. The edge of the box under her right foot crumpled, and she dropped to the cement floor. She caught Van's arm before she opened the door.

"No! How are we going to explain being in here? They won't know anything about my mom or the school. They'll think we're trying to steal or something, and if they take us to the station Tom will never know where we are. He'll be alone."

For a moment she wavered, thinking that might be best for him. If he came back and found them gone, he could put the gas in the car and make his way home, where he'd be safe. Away from her. The police would probably send Van home, too. Then Kelsey could shed the burden of responsibility for her friends. Shed the fear they'd be hurt, or worse, as long as they were with her.

But Van, who'd only known her for a couple of months but seemed to be able to look straight into her head, shrank away from the door and into the darker shadows at the back of the shed.

"Forget it, girlfriend. I'm in this for the long haul. So's Tom."

"Fine." Kelsey hunkered down behind a tarp-covered lawnmower and a kid's battery-powered Jeep. "Don't say you never had the chance to get out of this."

She folded her arms around her knees and listened hard. She heard the squawk of the police radio but no clear words. Two voices, a man's and a woman's, were low but calm. The clear, still, predawn air carried sound well. Kelsey could only make out a phrase here and there, but was afraid to move and give them away.

"…plates stolen in California…local vehicle…call owner?"

"…the tow…and Captain…not…canvass the neighborhood."

Kelsey's heart started to race again. Had he said

they were going to canvass the neighborhood, or that he didn't want to? The woman said something sounding like "abandoned car" and Kelsey held her breath, hoping. A few minutes later she heard two car doors close. The engine didn't start right away.

She tried to plan. If the cops waited for a tow truck and the car got hauled away, they'd be on foot. She and Van would wait for Tom and then they'd have to find their way to another public area where they could lose themselves. That could be a good thing, because the fake cops would still be looking for their car. But it was a very bad thing, because she was exhausted and her friends must be, too. Tom most of all, after walking for miles. Plus…

"Shit," she breathed.

"What?" Van whispered back.

"Our bags."

Van gasped. "Shit."

Their bags were in the car. Kelsey's ID and a couple of emergency credit cards were in a card case in her back pocket. She had Van's phone in her hand. But everything else they'd dragged along was in the car, including her math notebook with her name and dorm address on the inside front cover. She wanted to cry. Her mother never would have let her label stuff. Why hadn't she taken it out of her backpack when she left?

She'd thought she was so tough, so prepared. Especially because she'd believed her mother was crazy. But she wasn't. This was real. People were after her, she had almost no one to trust, and she was making mistake after mistake. Kelsey dropped her head onto her arms and took a deep breath, trying not to fall apart. She didn't have the luxury.

She lost track of how much time passed. It couldn't have been much, because the sky hadn't started to lighten. At least, not what she could see of it through the tiny windows in the shed. After a while there was a sound like a screen door opening, then slapping shut. Scuffing footsteps, maybe in bedroom slippers, scraped across the sidewalk. Then she heard a man's voice.

"What's going on, officers?"

A car door opened but didn't close again. There was clinking, and Kelsey imagined the male cop hitching up his pants, making his belt rattle the handcuffs and stuff hanging from it. But the voice was the woman's.

They must have been on the lawn, closer to the shed, because Kelsey could hear them talking clearly now.

"Do you recognize this car, sir?"

"No. I don't think so. Why?"

"Did you happen to notice when it appeared?"

"Um…" Kelsey imagined him scratching his head. "Nah. Don't think it was there when I let the dog out. 'Bout ten last night. Someone call you about it?"

"You're up early."

"Yeah, I leave for work at five. Early shift. Look, am I in some kind of trouble?"

"No, sir. Thank you for your time." Shoes scratched against concrete.

"Is the car stolen?" the guy from the house asked.

"Best get to work now, sir. Thank you."

"Hey!" The man didn't sound pleased at being given the brush-off. Kelsey smirked.

The police radio squawked again, something about a burglary in progress. The man cop shouted to his partner and started the engine. A moment later the door slammed and the car moved off, fast.

Van started to get up. Kelsey caught and held her until they heard the screen door open and close again. They rose to their feet and edged to the door, cracking it just a little and squinting through.

"Dog," Van whispered, and they closed it quickly again, listening to the animal snuffling around. Praying it didn't sense them in the shed.

It did. First it gave an excited little yip, then a sharper bark. Kelsey wedged her fingers into the trim around the edge of the door to hold it closed. She jumped as the dog started to scratch at the siding, and clung tighter. Van stared at her, eyes wide, lips pressed together. Her chin trembled when they heard the screen open yet again.

"Kinky! What are you doing? Get over here."

Kelsey let out a snort. Kinky? Luckily, the dog's bark covered the sound. His feet rustled against the dry grass.

"Kinky! Come!"

The dog gave one last bark and ran off, receiving praise from his owner. Kelsey covered her mouth to hold in her laughter, but Van started coughing with her effort. Kelsey shushed her, which made the laughter worse for both of them.

Until the shed door opened.

Sheer nerve kept Kelsey from screaming as the door jerked out of her hand, ripping two fingernails. She barely felt it, clenching her hand in a fist and swinging. Van let out a stifled yelp and fell back into the shed, away from their attacker.

"Whoa!" The man in front of her caught Kelsey's right fist in his hand, but his instinct to dodge threw him off balance. She followed with a left upper-cut before she realized it was Tom. She pulled the punch, but it clipped the underside of his chin and he sprawled onto his back.

Kelsey leaped out next to him and crouched at his side. "Tom!" she whispered urgently. "I'm so sorry! Are you okay?"

He groaned and worked his jaw with his fingers. "I think I bit my tongue."

"God, I'm sorry. I thought you were—"

"I know." He let her help him sit up. "You've got to stop doing that to me."

Van, who'd followed Kelsey out of the shed and closed the door, wrinkled her nose. "Hon, I hope you didn't land in what I'm smellin'."

Kelsey leaned to look at Tom's back. "Ew." He'd definitely landed in Kinky's fresh poo. "Van, see if there's anything in the shed to clean him off. At least it's your jacket," she tried. "Could have been your shirt."

Tom grimaced. "You know how hard it is to clean leather?" He pushed to his feet. Kelsey took the wad of paper towels Van handed her and scraped off the bulk of the mess, which luckily came off in one chunk. The dark stain left behind was still going to stink, though. She barely stopped herself from apologizing again.

"How did you know we were in there?" Van asked.

"I saw the cop car and backtracked through the neighbor's yard." He pointed to a thicket of trees separating the yard they were in from the house behind. "Crawled through there and watched until they left. I heard the dog scraping at the shed, and since you weren't around, I figured you were in there."

"Or gone," Van said.

Tom looked directly into Kelsey's eyes. "I knew you wouldn't leave me."

A frisson went up her spine and something seemed to burst inside her chest. "No." She wanted to hug him, but her sense of self-preservation told her they were wasting time. "Did you get the gas?"

"Yeah, the can's next to the car."

"Let's get out of here. The cops might still call for a tow on their way to that burglary or whatever."

"Where are we going?"

They followed Kelsey to the car and watched as she filled the tank. She took the keys from Van and dumped the can into the trunk.

"Wait." Tom stripped off his jacket. "Better put this back there, too. Keep the stench out of the car." He dropped it in and quietly closed the trunk lid. "Where to?" he asked again.

"You'll see." She'd remembered something her mother had taught her when she'd been learning how to drive. She wished she'd thought of it earlier. They could have been resting instead of hiding and walking miles and miles for gas. And the car wouldn't reek so friggin' much. Putting the jacket in the trunk hadn't helped.

But lamenting poor choices didn't make the results any better. She started the car and put it in gear with a spark of optimism. They were going to be okay.

She hoped.

"WHAT NEXT?" Tyler asked Regan quietly after he'd driven aimlessly for nearly half an hour. Restraint tightened his voice, but his frustration had been building for the past quarter hour.

"I don't know yet."

"We can't drive around all night. What's left of it." The sky had already turned gray on the eastern horizon.

"I know."

"So—"

"Just shut up and let me think, Tyler."

His mouth clamped shut and his hands clenched and released on the steering wheel, and she felt bad for her outburst. Logic said the likeliest explanation for the guys showing up at the motel was that Tyler had called them. But she was still here. She was beginning to trust him. Eighteen years of conditioning were hard to break, but she hadn't run from him.

Nor had she come up with a plan. Fear for Kelsey and uncertainty of her whereabouts made it hard to think of a strategy. Every few minutes she tried Van's phone and got voice mail every time, usually after a recording stating the network was trying to find the subscriber she was calling. She hoped that only meant there was no signal.

She was not prepared for this. For eighteen years she'd been training and planning escape routes and survival techniques, but never on the fly. Time was not a factor in her planning. Now all she could do was react, and her tired brain wasn't up to the task.

"We should find another place to rest," Tyler suggested. "I'm whupped, and you've been through a lot more than I have tonight."

She couldn't believe it was still the same night. It seemed they'd been on the run for months. "I need to find Kelsey."

"She might not even be around here. They probably kept going."

"If they had, they'd be home by now and at the police station. They would have called. They got off the highway." She looked around, her instincts almost screaming that her daughter was close. She knew getting back on the highway would be leaving her behind, and she'd never do that.

She turned back to Tyler as he approached a stop sign. "Drop me here. I'll find my way."

"Screw that!" He threw the truck into park and let it idle. "I doubt you can even stand. If you can't make the decision, I will."

Feeling as though she was drowning in inertia, Regan looked out the side window at the house they were next to. It looked like a parking lot, with six cars crammed into the driveway and the yard next to it.

Then it clicked. She knew what Kelsey would have done.

"Turn the truck around." She directed Tyler back to the commercial strip near the highway, then up and down cross roads, looking for the right place. The sky had lightened considerably and they were close to dawn, but all the retail parking lots were empty. Even the twenty-four-hour superstore's lot only had three cars, probably belonging to employees.

Finally, she spotted it.

"There. Pull in there." She pointed across the street. Tyler gave her a quizzical look but complied, making a left turn and cutting through a furniture warehouse lot to get back on the road. A second later, he pulled into the car dealership she'd indicated.

"Just park. Driving around might spook them."

He didn't say anything, just pulled the truck up to the side of the lot and shifted into park, waiting. Regan climbed out and started walking up the aisle of used cars. Kelsey would park there, instead of where the shiny new ones gleamed under bright lights. If she remembered what Regan had taught her during her driver training.

Driving around can draw the attention of those who are after you. They'll be searching the streets, maybe checking fast food places or gas stations where you might stop for supplies or directions. You'll blend in here.

Kelsey had been a sponge, soaking up lesson after

lesson. But if Regan was having trouble planning on the run, how could she expect her daughter to remember one detail from two years ago?

But then there it was. The car she'd seen at the side of the road, parked at the end of the row between an ancient Datsun and a Saturn sedan. Regan walked faster, her heart pounding. She couldn't see anyone through the glare on the rear window. If they'd left the car and moved on, she would have no idea where to go next.

The rear door on the passenger side opened. Regan tensed, prepared for it to be someone else, another goon playing with her mind and emerging to kill her or taunt her with her daughter's capture. She held her breath and stopped, ready to run or fight.

Then Kelsey's dark, beautiful head popped up over the side of the car.

SEVEN

"Mom!" Kelsey started running, and so did Regan, the pain in her bare feet and hip disappearing in her overwhelming relief.

Kelsey body-slammed her, her arms wrapping tight around her. Regan clutched her daughter to her with her good arm, trying to hold back the sobs. Kelsey was openly crying.

"I'm glad you're okay, ma'am."

Regan looked up to see Van, holding a hockey stick and looking like she'd played a full tournament, standing next to a tall, handsome boy braced for a fight.

"Thank you for helping my daughter." The words came thickly. She released her headlock on Kelsey but didn't take her arm away. Her daughter twisted in her embrace.

"Mom, this is Tom. Tom Johnson."

He held out a hand. "How do you do."

Regan laughed and let go of Kelsey to shake it. "I do pretty damned poorly at the moment. We've got to get out of here." She looked back. Tyler had gotten out of the truck but remained beside it, watching. Ready.

"What happened to you, Mom?" Kelsey seemed to notice her mother's state for the first time. Her eyes cataloged the filth on the navy hospital scrubs. The sling. The dark patch of blood on her hip over her knife wound. Her bare feet. When she looked up, she was frowning mightily. "You should be in the hospital."

"Yep. But I'm not, and we can't stay here. Come on." She waited while Van pulled backpacks from the car and Tom retrieved his jacket, and led them back to Tyler's truck, mercifully a crew cab with a back seat. It would be a tight squeeze, but they'd all fit.

"Where to?" Tyler asked once they'd all crammed in.

"The first hotel you find."

"They'll—"

"Trust me. I know what I'm doing." Now. Her relief seemed to free her mind, which was firing on all cylinders again.

"The nearest hotel is the one we were in before."

"Perfect."

"If you say so." He said no more, simply did as she'd asked.

"I'm cleanest," Tom said as Tyler pulled up in front of the Red Roof Inn lobby. "I'll go check us in."

"No. Thank you." Regan opened her door. "We need to use my credit card." She started to put one foot down, wincing. "Can I borrow someone's shoes?"

Kelsey quickly toed off her sneakers and contorted herself to pick them up and hand them over the seat back. "I don't mind going in, Mom. You're hurt."

"I have to go. You can get the next one." She grinned at her, almost euphoric at being able to see and hear her and know she was okay. They weren't even close to being safe, but "safe" felt a lot more possible now that they were together.

The desk clerk barely looked up when Regan went in and asked for a room. She didn't seem to recognize her from earlier, though she'd told the cops "those two" didn't look like terrorists.

"Single?"

"Double, please."

"How many people?"

"Two." She filled out the slip the clerk gave her and handed over her credit card. She didn't know Tyler's license number, so she made something up. She probably shouldn't give the right one, anyway. Any little bit of effort she forced their enemies to make would help.

"Drive around back. Unit's at the end." The clerk slid a sleeve with two key cards across the counter, added the credit card, and went back to the far end of the reception desk without another glance.

Interesting. Tyler had said the only room available was the one next to the office. The trust pendulum swung yet again.

Regan went out the front door and climbed back into the truck. "Around back."

Tyler put the truck in gear and drove around the end of the building, stopping in front of the unit Regan pointed to.

"Wait here." She hopped out, opened the room, dropped the key cards on the table, and returned to the truck.

"What are you doing?" Tyler asked.

"She's being smart." Kelsey's eyes shone in the darkness, and Regan could see the pride in her face, despite the shadows.

"Your mother's not such a paranoid old pain, is she?" Regan grinned. Kelsey rolled her eyes.

"What are we doin', then?" Van piped up.

"Going to another hotel."

"We'll use my credit card," Tom offered, clearly getting it. "They might not be looking for my name."

"Thank you. We'll pay you back." Regan tried not to see Kelsey squeezing his hand, or the possessive arm he'd slung over her shoulders.

"It would be better to get them to the police," Tyler murmured to Regan.

"I know. We will. Let's just regroup first."

They went back to the superstore and Van went inside this time. Regan was okay with what Tyler had gotten her before, except he'd forgotten underwear. Van collected packs of underwear for everyone, a new shirt for Tom—who smelled mysteriously of dog shit—and some toiletries and food. Then they drove down the highway two exits and found another hotel. This one was nicer, and Regan allowed Tyler to book a suite with Tom's credit card. She watched them through the entryway, considering taking the truck and the kids and leaving him behind. A couple of hours ago, she would have.

Now, she didn't want to.

They trooped into the suite a few minutes later. Van dropped onto the sofa in the center of the living room, still gripping her stick. Tom settled next to her, his movements more controlled. Tyler flipped the deadbolt and swing-arm latch across the door, then surveyed the group.

"Regan, you need a shower. Very badly. After that, I think—"

"We need some answers," said Kelsey, eyeing him. "Like why *you're* here, for starters."

"We'll talk about everything. But I think your mother needs—"

"I'll deal with my needs, thank you."

Tyler looked ticked at being interrupted again, but Regan was about to fall down.

"We'll rest, then talk. We should be safe for a few hours. Right?" She stared at Tyler, challenging him. Trying not to let him know how things had changed, because not *everything* had.

"Right."

"Okay, then. I'll be right out."

Tyler started to cross the room. "You'll need help." His eyes met hers, and something sparked between them, completely unexpected. It sprung from the awareness that had annoyed her since he asked her out, compounded by intimacy forced by their circumstances. And something else—something she hadn't been aware of all night, but which hit her hard now that circumstances had shifted.

Tyler paused, waiting, but didn't take his eyes off hers. Regan couldn't suppress a shiver, but found the ability to ignore it.

"Kelsey can help me," she finally said.

"Sure." Kelsey preceded her mother into the large bathroom. Regan forced her gaze to break from Tyler's, and shut the bathroom door.

Kelsey had already started the water in the shower. Regan removed the scrub pants and reached for the clip on the sling.

"What happened to you?" Kelsey asked her, removing the fabric from around her arm and then the shirt.

Kelsey moved Regan's shoulder as little as possible as she helped her, but Regan rotated it slightly, testing her strength and pain level. She'd need both arms over the next few days. She stepped into the shower, sighing at the soothing warmth. All her muscles relaxed, tension draining away. While she soaped her hair with one hand and marveled at the dirt swirling at her feet, she briefly relayed the attack at the house and what the man had said to her before she lost consciousness. She glossed over why Alan was in her bed, but with everything that had happened, Kelsey didn't seem to pay attention to that detail, anyway.

"Alan's dead?"

Regan heard a thunk and peered around the curtain. Kelsey had apparently landed hard on the closed toilet. There was pain in her eyes when she looked at her mother. "He didn't do anything."

Except care about us. Regan pulled her head back into the shower, unable to talk about it. It had been easier not to even think about Alan when she'd been searching for Kelsey. She didn't want to start now, no matter how safe they might be for the moment.

She didn't have the luxury of wallowing in grief and regret. Not yet.

"What's Tyler doing here?" Kelsey demanded again.

"He found me, and helped." Regan left it at that for now. Tyler could tell his story later.

While Kelsey updated her mother on her own adventures, Regan let her help her dry off, redress her hip wound and the cuts on her arm and leg, and put on the button-down shirt and jeans Tyler had bought earlier—assessing Regan's size and preferences amazingly well. They left the bathroom to doctor her beat-up feet, and Van took the next shower, declaring herself "stinky as a neglected hen house." Regan thought Tom probably needed it more, but didn't say anything. He'd get his turn.

"We need sleep." Regan looked around at the group, minus Van. Tom was attentive to Kelsey but his eyes kept drifting closed. Tyler stood against a wall, and Regan was certain it was because he, too, would have trouble staying awake if he got comfortable.

"Do you think we should set a watch schedule?" Tyler asked her. She looked around for a clock. It was after six in the morning.

"We should, but we don't have time to rotate."

Van came out of the bathroom. "Next."

"You go ahead," Tom told Kelsey. "Then you three can take the king bed in there." He aimed his chin at the larger bedroom. "Tyler and I will share the double in the other room."

"Okay." Kelsey capped the antibiotic ointment and gathered bandage wrappers in one fist. "Come here a minute?" she asked Tom, who nodded and followed her to the bathroom. Van disappeared into the big bedroom.

Regan had to ignore her instinctive need to keep Tom and Kelsey apart, or at least keep them from being alone. She already knew they had an intimate relationship, and now she knew a lot more. Tom loved her daughter. He'd run with her, protected her. More, he respected both her and her mother, and showed a dozen ways in the last hour that he was in this for the long haul. Regan could do no less for him. But she needed time to adjust.

To distract herself, she stood and went to Tyler. He hadn't moved since they'd arrived.

"I'm putting all of our lives in your hands, Tyler." She kept her voice low, her eyes angled away from his. "I still don't know if I can trust you." Not the truth, but admitting that would open up too many new possibilities. "At the moment, I don't have much choice. Convince me."

Tyler's expression was inscrutable. "I'll tell you what I can. You decide what to do afterward."

"I will." She hesitated, sensing something else going on. "What's wrong?"

"Nothing." But his jaw flickered.

Regan grabbed his elbow, watching the flare in his eyes but not comprehending what it meant. "Tell me what's going on. What did you do?" She tensed, expecting someone to come bursting into the suite, or worse. But Tyler didn't move except to shake his head.

"It's not that. Just…please just go into your room."

Her eyes narrowed. "Why? Do you need to contact someone?"

"I should, yes, but that's not what—" His head thudded against the wall, once. "I'm not your enemy, Regan. Parts of me want to be a lot more than 'not your enemy,' if you get my drift."

Heat washed over her as if he'd burst into flames, and she released him to back away. "This is so the wrong time." *But not the wrong thing*? a voice teased. *Shut up*, she told it. She stopped moving when she reached the opposite wall. Since they were in the suite's short foyer, it wasn't far.

"I don't know how you can even think about that with all this going on," she said. One side of Tyler's mouth curled up, and she couldn't resist smiling back at him. "Dammit."

"Go sleep. We'll deal with this later."

"No, we won't." She pushed away from the wall, but stopped and rested her hand on his crossed arms again. "Thank you, Tyler." She hesitated, trying to hold back, but couldn't stop herself. "I owe you a helluva lot."

Now his smile approached his old carefree grin. "Don't be saying stuff like that unless you intend to follow through."

Despite everything, Regan had to laugh, and it felt good. She held on to the feeling, knowing it was going to be the last one for a while.

SHE FELL ASLEEP before Kelsey came into the room, but woke briefly when the side of the bed dipped. Van, on her left, didn't budge. Regan considered making Kelsey sleep in the middle, the safest position, but the idea of shifting them all around was excruciating. Plus, she had to sleep on her right side. This way she could keep her hand on her daughter and know she was safe, even in sleep.

"Tom okay?" Regan murmured.

"Yeah, and he and Tyler were on their way to bed, too." Kelsey kept her voice to a whisper as she slid under the covers with a sigh. "Tyler said he's setting the alarm for noon."

"Too long," Regan managed, but drifted off again before she heard Kelsey's reply, if she gave one.

When she awoke again both girls were gone. She panicked, wondering why she hadn't sensed them leaving, afraid they'd been taken. Then she heard laughter through the door, which was open a couple of inches, and relaxed.

Her body seized in protest when she tried to get out of bed. She sat on the edge, assessing the damage. Her shoulder was a dull ache, sharpening when she tried to move it, but she thought she could start using her arm. Carefully. The various cuts and bruises made themselves known, and she swore not a single muscle in her body didn't hurt. The only thing slightly improved was her face. Her cheek no longer throbbed when she opened her mouth.

She eased down onto her feet, which felt okay themselves. She went barefoot a lot and had built calluses that had protected her from too much damage. Socks and tennis shoes should be fine.

But as soon as her weight settled on those feet, a shockwave of pain went up her body. She moaned, closing her eyes and trying to straighten her tight back.

"Here."

Her eyes flew open. Tyler stood at the door a few feet away, holding out a little blue pill.

"I don't need that, thanks. Erectile dysfunction is the least of my concerns at the moment."

"Ha ha." He came into the room and she saw he also had a tall glass of water. "It's naproxen sodium. Aleve."

"Thank God. And thank you." She tossed the painkiller into her mouth and drowned it with the full glass of water. "What time is it?"

"Nearly two."

Shock swept over her. "No way."

"Yeah. Tom and I slept through the alarm. We've all trickled out over the last half hour."

Regan looked down at her rumpled clothes, abashed that she'd been the last one up when she was supposed to be leading this motley group.

"Hey." Tyler lifted her chin with a finger. "Cut it out. You were injured. The rest of us were just tired."

She thought about protesting, but decided to cut herself some slack. She *had* fought off a lot of men last night in addition to climbing ditches and running through woods barefoot.

"Okay. What's the plan?"

Tyler raised his eyebrows in unconvincing innocence. "Plan?"

"You've been up for half an hour. There's got to be a plan. Hold that thought," she added, raising a hand. Her bladder had reminded her of priorities. "I'll be out in a minute." She retreated into the suite's bathroom and took care of business, then started to wash her hands.

"Gah!" Her appearance in the mirror was so shocking she couldn't suppress her reaction. Her hair, as long as Kelsey's but not as dark a brown, had been wet when she went to bed. Now it rioted all around her face, which still looked gray and was covered with tiny nicks and scratches. Her eyes drooped with fatigue and sported dark circles.

Tyler *had* to have been lying last night.

Regan dismissed the thought, along with her frightening appearance, and used clips Van had bought to get her hair out of her way. After washing up and brushing her teeth, she packed the toiletries the others had left for her and went out into the main room.

She took a moment to look them over. Kelsey and Van sat at the table next to the kitchenette area. Kelsey appeared subdued as she ate a croissant and sipped from a takeout coffee cup, while Van seemed to be fully recovered and back to her spiky-haired, perky self. Her eyes sparkled and she looked adorable, despite the butterfly tape closing a gash on her cheek.

Tyler and Tom sat on the couch, deep in conversation. Regan realized how alike they were—both with shaggy blond hair and blue eyes, long legs, solid torsos…

And identical grim looks.

"What's going on?" she asked. The men looked up—and though she hated to think of her daughter's boyfriend as a man, that was what he was. His jaw firmed with determination and he shifted away from Tyler. Neither of them looked as tired as she still felt, despite the additional sleep she'd gotten.

"Nothing," Tyler said, but Tom shook his head and stood.

"Tyler thinks we need to get out of here immediately but won't say where he plans to take us. And Kelsey wants to know his story before we go anywhere."

It was clear Tom sided with Kelsey.

"We need to compromise." Regan crossed to the little table and took a croissant. "Who went out and got this?"

"I did," Van answered. She leaned to open the microwave and handed Regan another paper coffee cup. "It's just from downstairs. Kels said you like it black."

"I do, thank you." The coffee's temperature was just right for drinking. She drank half the tall cup, and right away her lethargy began to fade and her thinking cleared. She walked around the perimeter of the room to help get her blood flowing and ease the cramps in her muscles.

"I'm just as eager as Kelsey to hear what Tyler has to say. But we can't stay in one place for long, especially in this area. We need to put some distance between us and those men." The back of her neck prickled, as if she could sense them bearing down on her.

"Who are they, Mom?"

"I don't know." Frustrated, she ground her teeth together. "I've never known. I have some explaining to do myself," she admitted. "But not here. Not now."

"Where?"

She'd been mulling it over since she woke up. "North. We'll be harder to find in a city. Columbus is too close, and Cleveland is bigger. We need to make a stop first," she told Tyler, who nodded.

"I'm still in, then?"

"I think you have answers we need. Plus, it's your truck."

"Ouch." He gave an exaggerated sigh. "I had to ask."

"Is everything packed?" Regan asked. They all nodded.

"Then let's move out."

She resisted Kelsey's badgering to talk in the truck and directed Tyler to a tiny town north of Columbus. The bank she needed was across the street from a park. Everyone wanted to go with her into the bank, but she knew they'd attract attention and refused. She only let Kelsey come, because she couldn't turn off her need to train her daughter. Who knew when, if ever, this would be over?

"You always need to have an escape plan," she lectured, trying not to limp as they walked uneven brick pathways. "Be prepared for anything. Including getting hauled away from your stuff naked and unconscious." She stopped next to a statue of the town's founder. "Anyone around?" It was late afternoon now, and traffic rumbled by but there were no pedestrians.

"No, we're clear."

Third brick from the right on the right, Regan remembered, studying the walkway. She found a small stick and used it to dig out enough sand between the bricks to pry up the third one near the base of the statue. Then she had to get low to reach into the hole and deep under the statue. But her fingers closed over the leather coin purse, right where she'd left it. She came up grinning.

"What's that?" Kelsey stared at her. "It's too small for ID or anything."

"You're right." Regan replaced the brick and stood without Kelsey's help. She unzipped the purse and shook out a key. "Safety deposit box." She aimed her chin at the bank. "ID and money are in there."

"Holy crap, Mom."

"Hey!"

Kelsey ignored her. "What if they'd decided to replace the walkway?"

"There's no place to hide something with zero risk of discovery. But I shoved it as deep as I could, hoping no one would find it. New bricks or cement would have made it harder to get to, though." She started to cross the lawn to the road on the far side of the park. She'd approach the bank around the other side to scope out the area and make sure no one was watching them.

Kelsey matched her purposeful stride. "See that guy at two o'clock?" she asked quietly.

Regan cut her eyes that way. A hunched-over man in a green Army jacket pushed a battered grocery cart, about forty yards away and around the corner of the square.

"Yeah."

"Just checking."

Regan caught Kelsey's smart-aleck grin and smiled back. God, she'd missed her. She wrapped an arm around her shoulders and squeezed, then let go right away, not pushing the moment.

Kelsey moved ahead to open the bank door and hold it for her mother. Regan went straight to customer service—the branch hadn't changed an iota since she was first here six years ago—and asked for access to her box. A few minutes later, she and Kelsey left the bank, a couple thousand dollars more comfortable and carrying driver's licenses and credit cards declaring them to be Hestia Wallace and her daughter May. The documents weren't exactly legal, but she'd pre-paid the balances on the cards, so at least she wasn't committing credit card fraud.

"Passports?" Kelsey questioned, studying her old photograph. "I can't believe I still match the picture. I was *ten*."

"Doesn't matter since it expired, but we're not planning to leave the country, anyway."

"I know. Still, it's kind of exciting." Regan eyed her. She shrugged. "You know, besides the whole being-chased-'cause-someone-wants-to-kill-us part."

"Yeah." Regan stopped walking. No one was nearby, and there was something she should say before they were back with the others. "Kelsey, you know we have to get Tom and Van home. Or at least back to school. They can stay with us for now because they deserve to know what's happening." It was difficult for her to allow, as it went against everything she'd believed for eighteen years. But it was too late to keep them out of their lives. They'd adopted the damned puppy.

"Well, gee, I appreciate that." Kelsey's sarcasm was a precursor to anger, Regan knew.

"They're good friends. I understand, Kels. And as I said, they should know why they've been running through the woods and driving all over kingdom come. But they're in danger as long as they're with us." She took a breath to say more, but Kelsey surprised her.

"I know, Mom. We won't argue when the time comes. Well, *I* won't. I can't speak for Van." She smirked, but Regan saw the loneliness behind it. Her heart cracked. For the first time, her daughter had true friends. In two short months, they'd become close enough to endanger themselves for her. And here her evil mother was, sending them away.

"I wish they could stay with us, honey."

"It's all right, Mom. I know why they can't."

The white truck, splattered with dried mud, rumbled up to them. Tyler had circled while they were talking. Tom sat in the front seat now. Kelsey ran around and climbed in next to him, crowding the front of the cab.

Regan raised an eyebrow at Tyler. He lifted a shoulder. She bit back a response and climbed into the back of the cab.

"Still heading north?" Tyler asked.

"Yeah, let's find a hotel in Cleveland. We'll share information and rest some more. After that, though, we have to get Van and Tom back to school somehow."

Their protest was immediate. Tom twisted to look over the seat, his expression earnest though she couldn't hear his words over Van's strident argument.

"I can't understand either one of you," Regan said, "and it doesn't matter. You're not safe with us. We'll go to Cleveland, stay the night so everyone can rest properly and eat a couple of real meals, and then we'll send you back to Whetstone. And Tyler, you'll move on, as well."

"And what are you and Kelsey going to do?" Tyler asked.

"Doesn't matter, because they're not ditching us," Tom said.

"If you think I'm leavin' my best friend to those assholes, you've got another think coming!" Van added. "She wouldn't even have gotten away if it weren't for us!"

"It's out of the question," Regan said. "Your help has been invaluable, but she would have been fine without it. More scared, I'm sure, and much more lonely. But she knows what she's doing. It's irrelevant, anyway, because *we are not putting you two back in danger.*"

"Making me leave you will put me in danger," Tyler asserted. "My boss will murder me if I leave you alone."

Anger flared in Regan. "What else does he expect of you? What do you have to do to us to avoid that fate?"

Silence descended in the truck, and no one spoke for several miles. Then Tom and Kelsey started murmuring to each other in the incomprehensible way teenagers have even with adults within hearing range of a whisper. Van leaned forward and joined in the debate. Regan watched unabashedly, not caring if they thought she was invading their privacy. She couldn't read their lips or hear more than mumbles, but she could tell Kelsey was trying, and failing, to stand firm.

Regan sighed and closed her eyes, easing down in the seat until her head rested on the back of it. "How far to Cleveland?" she asked Tyler.

"About two hours."

"Wake me up when we hit the beltway, please." She shouldn't fall asleep. It would give Tyler an opportunity to alter their course or hand Kelsey off to someone before Regan could react. But she was tired, and though the pendulum hadn't swung all the way back to "trust him," it hovered somewhere in the middle. He had to prove himself, but if he was against them, he'd worked awfully hard to help and protect them instead. It seemed too much effort to win them over, even without knowing why he might do such a thing.

Besides, even dozing, Regan kept part of her brain and attention on the movement of the vehicle and the sounds inside it. She was still in charge, even if no one knew it but her.

EIGHT

KELSEY ARGUED, BUT Van was wearing her down.

"You need help," she insisted for the third time.

"I've got my mother now, Van. I keep telling you, I didn't intend to drag anyone into this."

"You didn't even know it was coming!"

"I can't be responsible for anything happening to you," Kelsey argued. "Your parents—"

"Have nothing to do with it." Van's eyes narrowed, but Kelsey saw hurt behind the lids, anyway. "I thought we were friends."

"Oh, for God's sake, Van." Kelsey rolled her eyes. "You know we are. I've never had a friend like you." She flicked her eyes up to see her mother watching them, and lowered her voice even further. "Let's hear what my mother and Tyler have to say, at least. We don't even know what the danger is."

"We've kicked ass so far," Van said. "Tom, back me up."

"She's right. I know you have your mother, but what do you know about Tyler? She doesn't trust him very much. You should have someone watching both your backs."

She bit her lip. It sounded so logical. "My mother

won't go for it," she said reluctantly. "And I really want you guys to be safe."

"There's no guarantee we'd be safe back at school, either."

Kelsey's insides froze. She hadn't thought of that. Her imagination dutifully provided rapid-fire images of Tom and Van being slaughtered with knives.

"They know we were with you," Tom pressed. "They'll figure out who we are, and it wouldn't be hard to take us at school."

Van jumped on that. "Yeah, they could use us as bait to get you. Or hurt us to make you come in."

"Van, sit back and put your seatbelt on, please," Regan said. Van scowled but obeyed. Kelsey and Tom turned to face front. Kelsey laid her head on Tom's shoulder, torn.

Tom slung his arm around her and dipped his head to murmur in her ear. "I'll do whatever you want me to, no matter what your mother says."

His words comforted her, though she knew he didn't have a chance against her mother. "Don't underestimate her."

When they neared the city, Regan directed Tyler to find a hotel with suites and an underground lot. Regan checked in at the lobby, paying cash, and led them all to the suite she'd booked.

"I think we all should rest some more before we do anything else," Kelsey said as soon as they walked in the door. She wasn't ready to face leaving Tom.

No one answered her. Tyler and her mother cased the suite, checking every room, every doorway and window. Tom went immediately to the information folio and flipped to the room service menu.

Van came out of one of the bedrooms. "Looks like we're sharin' again."

Kelsey pressed her lips together. She was already tired of being surrounded by bodies. The only body she wanted to lie next to was Tom's.

Not that she was going to tell her mom that.

They collected in the sitting area, a black-and-white room with rectangular furniture and plain vases on shiny tables.

"What do you want to do?" Tyler asked her mother.

"Anyone else hungry?" Tom asked. "I'm gonna call for some chow."

"Let's eat and rest," Kelsey said again, trying not to sound desperate.

"I thought you wanted to know what was going on." Her mother had a knowing look.

Kelsey swallowed, wondering why she felt guilty. "I do. But I think we'll all feel better if we eat and rest."

To her relief, her mother chuckled. "You're either trying to prolong being with your friends, or you're afraid of my mood."

Kelsey raised her eyebrows hopefully. "Okay if I say both?"

Regan smiled. "Nice try. Food, we can do. Then we'll tell you what we know and move on."

"Okay except the moving on part," Van grumbled, but accepted the menu from Tom to make her choice.

While Tyler called their order in, Kelsey slumped onto the couch next to Tom and rubbed her eyes.

"I'm so tired." She wiggled on the hard cushion. "Who bought this furniture?"

"You can sit on my lap," Tom leered, making her laugh.

"Yeah, with my mother right there." She studied her for a minute, trying not to be concerned. She didn't look any better now than she had when Kelsey first saw her just before dawn. The shadows under her eyes had darkened and though she was using her left arm, it was clear it still hurt her.

Van came out of the bathroom and bounced onto the sofa beside her. "Ouch. Not very soft." She bounced again. "Could be fun, though."

Tyler hung up the phone and perched on the arm of a chair. Regan remained standing behind the love seat opposite the couch where Van, Tom and Kelsey sat.

"Where do you want to start?" Tyler asked.

"At the beginning." Regan sighed. "It's about time."

Kelsey held her breath. The beginning meant her father. She leaned forward and dug her fingers into Tom's leg. He flinched and gathered her hand gently into his.

"Chelsea Conrad met Scott Harrison at Blaydes Academy when she was seventeen," Regan began.

"What?" Kelsey burst out. That wasn't what she'd expected to hear. "Who's Chelsea Conrad?"

"I was."

Kelsey stared at her, barely hearing Van's noise of

interest or feeling Tom's comforting squeeze. "You changed your name?" She couldn't believe she hadn't known. Now it seemed obvious, with the little bit she knew, but… She pressed a fist against the betrayal in her gut. It was stupid, just a name, but it skewed her view of her mother, already. How much more would the story change?

"You don't look like a Chelsea," Van said.

Regan's smile was sad. "No. I haven't been for a very long time. But that's who I was then. My parents had been killed, and I wasn't doing well in foster care. An excellent social worker found Blaydes for me, and everything changed." Something flashed in her eyes and she looked distant, but she brought herself back to the apartment and focused on Kelsey.

"I fell in love with your father immediately. He wasn't perfect—he partied pretty hard and he had some friends from the football team who were jerks—but he was smart and sweet and fun, and when he was determined to do something, he succeeded."

"Like taking the team to State his junior year." It was one of the few stories her mother had told her.

"Yes." She blew out a big breath and tucked her left hand into her pocket, wincing as she shifted her shoulder. "I found out I was pregnant when we'd been together nearly two years. I was terrified, but Scott was positive we would get through. He was so excited." Her eyes welled with tears, and her eyes met Kelsey's, earnest and pleading, though Kelsey didn't understand why. "He wanted you so much, Kels."

She sniffed and jerked her hand up to swipe at

the tear dripping down her face. She felt like a tower loomed over her, a jagged, tilting pile of everything she'd missed, not having a father. For a moment it overwhelmed, about to bury her. She took a deep breath and pushed it away.

"You've told me that, Mom." She cleared her throat when her voice came out thick. "But you never told me what happened next."

"He went to tell his parents. I didn't want him to go. They were career military and very controlling. I was afraid they'd make us give you up, or worse. Or take you from us to raise 'for our own good.' Or Scott's, anyway. I knew they saw a brilliant future for him."

"Did you ever meet them?" Kelsey asked. She'd always been curious about the only grandparents she had alive, out there somewhere, perhaps unaware they even had a grandchild. But her mother rarely talked about them.

"I did. They were very nice to me and seemed glad Scott was happy. They let me join them during parents' weekends since I didn't have any. They cheered me on during my karate competitions."

Kelsey gaped at her. "You did martial arts?"

"Yep." She grinned, a hint of pride in the expression. "First place, six times in two years."

"Awesome!" said Van. Kelsey turned her head. Her friend's eyes were wide, her hand clutching the side of the sofa.

"But you don't do martial arts now," Kelsey accused.

Regan shook her head a little. "It's hard to keep it up without a partner, and joining a dojo wouldn't have been smart. It would have connected me to Chelsea."

"How come you didn't go with Scott—I mean, Dad—to tell his parents?"

Her mother's indrawn breath shook, as did her voice when it came out. "I was afraid, and he knew it. He was going home for the long weekend and knew he couldn't keep it from them. He was too happy. He wanted me to go, but told me to stay at school until they knew and he'd proven to me everything would be all right. It turned out," she choked, "to be the best thing he could have done. For us." She indicated herself and Kelsey.

No one moved, waiting for what they knew was coming.

Her mother's face tightened. Her shoulders squared, and her voice came out stronger this time. "I talked to him on the phone Monday morning. He said things hadn't gone as planned and I should pack a bag. He was coming to get me. He sounded scared but determined. I didn't hesitate. I packed everything I could into one suitcase and waited outside my dormitory. Two hours after he was supposed to have gotten there, I had to go to the bathroom. When I came out I heard a voice, a man's voice, in the common room around the corner. Something made me stop—I never figured out what. But he was asking one of the other girls about me. She said she'd seen me outside with my suitcase and that I must have left.

"When I went back outside, even though it had gotten dark and there was no one around the entrance or the parking lot, I hid behind the bushes. Scott drove up in his Mustang an hour later. I ran out and started to get into the car, but he opened his door and fell out onto the pavement." Tears began streaming freely down her face, though she continued in the same strong voice. "He was bleeding. All over. I couldn't tell from where, but I think he had at least a shoulder wound and probably his kidney."

Kelsey released Tom's hand and wrapped her arms around her freezing body. "From what?"

"I don't know. Gunshots, or knife wounds." She thanked Tyler for the box of tissues he handed her. "I don't know how he managed to get back to Blaydes. Sheer force of will, I guess. He fought off my attempts to help him and clutched my shoulders. His eyes burned with intensity." She closed hers, as if lost in the memory. "He said I had to run. They wanted the baby and would do anything to get her—he always believed you were a girl." She dragged in a hitching breath. "They'd tried to kill him."

Her mother's eyes opened, and the anguish in them was more than Kelsey had ever experienced. She pressed the heel of her hand against her chest, against the sharp pain that had grown there over the last fifteen minutes.

"Then what?" she whispered.

"Then he told me he loved me. Loved both of us. And died."

Van gasped. "He died? In your arms?"

Tom's hand wrapped around Kelsey's again. She

was having difficulty breathing, as if the room had turned into a sauna.

"What did you do?" Tom asked.

"I did what he said. I ran."

"You left him there?" In a second grief flared into outrage, and Kelsey leaped to her feet. "You left his body in the parking lot?" She could barely hear over the roaring in her ears.

Her mother didn't look the slightest bit apologetic. "I didn't think I had a choice. Someone had murdered your father and he believed you were in danger. And someone—maybe even the same someone—was looking for me."

"Why didn't you go to the police?"

"I was too scared." She flattened a hand over her abdomen, as if remembering the baby she'd been carrying. "Even then, when I was only a few weeks pregnant, I was fiercely protective of you. I had bad memories of the police from when my parents were killed—I didn't trust them. What if whoever killed Scott could get to me through the police? Worse, what if the police thought *I'd* killed Scott? So I ran."

"To Ohio."

She laughed, a bitter sound. "Oh, hell, no. I wasn't very smart in the beginning. Scott's parents lived in Northern California, so I went south. Got a lousy job, found a lousier place to live, gave birth to a beautiful, delicate baby girl, and decided it had all been nuts. I convinced myself Scott had been in an accident or something, and was delirious. It was too late to go back, but I fooled myself into believing we were safe."

Kelsey couldn't remember a time when her mother had felt safe. "What happened to change that?"

"They found me and tried to kidnap you when you were only a few weeks old. Two men came in. I fought one, but my karate was competition-oriented and his training wasn't. He pinned me to the floor while the other guy got you from your nursery. They left me there, carrying you out with your diaper bag slung over one shoulder, like you belonged to them."

"But you got me back!"

"I did." Her smile was a fraction of what it had been when she mentioned her wins, but it bore the same mark of pride. "I had bought a gun, when we first moved down there. I pulled it from the towel drawer where I had hidden it and shot one of them. I got you away and left, and never took anything for granted again. Any time I got too tired or too over-whelmed, or felt silly for my paranoia, I remembered what it had been like to see them carrying you out the door."

Tyler, who had remained still and silent until now, asked, "Where did you go?"

Regan's eyes narrowed on him, and Kelsey could see her brain working.

"Wondering how I evaded you?"

He shook his head. "I never knew you existed until right before I moved in next to you."

"Why don't you tell us about that?" Regan circled the love seat and sat on its arm, facing Tyler on his chair arm. They reminded Kelsey of the old adversaries in black-and-white movies, the couple who were at odds but loved with a fiery passion in the end. She looked back and forth between them, her mind flashing over romantic scenarios.

What the hell are you doing? Her musings came to a screaming halt. They were on the run, and Tyler could be the enemy. But she knew what was going on—subconsciously she was trying to escape from the agony of grief over the father who'd died to save her. The father she'd never known. It was unfair to blame her mother for that, and she gulped back the fury trying to spill over. She wanted to stop all the talking, make everyone go away and let her process what she'd just learned, but there was no time.

"Finish your story," Tyler told Regan. "Mine takes up where yours leaves off."

Kelsey thought her mom would argue, but she only folded her arms and continued. "I went to Illinois first, where I became Regan Miller. Then to Michigan, down to Texas, up to Maine, and finally, when Kelsey needed stability for school, to Ohio. Nothing had happened in nearly five years, and I took a chance I obviously shouldn't have taken."

Tyler shook his head. "For someone without a clue how to disappear—a teenage mother with an infant, no less—you did an admirable job."

"So? Your turn."

Tyler took a deep breath. "My employer had been searching for you since the day your—Scott died. He finally tracked you down about two years ago and sent me to check on you. I reported that Kelsey was healthy and happy and you seemed to be a typical single mother, and I thought that would be the end of it. But he assigned me to watch you, which I did."

"Who is 'he'?"

Kelsey knew the question was pointless, and no doubt her mother did too, but she watched Tyler carefully when he answered.

He gave nothing away. "All I can say is that he's on your side. But I'm not authorized to say who he is."

"You make it sound like special ops or national security," Regan accused.

"In a way, it is."

Stunned silence filled the room. Kelsey found her voice first, rough as it was. "What part? My father's death, my mother's disappearance or my existence?"

Tyler turned to her. "All of it."

"Whoa," Van said, behind her.

Kelsey's mind spun. She'd thought none of it would be a surprise, thought she'd figured out what her mother hadn't told her. But in a few short minutes, her world had flipped and thrown her on her ass.

"So you've been spying on us all this time?" Regan asked, her lips tight and her eyes burning with anger.

Tyler nodded. "Sending very dull reports every month. Nothing ever happened."

"Must have been a boring two years," Kelsey said.

"No." Tyler answered her but kept his gaze on her mother, who couldn't look away, either. "Far from it."

Regan shook herself a little. "What's different? What happened this weekend? I don't remember you going away before."

"No. I never did. But I got called in to receive

sensitive information they didn't want to relay electronically." He shifted and looked down at the floor. "They learned someone else knew where you were."

Kelsey didn't understand. Why would someone send him to watch them, if he wasn't supposed to protect them? But if he was supposed to protect them, leaving his post left them vulnerable.

"Would those be the same people who killed Alan and tried to kill me, and went after Kelsey?" Her mother's voice had hardened.

Tyler's jaw flexed, and he was clenching his teeth when he admitted, "Yes."

"Who conveniently showed up while you were gone?"

"Yes." He hunched his shoulders. "They sent someone to watch out for you, but he…well, he's been fired."

"And what was your purpose in being a few dozen yards away from us at all times?" her mother asked, the question coming fast and hard, like a cop interrogation.

"My purpose—is irrelevant. I failed."

"What are your orders now?"

"I don't have any. I'm here on my own."

NINE

REGAN DIDN'T BELIEVE him. No one spent two years on a tedious undercover assignment without being completely dedicated to his job and loyal to his employer. That kind of man didn't go rogue when things changed. He dug in deeper, held tighter to the beliefs that drove him.

But she knew by the set of his jaw and the knot of his folded arms that he wasn't going to say any more. She hadn't heard nearly enough, but she didn't know how to make him tell her the rest. *She* didn't have that kind of training.

She wondered if he still worked for the government. But why would they have any interest in her or Kelsey? She couldn't think of anyone who would, except the people who'd killed Scott and tried to kidnap his daughter. She'd always believed it was his parents, or at least someone connected to them. But Tyler said his employer wanted them safe, which didn't fit.

Her attention shifted to Kelsey and the more immediate worry of her daughter's reaction to the story of her father's death. She'd sat back down on the sofa. Tom cradled her against him, stroking her hair while she cried.

The pain in Regan's chest rivaled that of a heart attack. *She* was supposed to be comforting Kelsey. Not this stranger who'd only been a part of her daughter's life for two months. Someone who had never suffered a parent being killed in an unspeakably violent way. Regan knew what it was like, knew what Kelsey was probably feeling. Wanting to spare her those emotions was one reason she'd never talked much about it.

A knock on the door was followed by a man calling, "Room service." Regan and Tyler confirmed it, didn't let the server into the room, and checked the cart before wheeling it in. The kids fell on the food immediately, Kelsey's tears forgotten, at least for now.

Regan went to the kitchenette. The open plan of the suite made it impossible to hide, but she could at least distance herself a little. She fussed with the coffeepot so she could turn her back. Every parent faced the transition of their child's focus from parent to new love. The smart ones prepared themselves for it, and Regan had. Dammit, she had worked hard to counter her own programming.

But this situation had thrust her back into old habits, old needs. She had wanted to rip Kelsey out of Tom's arms and send him on his way.

She wanted history to not repeat itself.

"Can I help?" Tyler came up beside her and reached for the packet of coffee she couldn't open. His voice was low, understanding.

Regan blinked hard against the tears. "I've got it, thank you." She bit the top of the packet and tore it. The rich aroma of ground coffee calmed her, and her movements smoothed with the routine of preparing the coffeemaker.

"She's not abandoning you." Tyler retrieved mugs from the small sink and rinsed them. "And he's certainly not trying to take her away from you."

"I know," she snapped. "Stop trying to therapeut me."

"Therapeut?" He laughed. "What the hell is that?"

Regan couldn't help smiling. "You're not analyzing me, you're trying to fix me. Offering amateur therapy. I don't need it." She tuned in behind them but couldn't hear anything, not even Kelsey crying. She looked over her shoulder, but the room was empty.

Abandoning pretense, she slumped against the counter and pressed the heels of her hands to her eyes. "Did you see her face when I said I left him there?"

"No. I wasn't looking at her."

Shit. Regan dropped her hands. "Tyler, that's got to stop."

"What does?" But he had his intense, unblinking gaze on her face again. Like he was trying to send her a message without words.

"That." She pointed at his eyes. "I. Don't. Trust. You." She poked his chest with each word. "Trying to make out like you care about me isn't going to change it."

"You've trusted me to get you this far."

She couldn't dispute that. "And I'm grateful for the help you've given us. But you're still not being honest with me."

His hand balled into a fist and he thumped it on

the cabinet above them. "I can't help that. I'm under orders not to tell you who I work for." He stood like a man straining against bonds, his jaw flexing as if he were chewing back whatever he wanted tell her.

"You said you're not under their orders now," she reminded him.

"They haven't ordered me to stay with you."

"Tell me who they are, Tyler."

"I can't," he practically growled, not looking directly at her. "He—they—are afraid of what you'll do if you find out. They worked hard to find you, to protect you, and don't want to lose you again."

Regan slowly shook her head. "That's why *they* don't want you to tell me. But you have your own reasons."

His entire face tightened, as if he knew what she was going to say and it pierced him.

She said it anyway. "You won't tell me because if you did, I'd know why I can't trust you."

He flinched, the barest of movements, and her heart sank. She *wanted* to trust him—even admitted, in weak moments, that she did. And now he'd indicated that she shouldn't.

"Ms. Miller?"

Regan raised her head. Van stood at the counter dividing the sitting and kitchenette areas. "What is it, hon?"

"I need to call my parents. It's Sunday, and if I don't call, they'll freak out."

Lord, Regan had lost track of what day of the week it was. "How many classes do you have tomorrow?"

She wasn't sure they could get the kids back in time for tomorrow's classes.

"Three. But it's okay if I miss them. They're not my major, they're just distribution requirements, and I mean, this is more important. I just don't think it's a good idea for my mother to lose it and call the cops and put a nationwide APB on me. You know, in case the bad guys have access to that stuff. Then, knowing her, she'd go to the media and—"

"I get it, Van."

The girl grinned. "Sorry. I haven't had time to babble this weekend. It was building up."

Regan smiled back at her but felt little humor. "Call them. But *please*, don't tell them what's going on." She couldn't believe she'd just told a kid to lie to her parents.

Van shot her an "I'm not an idiot" look and pulled her cell phone from her pocket. Regan watched her wander across the sitting area and start chatting animatedly. She wanted to hover over her and make sure she didn't give anything away. The Leighs would probably call the police and make everything more complicated. Like Van said, an APB would reveal their location to whoever was after them. But teenagers were excellent at keeping things from their parents, and after a moment of listening, Regan knew it would be okay. At least, from that perspective. Now she was looking at it from Van's and Tom's parents' side of things, and how she'd feel if she knew her child was missing school *and* in danger. The tension vise tightened around her head. She had to get them back.

Tyler's hand came up to rest on the back of her neck. His fingers dug into her right shoulder a little, eliciting a moan.

"You want a rubdown?" He shifted her toward him to get a better grip. "You're all knotted up."

"No kidding." Regan let him do it because as soon as his long fingers touched her, the tension loosened. The knots he'd mentioned seemed to melt, and as the muscles relaxed, all her other aches eased, too.

Van kept her conversation short. "All done! They're happy. And don't worry about tomorrow. The school won't even notice I'm not there for days."

"Thanks, that makes me feel better."

Van flashed her grin again at Regan's sarcasm, accompanied by a knowing wink as she disappeared into the bedroom.

"What next?" Tyler asked. His left hand gently rubbed her tender shoulder while his right ran up and down her neck.

"What do you think?" She wouldn't follow his advice, but knowing what he planned might give her insight into his intentions or—well, she had to admit, she didn't know what to do at this point.

"I think we're still safe here, at least temporarily. We should stay tonight and get some more rest." He didn't say Regan was the one who needed it, but she knew that was what he meant. She tilted her head and closed her eyes, trying not to let relaxation become arousal under Tyler's ministrations.

"Tomorrow morning," he continued, "we take Van and Tom to the train station and send them back to

Whetstone. Then we head for my employer in California."

She tried hard not to tense, but Tyler either felt her reaction or realized his slip, because his hands paused. She didn't say anything, because that would confirm she knew the significance of his words. He continued the massage, his knuckles gliding down her spine to the small of her back, where he spanned her hips and dug in his thumbs.

Heat flared from deep in her center and burned her skin under his fingers. She drew in a quick breath, and before she could step away Tyler spun her. A matching heat blazed in his eyes. He held her gently by the shoulders, leaned in, eyelids dropping, until his mouth met hers.

As diversionary tactics went this was a good one, Regan thought. She moved closer and lifted her right arm up around his neck. Her left shoulder protested, so she rested her hand and forearm on his chest, her fingertips tracing the cord at the side of his neck. Tyler's mouth was firm on hers, his technique adequate, but his obvious distraction interfered with the effect he was going for.

Still in full possession of her faculties, Regan opened her mouth and touched her tongue to his. That startled a grunt from him and his arms reflexively pulled her closer to his body.

It was a good body. He was hard everywhere that mattered—and "everywhere" was an inclusive term. She rocked her hips once and he groaned, bracing the back of her head with his hand and diving in to kiss her with full involvement.

Regan's intentions went out the window. The heat in her belly flared into desire and she began to ache in places she hadn't ached in years. Not even with Alan. Her bra suddenly felt too tight, her nipples contracting painfully. She lifted one leg to cradle Tyler more intimately, and he pulled back, gasping.

"Holy hell, woman." He stared down at her. "I wasn't expecting that."

"Clearly." She dropped her foot to the floor and her hands to the hem of her T-shirt to tug it down. She schooled her breathing and willed away the flush she knew stained her cheeks and chest. Absentmindedly, she put the back of her hand to the bruise on her left cheekbone. It hadn't hurt while she was kissing him, but it pulsed now. "Next time you want to distract me, you might want to try a grenade or something else more potent."

He stroked his fingers gently across the bruise, but his eyes narrowed. "Nice try. My ego's not that big. Besides, I know you were more into it than you're showing."

She shrugged. At least it wasn't showing. "All right, we'll go with part of your plan. We'll rest here tonight. Tomorrow you can go to California and I'll take care of getting the kids back. You're not coming with us." She forestalled his protest by raising her hand in front of his face, and tried not to touch his open mouth. "I'm not arguing about it. I appreciate all you've done for us until now, but from this point on, it's me and Kelsey. Like always."

"You can't protect her forever," Tyler said softly. The kids were coming back into the room.

"I have for eighteen years."

She moved away before he could point out that if she'd done such a good job, they wouldn't be where they were now. After announcing the plan, she asked to talk to Kelsey alone so Van and Tom wouldn't argue again. Not that Tom looked like he was going to. So far he'd demonstrated a level head and plenty of concern for Kelsey.

She led her daughter into one of the bedrooms and closed the door.

"Mom, I'm not sure sending them back is a good idea," Kelsey started.

"We'll talk about it in a minute. Sit down." Regan waited until she joined her at the foot of the bed. She began to put her arm around her but stopped, not sure how it would be received and not up to rejection. "We should talk about what you just learned."

A curtain of soft brown hair shielded Kelsey's face from her. She waited, letting Kelsey choose where to start. After a moment, she raised her head and slipped her hair behind her ear, looking, to Regan's relief, like the steady, accepting girl she'd raised.

"You think it's my grandparents, don't you?"

Regan's eyebrows shot up. That was the part prominent in Kelsey's mind?

"I don't know. I have nothing to go on except that your father went to see them."

"So you think they're after me for some reason."

Regan honestly didn't know. She'd thought about it all this time, and had never come to any conclusions. "I would be surprised if the people I met would want to harm you."

"Which doesn't answer my question." Kelsey sighed and leaned her shoulder against her. "I wonder if they knew what happened to Daddy."

Regan's heart spasmed at the word. Kelsey had never referred to him that way, on the rare occasions they had discussed him.

"Was it in the papers?" Kelsey asked.

"Some. It was hard to track newspaper reports when we were on the run. I was focused on getting away, being safe. On not being found. And the internet didn't exist back then, not for people like me."

Kelsey stared at her. "But it does now. It has for, like, ever. You never looked? What if it was a random thing? If they caught his killer, we *would* have been safe."

Regan slanted a look at her. "We're not safe. Obviously. So even if they 'caught' his killer, there was no guarantee someone wouldn't still be after us. But—" she continued to keep Kelsey from arguing more, "—I did track down old articles and learned what I could. It wasn't much, even once newspapers started putting their archives online. As far as I could tell, they never found out who did it. I don't even know if they considered me a suspect."

"I want to see."

Regan huffed a laugh. "I don't *have* them. I didn't keep a portfolio."

Kelsey jumped up. "No, I mean, Tom has his laptop in his backpack. We can look them up now. And I bet he can find more than you did. He's a whiz, and you're—no offense—not that good at searching for stuff."

"Wait, Kels." Regan caught her arm before she ran out of the room. "What about your father?"

"What about him?"

"I want to know how you feel about all this."

Kelsey rolled her eyes. "How do you think I feel, Mom? Gawd."

It was such a teenager response, and so *not* Kelsey, Regan dropped her arm. Her daughter walked out quickly, not looking back.

"I'll get the computer!"

Regan sighed and followed her out.

"WE'RE ON," TOM said once he got his laptop connected to the hotel's WiFi and the main search window popped up on his screen.

Kelsey bent over his shoulder while her mother paced on the other side of the table. She wished she'd stop. She was making her dizzy. She kind of understood, though. Her mother was used to being in control, and Tom wouldn't let any of them use his laptop. He was protective, he'd told her once when she wanted to look up an assignment, because his roommate had crashed it and cost him hundreds in repairs. But it wasn't easy to have to watch him log

on to the hotel's wireless connection and start surfing
when her own fingers wanted to fly over the keys.

"What town was the school in?" he asked her
mother.

"Westbrook."

He typed. "No newspaper for Westbrook."

"No, it was too small. It would have been the
Fresno paper."

He typed again. "Here it is. Free archives, sweet.
How do you spell the name of the school?"

"B-L-A-Y-D-E-S." She gave the date of Scott's
death before he asked. Tom finished typing and they
waited, Kelsey holding her breath, while the page
loaded with results.

"Winning essays, honor roll, fraternity party
raids...let's see." He scrolled, reading the screen
faster than Kelsey. "Soccer playoffs...a rape on campus...professors being honored...here." He clicked a
link, and for the first time Kelsey saw her father's
face.

It was a football photo shot from the waist up, a
scan of a black-and-white newspaper article. Since
he wore his full uniform he looked enormous—tall
and wide and muscular. But what riveted her was his
smile, both his mouth and his eyes. He was happy.

And he looked just like her.

Her mother came around the table and was close
enough Kelsey heard her gasp when she saw the picture. Her hand lifted to her mouth, and Kelsey felt a
fine tremor go through her. But she couldn't tell if

she was crying because she couldn't stop looking at her father.

"I don't have any pictures of him," Regan said, her voice cracking. "When he called and told me to pack, I left all my school stuff behind, including the school directory where I kept his clippings. I didn't have a camera and he didn't care about taking pictures. It would have been too dangerous to keep around, anyway," she finished softly.

All of them were silent as they read the headline. Van crowded up on Kelsey's other side to see, and she sensed Tyler behind them, looking over their heads.

The headline read Blaydes Academy Football Star Murdered. Kelsey leaned on Tom to read the article below.

Late Monday night freshmen students at Blaydes Academy, the exclusive private school in nearby Westbrook, were returning to their dormitory after an evening of study when they came across the body of Scott Harrison, senior captain and quarterback of the school's football team.

Shot twice—once in the shoulder, once in the lower back—Harrison didn't have a chance, according to Lawrence Cardory, county coroner. "The shoulder wound was not fatal but bled profusely. The wound in his lower back damaged the right kidney and renal artery and would have been the cause of death." Dr. Cardory went on to say that the wounds were inflicted long before death.

That factor, combined with the blood in a vehicle registered to Mr. Harrison that was present in the parking lot where he was found, lead police to believe the injuries could have occurred anywhere.

Anyone with information about this tragedy is encouraged to contact the Westbrook police department.

Kelsey's eyes kept reading, but her mind didn't process the football statistics and Blaydes publicity crap in the rest of the article. It hardly seemed possible that her father's death could be made more real—she'd lived with the knowledge of it her whole life—but it was. She found herself feeling sorry for her mother, who had been about Kelsey's age when this happened. But she was also angry she'd kept the details from her, that she hadn't given her a sense of where she came from and why they lived the way they did.

Worse, she was suddenly filled with fear as she imagined the article being written about Tom.

Her mom was right. They had to get him out of here. She bent back over his shoulder to look at the next article in the search results. And the next. For an hour they took turns reading the stuff they found. One article talked about her grandparents, their roles in the Sacramento community where her father had grown up, and their grief over the unsolved murder of their son. Another very short piece said the police department's progress had stalled and the case was officially being remanded to the cold files. Blaydes had a school paper, but it wasn't available online before 2000. The Sacramento paper had a few more stories and a little more depth, but they said essentially the same thing.

Which was really nothing. Exactly what her mother had said.

The final article they found was published ten years after Scott's—her father's—death, on his birthday. It was a tribute in the Sacramento paper, basically reiterating everything the old articles had said, but it contained an interview with the detective in Westbrook who had been in charge of the case.

"You always hate to let 'em go," he'd been quoted as saying. "But that one was particularly tough. We always thought there was more to it than the usual drive-by kind of thing, on account of the girlfriend being missing."

It was the only mention there ever was of her mother. Kelsey figured that was a good thing, but it made her feel like a non-entity in a weird way. Like if her mother didn't exist, she didn't, either.

As if reading her mind, her mother squeezed her shoulder. "They probably did suspect me, and kept my name out of the papers to try to keep me from running too far."

They all sat in silence for a few minutes after reading the last article. Kelsey was sitting on Tom's lap since he hadn't been willing to move away from the computer while she scrolled, and her mother kept casting them inscrutable looks. She hated that. She'd always been able to read her mother, and now she had no clue what she was thinking.

Van popped up from where she lay on the floor. "It's ten-thirty. I'm gonna take a shower and hit the bed."

"You don't strike me as the early-to-bed type," Tyler observed from his perch on the arm of the chair, which had become his spot over the last several hours.

Van grinned. "We're getting out of here early tomorrow, right? Don't linger too long in one spot. Now that we know, you know, nothing." She grinned again. Kelsey loved her for finding this all a huge adventure and wished she didn't have to go back to school. Man, she could barely remember what school was like, way back last week when she wasn't running for her life. For a second, she was jealous of her friends for being able to just go back and forget all this, return to their normal lives. She'd only tasted that for a few weeks, barely two whole months.

"We're sending you and Tom back to school first thing," Regan said.

Van whirled on Kelsey, her eyes wide with significance.

"It's safest," she apologized, amazed when Van's face darkened.

"After all that's happened, you're letting her send us back? Without even arguin'?"

"It's safest!" she repeated. Tom, who'd been rubbing her back the whole time she sat on him, now stopped to pull her fingers off the curve where his neck met his shoulder. She saw red marks where her nails had dug in. "Oh! I'm sorry."

"It's all right." He folded her hands into his, where they wouldn't hurt him. But Kelsey couldn't talk without her hands when she was agitated, so she climbed off his lap and turned to face her roommate fully. All thoughts of adventure and jealousy had fled under the pressure of reality.

"You saw those pictures!" She pointed at the laptop. "You read some of those articles to us. You know what these people are capable of. You saw what they've done to my mother, who was ready for them and knows how to kick ass."

"Kels," Tom tried.

Van grabbed her hockey stick from where it rested against the wall and brandished it. "You don't think I can kick some ass? You haven't seen me use this."

"Come on, girls." Tom rose to stand between them, but he'd said the exact wrong thing. Both turned on him.

"Back off!" growled Van.

"Don't call us girls!" yelled Kelsey.

"You gonna do anything about this?" Tyler asked in the background, apparently of her mother.

"Nope. If they're mad at each other, it will make tomorrow easier."

That shut them up. Van dropped the end of the stick to the floor. "I'm sorry," she mumbled. "I can't stand the thought of not knowing where you are, or what's goin' on. I might never see you again." Her eyes shone with unshed tears and Kelsey rushed over to hug her.

"I know. I don't want you to go. But…" She trailed off, but Van finished for her.

"It's safest. You said that."

"I'm not sure that's true," Tom said. He stood with his hands in his pockets, looking relaxed, but Kelsey recognized his determination. It was the same look he wore on the field when the team was losing.

"Tom." Her heart rate sped up and her breathing started to quicken.

But he stepped closer to her mother and away from her. "Whoever these people are, they know Van and I were with Kelsey. We might not be safe at school, either."

"But you might be. And you're definitely not safe with me." Kelsey tried to counter her panic by breathing deeply, but all that did was put spots in her vision. "You're a math whiz, Tom. Figure out those odds. It's a better bet for you to go home."

"It's not about odds." He still didn't look at her. Kelsey jerked her gaze to her mother, who watched Tom thoughtfully. Oh, God. She was listening to him. He explained, "Math doesn't apply here. The variables are too many and too unquantifiable. If we don't know how far these guys will go to get to Kelsey, or what they want with her, then we could be ideal targets for them."

"If you're not with me, and I'm not at school, it will

be obvious I wouldn't even know if they did something to you." Kelsey's mind raced desperately and latched on to the only other thing Tom cared about more than her. "You'll miss practice! And the game Saturday! And then—and then you won't have play time, so the scouts won't see you, so you won't get drafted!" His look when he finally faced her was amused and affectionate, and she wanted to scream. "Mom, tell him. Tell him he can't come."

"You have a point," her mother said to him. Kelsey let out a low moan. Van came over and held her up when she would have sunk to the floor, but didn't say anything.

"I'm not trying to make a point, Ms. Miller. It's important to me to stay with Kelsey, and evaluation of what we know supports that action."

"I don't think it does. You're not wrong, but we'll alert the campus and town police to watch over you both, and I don't think they'll risk coming after you. Kelsey's right. It's safer there than here, even if it's not completely safe." She raised her eyebrows. "Or we could send you both home."

"No!" came in stereo from both Van and Tom, but a band released from around Kelsey's chest. Her mother wasn't going to give in. Her legs gave out completely and Van couldn't keep her on her feet anymore.

"Kels." Tom was next to her, full of concern and gentle comfort. "Are you okay?"

"I can't let you wind up like my father," she whispered. "Please, please, just go."

His jaw flexed, and she could see it took a lot for him to agree. But finally, he nodded. "All right. If that's what you want."

"I want you to be safe."

Yet, as she lay in bed an hour later, staring up at the swirly ceiling, she couldn't shake the feeling that there was no such thing.

TEN

"I NEVER knew Whetstone was so hard to get to," Regan complained, slamming the phone book shut. "No trains, no buses, no airports less than two hours away from the school."

"We can rent a car," Tom said. "It's only four hours, and no one can track us."

"Wish we had my cousin's car," Van said without a hint of complaint in her voice. "I wonder what happened to it."

"The police had it towed back to Whetstone," Tyler said. Everyone turned to stare at him. "I called them yesterday while you were all sleeping."

Wonderful. Regan wondered who else he'd called. "And?"

"And what?"

"What else did you talk to the police about?"

"I notified the police back home you'd found Kelsey so they could finalize the report. I called the campus police and said she was fine but they should keep an eye out for suspicious people on campus. They were already doing that because three women had called in complaints about two guys roaming the dorms, and in combination with our calls it put them on high alert."

She appreciated that he'd thought of those things, but didn't like that she hadn't known. "When were you going to tell me this?"

He didn't respond, but his clear amusement irritated her. At least he hadn't said "I'm telling you now" or "You didn't ask."

"Okay, here's the plan." She stood and replaced the phone book in the drawer where she'd gotten it. "We'll drive over to the airport, which isn't far from here, and rent a car for Van and Tom. The car rental hub is right off of I-71, which will take you to Columbus, and then you'll take—"

"Twenty-three, I know." Tom nodded. "I've driven it."

"Of course you have. We'll stop and buy a few prepaid cell phones so we can keep in touch off the grid and you all will have a way to contact the police if you need to." She paused. Something felt really off about the plan, but she couldn't put her finger on what it was. Maybe she just didn't like sending these kids off on their own when she was responsible for the danger they were in…even though they were in more danger as long as they were with her and Kelsey.

Or maybe it was because she wasn't following her instincts and leaving Tyler before they went to the airport. His truck was the simplest way to get there, and the least expensive. But all the discussion about whether Van and Tom were safer with Kelsey and Regan or away from them applied to Tyler, too. Regan didn't want to be responsible for something happening to him. The less he knew about where she and Kelsey went, and how, the better.

An idea came to her, and she mulled it over while everyone gathered up their things and Tyler checked out via the television system. By the time they were on the approach to the airport, she knew what she wanted to do.

"Tyler, drop us at the terminal," she ordered. "Park the truck in long-term parking. We'll all take the shuttle to the rental hub and get two vehicles." She planned to be on her way long before Tyler caught up with them, but she didn't say so. "Your truck was spotted by the fake cops a few times and I'd rather not be in it. We don't know how well-connected they are."

Tyler looked at her through the rearview mirror. She knew he didn't believe her, but it didn't matter as long as he did what she asked.

He pulled up a few minutes later in front of the main terminal upper level and they all climbed out, hauling backpacks and Van's ever-present hockey stick. Regan waited for Tyler to drive away. He studied her for a long moment through the truck window, until a security officer waved him on. *It's for his own good*, Regan thought, but felt a pang of sorrow both for ditching him, and that he was letting her.

"How long will it take him to get to the parking lot?" Kelsey asked.

"Assuming he does what I said and goes to long-term parking? Ten minutes to get there, another ten to walk back, more for the shuttle to the rental hub—could be up to a half hour. Let's go." She hurried through the doors into the terminal, the kids trailing behind her, and scanned the signs for the elevator. The shuttle should be on the lower level.

"We're ditching Tyler?" Van asked. "Why?"

"We don't trust him," Kelsey answered. "Mom, you okay? You're limping."

The cut on her hip was pulling, making her take shorter strides with that leg. "I'm fine. Hurry." She hit the button for the elevator, happy when the door opened immediately. So far, so good.

"Good" went bad as soon as they got downstairs, though. The door opened and they stepped out, Regan automatically scanning the crowd. She didn't see anyone suspicious, but Kelsey grabbed her arm and pulled her around the corner.

"They're here!" Her eyes were wide, her pupils dilated in fear. "The fake cops. I saw them." She pointed back toward the left end of the terminal. Van and Tom turned, but the angle of the wall they now leaned against blocked their line of sight.

Regan didn't waste time asking how the hell they knew to be there. "Tell me what you saw. Were they alone?"

"I'm not sure. I only got a glimpse of them." Anticipating Regan's next question, she said, "I know it's them. We fought them. They were right in our faces." She gestured down the terminal. "I saw them in profile, checking out the lines in front of the counters. They didn't see us. I think."

Regan turned to the other two. "Did you see them?" They shook their heads. She motioned them all further back along the slope of the wall, then inched to the corner and peered around it, trying not to be spotted or look like an idiot.

It had been too dark last night to get more than a glimpse of the two men, but she still spotted them right away. As Kelsey had said, they were standing conspicuously in the middle of the floor, searching the lines. They couldn't exit without entering the guys' line of sight.

"We can go outside over here and walk down to the end," Tom said. "But they still might see us through the windows."

"They're not being very stealthy," Kelsey said. "Did you see what they were wearing?"

"Yes." Bright red and green long-sleeved T-shirts with shiny jogging pants.

"They stand out an awful lot."

"They're not stupid," Regan said. "They're a diversion. We're supposed to head away from them and into a trap of some kind."

"How do you know?" Van asked. "They seemed pretty stupid to me."

"Instinct." She eyed the up escalator, but it was too open and too crowded. "Back to the elevator. Upstairs. Act normal."

They rounded the corner to the elevator and hit the button, but while they'd been deliberating it had gone back up. "Don't look at them," she warned in a low voice when the kids' heads all turned to the right. They swiveled back as one, making Regan sigh. Kelsey and Van fidgeted, while Tom positioned himself to block Kelsey on the right. Which was chivalrous and all, but now Regan couldn't see the fake cops, either.

"Excuse me."

The deep voice sounded behind her as the elevator dinged and the kids surged forward, battling the crowd of tourists coming out. Regan hung back, one eye on her crew, and turned to face the men they'd been trying to avoid.

Deciding to brazen it out, she smiled pleasantly. "Yes?"

Polite inquiry turned to satisfaction on the man's face when she turned. Dammit.

He grabbed Regan's right arm above the elbow. "Come with me, please, Ms. Miller."

"Yeah, right." She swung her arm up and over in a circle, breaking his grip, then shoved at his chest. Caught off guard, he backed into his companion, giving Regan just enough space to dart into the elevator behind closing doors. Just before she did, she caught a glimpse of several fast-moving shapes coming from her left. The trap they'd avoided.

She had no time for fear. Adrenaline spiked, a call to action. "Drop your packs." The backpacks didn't have anything that couldn't be replaced—Tom's laptop notwithstanding—and would slow them down too much. Three thuds sounded as the doors opened on the upper level. Regan shoved the kids out ahead of her. "To the left." They obeyed quickly. She overtook them and raced out the open doors. Traffic moved slowly in the pickup area. She held up a hand to halt a taxi and led the kids across the drive and onto the walkway to the short-term parking garage.

"Straight across!" she yelled, reading signs on the run. The long-term garage was on the other side, connected, she hoped, by another walkway.

"They're coming!" Judging by Tom's voice, he was taking up the rear. That would make Kelsey hang back. Regan stopped and motioned them to keep going. "Follow the concourse!" They didn't stop to question her. She glanced back and saw the two neon-dressed guys and at least four black-clad people dashing down the main aisle. They were still a distance back and had to stop for a car whose driver obviously didn't care about pedestrian right-of-way.

Regan kept running, glad she'd gotten some of her strength and flexibility back. The kids were so far ahead she could barely see them. They disappeared through the archway into the other garage. She picked up her pace to catch up and barely slowed when she reached the spot where they waited. Van had taken up a batter's stance with her hockey stick.

"Stairwell," Regan barked, urgency driving her.

"There!" Kelsey pointed to the corner of the garage and they headed that way, Regan once again taking the lead. They raced down one level and back into the garage, where several cars circled, seeking parking spaces.

"Watch for them," she instructed Van and Tom. To Kelsey she said, "You know what to look for."

They all split up, two on each side of the aisle, checking the cars. Regan paused at a sedan a few years old, a car seat visible through the rear window. She felt under the rear wheel wells, then behind the license plate and rear bumper. To Van, who was behind her and still watching for their pursuers, she said, "Check the front wheel wells and under the front bumper for a key box or a key tied to the frame." She could see Kelsey and Tom doing the same with an old Ford wagon on the other side.

They'd checked half a dozen cars and made it halfway around the garage before they got lucky.

"Here!" Kelsey shouted, and Regan and Van dashed over. Regan scanned the level and saw three figures two rows over.

"Duck down," Regan urged.

Kelsey was already unlocking the doors of the Taurus with the key she'd found. Regan made a quick decision and headed for the front passenger seat. "You drive," she told her daughter. "My shoulder will hinder me. Everyone stay down." Tom and Van, in the back, slid down in their seats. Regan stayed upright but flipped the visor down and over to the side window. "There are at least three of them behind us. They expect to see four people. Drive normally," she told Kelsey.

"I know." She checked over her shoulder and backed out, then put her seatbelt on as she put the car in gear and drove smoothly up the aisle.

It didn't matter. A faint shout was followed by a ping against the trunk. Kelsey pressed hard on the accelerator and the car surged forward.

"Shit, where's the exit?" she shouted, her tone

belying the calm and skill with which she handled the car.

"Circle around to the left," Regan told her. "Get all the way down, to the floor, you two." She turned and slid down herself, knowing a bullet through the rear window would penetrate the headrest, and peered between the seats and out the back window. The people behind them—two men and a woman—were running full speed. They closed in a bit when Kelsey took the corner but fell behind again on the flat.

That is, until they cut through the rows of cars.

"Mom!"

Wishing she had her gun, Regan faced forward to see what had Kelsey freaked. Her heart bounced up into her throat when she saw the rest of their pursuers outside the elevator, some of them kicking and beating on a figure on the ground. Tyler.

"What do I do?" Kelsey cried. They were nearing the exit ramp.

"Stop."

Regan caught herself against the dash as Kelsey hit the brakes. "Stay in the car."

She opened her door and jumped out, grabbing the hockey stick Van handed over the seat as she did. She came out swinging and clocked two guys in the head before they even knew what she was doing. The stick broke on the third man's back, but he stopped in the process of nailing Tyler in the ribs and whirled on her. She jabbed the broken end of the stick into his gut. He fell to his knees, his eyes and mouth wide open.

Regan lost the stick as he went down and didn't

bother trying to retrieve it. Adrenaline and rage gave her strength. She spun around the woman coming up behind her and slammed the heel of her foot into the back of her knee. She went down and Regan used her momentum to follow up with an elbow to the back of the woman's head. Pain radiated up her arm and she knew the strike hadn't done much damage, but she'd cleared the way to Tyler for a few precious seconds. Tom had followed her and he now grabbed Tyler's arms, half dragging, half lifting him toward the open rear door of the Taurus.

The people running across the garage had reached them, making up for the three Regan had temporarily incapacitated. A gunshot echoed in the confined space and Tom flinched, going down on one knee in reaction.

Regan pulled Tom to his feet and guarded him, readying herself for attack from all sides, opening her mouth to tell Kelsey to go and knowing with despair that she never would.

Amazingly, the attack didn't come. Half the people around her had hit the floor in reaction to the gunshot. Since it had come from behind the car, the others didn't know it was their own people firing. The ones who hadn't hit the deck were searching for the source.

Taking advantage of the moment of distraction, Tom shoved Tyler into the backseat and followed him in as Van pulled the big man completely into the car. Regan leaped to the front seat and fell inside. Kelsey gunned the engine again before Regan's door was closed. It caught her leg and bounced back, hitting the wall as the car soared onto the exit ramp. Regan barely got her leg in before the door slammed shut.

"Everyone okay?" Kelsey asked.

Regan couldn't answer. Her lower leg felt like it had been snapped in two. All she could see was a haze of red, and she chanted *it's not broken, it's not broken, it's not broken* in her head.

"I'm fine," Tom said. "Tyler's not doing so well."

"Not so bad," Tyler slurred. "Not dying."

"Mom? Mom, talk to me." Kelsey's voice grew more frantic the longer Regan didn't answer. She wanted to, but couldn't unlock her jaw against the pain.

Slowly the red receded, the pain in her leg subsided, and she lifted her head from the back of the seat to see where they were. The car rapidly approached the exit booth, where a sedan blocked their way.

"Go through," Regan managed to say.

"What? I'll smash that car."

"Follow it through."

"I—" Kelsey cut herself off and gripped the wheel tighter, her foot coming off the accelerator as the arm slowly rose in front of the vehicle ahead of them. Regan could see the attendant looking down, sorting cash into the drawer.

"Now!" Regan ground out. Kelsey floored the accelerator again. The car ahead of them turned left onto the access road. Kelsey flew past the booth and cut inside the other vehicle's wide arc. The Taurus scraped the other car's front left fender, but got by onto blessedly clear road.

Which lasted only a couple hundred feet before the access road ended at the main exit drive, which was not clear. Kelsey didn't slow down but did lay on the horn as she spun out into the traffic, slipped between lanes, and found her spot. A moment later they merged onto 237 heading for I-71 South.

The collective sigh in the car fogged the side windows.

"Awwwwwesome," Van breathed, patting Kelsey's shoulder. "You gotta teach me how to do that."

"Is anyone following?" Regan asked. A moment later Tom and Van both said no.

"The cops will be after us," she said. "We didn't pay."

"Not to mention the stolen car and hit-and-run," Van pointed out.

"That's secondary." Kelsey sounded matter-of-fact. "More important are Mom's injuries. Hers and Tyler's."

Regan bent and pulled up the leg of her jeans. A giant red-purple bruise already circled her shin and calf. A redder mark and a dent on her shin showed where the door had nailed her, while her calf burned when she touched it. But she could flex and point her foot, and though she wasn't sure, she didn't think the bone was broken. If her leg had still been outside the car when they hit the wall, things would have been much worse.

"Tyler?" Kelsey glanced in the rear view mirror, checked for traffic on the right, and zipped up the ramp onto I-71.

Regan looked into the back. Tyler was slowly making his way up onto the seat between Van and Tom. He held his ribs with his right arm, and his left wrist seemed swollen. A cut near his hairline oozed, and the strain of his movements showed on his face.

"Is your wrist broken?"

He shook his head and moved the wrist up and down. "Sprained. I caught myself when they knocked me over. Idiot," he sighed, easing back. "I never expected an ambush. They overwhelmed me."

How did they know we would be at the airport? Regan didn't voice the question. The obvious answer was that Tyler had alerted them, but if so, why did they beat him? There was no guarantee she would even see what was happening, so it couldn't be a tactic to fool her.

"What else?" she asked.

"Bruised ribs, maybe cracked." He drew in a slow, deep breath and winced but shook his head. "Bruised. Don't know how I managed to dodge that bullet."

"Tom got scared and fell," Van joked. "So the bullet missed you guys." Tom leaned past Tyler and smacked her lightly on the shoulder.

"I didn't see *you* getting out of the car," he sniped.

"I didn't have my stick. I'm a fraidy-cat without my stick."

"Thanks for stopping, by the way," Tyler said. "Ditching me *was* your original plan, wasn't it?"

"Of course." An unexpected pang of regret went through Regan. "I'm sorry" came out before she stopped it.

"I understand." He peered out the window. "What have we lost?"

"Some food," Kelsey said. "I had water and snacks in my pack, and some first aid stuff and toiletries."

"Same here," Van added. "Clothes. My old phone, but I have the prepaid." They'd bought five of them on the way to the airport, and Regan had insisted they keep them on their bodies, along with any money and identification they had.

"Geography and chemistry textbooks and my jock," Tom joked. "And my laptop," he added with a mournful sigh.

"I'll pay you back," Regan said, her heart sinking at the mounting expenses. When they abandoned this car, she would have to leave money for the repairs, too.

"Don't worry about it," Tom said. "At least we're all here."

Regan managed not to say it, but couldn't stop the words from echoing in her head:

For now.

ELEVEN

THEY LEFT THE car in a shopping center lot in Brook Park. Regan found an envelope and a pen in the glove compartment and, with her sleeves down over her hands, scribbled a note that she wrapped around the money and tucked into the steering wheel. She had Tom check the trunk for rags or something they could wipe down the car with, as they'd left fingerprints all over everything. He pulled out a bag of used kids' clothes, and they rubbed away the evidence of their crime with a few onesies.

As they headed for a McDonald's at the edge of the parking lot, Regan couldn't help lamenting to Tyler, "Through all of this I never broke the law. I changed my name legally, paid taxes—"

"You didn't work under the table?" he asked, limping across the cracked macadam. "How did we not find you sooner?"

She shrugged, her heart skipping a little at his use of "we." Who the hell did he mean? "I did work some questionable jobs. But as Kelsey's needs grew, I needed better-paying work. And I didn't ever use fake ID or commit credit card fraud or anything." Until now.

"I always expected it to be my downfall," she said,

"but they didn't find us for all that time. And now I start out with grand theft auto." She looked back at the scraped and dented car and prayed it didn't belong to someone who was worse off than she was.

"Look at it this way," Tyler said, holding the door to the restaurant. "The blame is all on the people who are after you. You wouldn't have committed the crime if they hadn't pushed you to it."

It didn't help, but she smiled at him for the attempt.

"What the hell do we do now?" Kelsey asked after they'd picked up their food and gathered at a table in the corner, as far from anyone else as they could get.

"I don't know," Regan admitted. She poked her plastic spork at the salad in front of her, not really hungry but knowing she'd be better off if she ate.

"How did they find us?" Van asked next. She munched a handful of fries but had declined a burger. "Tracking device?"

"I don't know how they'd have tagged anyone," Regan answered. "They left me on the ground, naked and supposedly dying. Did they get close enough to you guys the other night?"

"Yeah, but I checked all our stuff when we were in the motel," Kelsey said. "I didn't find anything. They didn't have enough access to hide it well."

"Someone knows something they shouldn't," Tyler agreed. "It wasn't me. I know you think it was," he said to Regan. "But I swear, I told no one we were going to the airport this morning."

"But you had your own cell phone," she said. "Your employer probably has its GPS."

Tyler looked grim. "Yeah, you're right. I left it in the truck, so we should be okay now." He sighed and admitted, "But it does look like someone on my employer's team is dirty."

Regan wasn't sure she believed him, but it was a reasonable explanation and he *had* just gotten beaten to a pulp.

"So what have we got?" Kelsey asked.

"No transportation, no shelter, no one to communicate with," Tom listed.

"No schoolbooks," Kelsey teased.

"No jock!" Van added, giggling.

Regan shook her head. "I can't believe you all still act like this is an adventure. Tyler was almost killed back there."

The kids sobered immediately.

"Now do you see why I want to send you back? I—" She shut up when a ringing cell phone interrupted her. They all stared at each other for a moment, then Tom pulled his prepaid phone from his jeans pocket—the one he hadn't used yet, the one no one but the five of them had a number for. It rang again, shaking slightly in his hand. He raised his eyebrows at Regan for instruction.

She reached over and took it. The display listed a number with a California area code. Tyler's employer was in California. Sick to her stomach, she thumbed the answer button and lifted the phone to her ear.

"Hello."

"Ah, so the young man is still with you, Regan Miller. Or should I say, Chelsea Conrad?"

Regan said nothing. The voice was mechanically altered so she couldn't tell if it was a man or a woman, but somehow the smug satisfaction came through. She didn't bother pelting the person with questions, knowing they wouldn't be answered. Nor would she give him—she just assumed it was a him—any cause to believe he'd gotten to her. To any of them.

Whoever it was got the message and lost the purr with his next words. "We need to see you. You and your daughter. You can let the others go on their way, but we'll know where they are. If you and Miss Kelsey do not do exactly as we say, we will obtain her friends and yours and show you we do indeed mean business."

Still Regan said nothing, though pointless words of hatred poured through her head. Words mixed with despair, because how had he gotten Tom's number? He couldn't have zoned in on the store where they bought them, not this fast. The only way was through Tyler.

"Are you prepared to write this down?" the caller asked.

Regan swallowed against the burn in her throat. "I don't have anything to write with."

"Then you'd better remember it, hadn't you? There's a flight leaving Cleveland for Los Angeles in two hours. Be on it. You will be met at the airport and escorted to my compound. If you cooperate, no harm will come to any of you, including your daughter.

"You've given me a merry chase for nineteen

years. That's an impressive record. But it ends now."
A beep signaled he'd disconnected.

"Who was it? What did they say?"

Regan didn't answer the kids. White hot rage burned inside her, but it wasn't directed at the idiot who had told her to get on a plane. She was such a fool. Ready to believe Tyler—to believe he cared about her and Kelsey, that his employer wasn't the person who'd killed Scott and tried to kidnap her baby. Since the hospital, she'd been anticipating his betrayal, second-guessing his motives, bracing herself for the inevitable. And of course, just as with Alan, it came when she let down her guard.

"I need to talk to you," she said to Tyler, who immediately rose and followed her to the back hall where the restrooms were. She tried the ladies' room, but it was occupied. She pushed into the men's room and locked the door behind them.

"Regan—"

She slugged him. Not in the face, where his strong jaw would have broken her hand, but in the ribs where he was already hurt. She had to use her left hand for the proper angle and the burning pain in her shoulder weakened the punch, but Tyler wasn't expecting her to hit him and he twisted away, falling to one knee with a gasp, his arms cradling his ribs. All the terror and helplessness of the last couple of days overwhelmed rationality, and Regan slammed her knee up into his chin, knocking him backward onto his ass.

"You gave us up, you son of a bitch!" She somehow managed to keep her voice low, despite her need to

scream her betrayal. She yanked him up by his shirt
and cuffed his ear with the heel of her right hand. He
grunted and fell sideways but didn't try to fight back.
She didn't care. "My *daughter!* She's going to die because of you! If she doesn't, her boyfriend will!" She
didn't even know what she was saying. All she knew
was that she'd trusted him against her judgment and
he'd handed them over to the enemy.

"I didn't," he managed to say before she swung
her joined hands at the side of his head. He ducked,
and she let out a roar of outrage.

"Mom!" The door rattled behind her. "Mom, stop!
Let me in!"

"Eighteen years I've been on the edge, afraid, determined. But I've kept her safe. Now you've ruined
both our lives!" She stumbled back when Tyler nudged
her in the bad shoulder, off balance because she wasn't
fighting smart. She was driven by something deeper
than anger, more painful than protectiveness.

The door banged in the frame harder and harder,
all the kids' voices now audible through it. Tyler
lurched to his feet, but Regan pushed off the wall
and launched herself at him. Her right shoulder hit
his midsection as the door flew open and hit the wall.
Tyler flailed and caught the paper towel holder, ripping it off the wall on his way down. His elbow went
into the urinal. Regan cracked her head on the side of
the toilet, but she had the advantage and she wasn't
giving it up.

"They won't get my daughter!" She punched him
in the side, the chest, and the face, panting with ex-

ertion. Someone grabbed at her but she evaded them and put her hands around Tyler's throat. His hand wrapped around her wrist but didn't pull, even as she squeezed. Instead he stared directly into her eyes, only inches away.

"I didn't, Regan." His voice rasped on her name as she started to cut off his air. "I swear, I didn't. I lo—"

"Don't!" She released him and jerked back, helped off him and to her feet by three sets of hands. "Don't you even say that, you son of a bitch!"

"Mom! For God's sake, stop it!" Kelsey turned her and shook her, hard. "They're out there calling the police. We've got to go. Come on."

Regan didn't know what brought her to her senses. Her daughter's calm, underlain by fear and shock? Or the words about to come out of Tyler's mouth—words she hadn't heard from anyone but her daughter since the moment Scott died? Whatever it was acted like a bucket of icy water cast over her. She stared at Tyler, already beaten before she'd pummeled him and now much worse, horrified at the person she'd become.

Tom slipped under Tyler's shoulder and supported him out the restroom door and the exit immediately outside it. Van followed, but Kelsey waited for her mother. Regan avoided her eyes. She was ashamed, but facts were facts. The caller had not only known who Tom was, and that he was with them, but had chosen to call his phone. Sending her a message, she was sure. Trying to intimidate her into turning herself in. Into giving up her daughter.

It was never going to happen.

"HOLD STILL."

Kelsey dabbed antiseptic on Tyler's cheek. She couldn't tell which of his injuries had been inflicted by her mother and which the gang who'd jumped him in the parking garage, but he was banged up good. While her mother told them what the caller said, Kelsey had cleaned Tyler's whole face and used butterfly bandages to close the big cut at his hairline. This split over his cheekbone was probably from her mother. It looked fresher.

She glanced over to where her mother sat, alone in the corner of the new motel they'd checked into. It had been an hour since the phone call. They'd gone to the grocery store in the strip mall and called a taxi, which took them to this hellhole where Van had gone inside to check them in, paying cash.

"That was some tackle," Tom said, trying to get a response from Regan.

But her mother still didn't respond to anything anyone said. Her eyes looked dead, which frightened Kelsey more than anything else had.

Tom turned to her, worried. Kelsey shrugged. She didn't know what to do, either.

"The bleeding on this one stopped," she told Tyler. "I don't think it needs a bandage. Anywhere else?"

He held up his elbow. Kelsey wrinkled her nose. "It smells like urinal cakes."

Tyler grimaced. "That would be because I stuck it in the urinal. How do you know what urinal cakes smell like?"

She glanced at her mother again, but she doubted

she cared. "I've used the guys' bathroom at the frat house."

"Gross."

"Big time. But I was too lazy to go downstairs to the women's room." She checked the scrape on his elbow and shook her head. "I'm not touching it. You need a shower."

He sighed. "I'm not sure I have time."

Kelsey gathered up the trash and chucked it in the tiny trashcan, then stalked over to her mother. "Mom. Come on. You have to tell us what's going on."

"I don't."

Kelsey stopped short. She hadn't expected her to respond. Now when Regan raised her head to glare at Tyler, she looked alive again, and full of the anger that had made her almost kill him. Kelsey had no doubt she would have done it if they hadn't stopped her.

Yet another thing to frighten her. She liked it better when they were just being attacked by the bad guys.

"Who was on the phone?" Kelsey demanded.

Regan stood and circled the bed to stand in front of Tyler. "You're the one who has answers."

Tyler didn't flinch away from her, or try to get away. If it didn't make her feel guilty, Kelsey would have been impressed with the way he looked up at her mother.

"I gave my number to my boss," he admitted. "All our numbers are consecutive. So whoever the mole is must have passed the information on."

"He knew it was Tom's phone specifically," Regan pointed out.

"Then he was guessing," Tyler shot back.

"That would be convenient. You can't prove it."

"You're right." Everything in the room stopped. "I can't operate under my old orders anymore."

"You said you weren't, anyway. That you didn't have orders."

"I didn't have new ones. I was informed it was imperative not to let you know who I worked for."

"And that is?"

Even several feet away, Kelsey could see the shadow crossing his eyes. Her mother didn't move.

"Benjamin and Jeanne Harrison."

Three beats passed before Kelsey processed what he said. Her father's name was Harrison. Those were the names in all the articles they'd read yesterday.

He worked for her grandparents.

But her mother thought her grandparents were the ones after her.

She backed up without thinking, adrenaline speeding through her system on the tail of fear of what was about to happen. She bumped into Tom, whose arms came around her and held her gently.

"I knew it!"

Kelsey thought her mother would start beating on Tyler again but instead she whirled away and limped around the room like she was searching for something.

"Good thing we lost my stick," Van whispered from slightly behind Kelsey. "Should we get out of here? She's scary."

She *was* scary. But Kelsey wasn't going to let

her commit murder. She broke away from Tom and caught her mother before she grabbed the heavy lamp on the bedside table.

"Let him talk, Mom. You can brain him later." She held her mother's shoulders, which heaved under her hands. Regan stared past her, not seeing her or even Tyler on the other side of the room. Kelsey swallowed hard, uncertain what to say to get through to her. "Mom. You can't kill him," she said softly. "I need you."

That did it. Regan set the lamp down and buried her face in her hands. Kelsey put her arms around her, wondering if she was going to cry. She'd never seen her cry before this weekend.

But she didn't. She straightened and glared at Tyler again, but the awful burning was gone.

"Speak."

"I've worked security for the Harrisons for ten years. They're good people," he started, but apparently decided now wasn't the time to go there. "Two years ago someone they'd hired found you. They sent me to watch over you and report in regularly. You know that part. And I did it, for two years, without having any clue why."

"I don't get it," Regan said. "How could you not want to know why?"

"I didn't say I didn't want to. I was STT in the Air Force. I'm used to operations where I know nothing outside the parameters of my job."

"What's STT?" Kelsey asked.

"Special Tactics Team," Van piped up. She

shrugged when everyone turned to stare at her. "It's spec ops."

"How do you know?" Tom asked.

"I read a lot." She grinned. "There's a website."

"Of course." Tom snorted.

"Anyway." Regan motioned at Tyler to continue.

"Anyway, I sent electronic reports and talked to them by phone."

"What kind of things did they want to know?" Regan asked.

"Your job, who you dated, your friends. Where Kelsey went to school, who *her* friends were, what the score of her soccer game was and how she was doing in classes. Basically, everything a grandparent wants to know, plus the kind of safety things an Air Force colonel and major would ask."

Kelsey still stood ready to hold her mother back if she went at Tyler again, but something warm spread inside her. She had grandparents who wanted to know about her soccer game. It didn't matter, just then, how one-sided it had been, or that maybe they'd tried to kidnap her as a baby. For a moment, she felt normal and loved.

But her mother kept asking questions.

"Why didn't they just contact us themselves?"

"I don't know. They must not have thought it would be safe to."

Regan made a face, but continued, "Are they still in the service?"

"No."

"What do they do?"

"I'm not sure. They're scientists, always have been, but the security team isn't privy to their business concerns."

"But you have an idea," Regan guessed.

He nodded, shortly. "They still have strong ties to military science. I think their company does work for defense, which would make sense. I don't know for sure—it was sometimes hard to tell the difference between business visits and social visits by military personnel who were old friends. But I worked in the house, and picked up snippets of conversations here and there. I think…" He hesitated, eyeing Regan. "I think something they were working on before Kelsey was born is the reason you two are in danger now."

That was it? Kelsey deflated. He hadn't told them anything her mother didn't already suspect.

"Why *are* we in danger now?" Regan asked. "Why did they wait?"

Tyler tried a shrug, but her mother would have none of it.

"Someone working for the Harrisons has to be leaking information. That's the only explanation, if it's not the Harrisons themselves."

Kelsey raised her eyebrows. There was something different about the way her mother said that.

Tyler gave a curt nod.

"So they must have known where we were two years ago."

"It's possible."

"Why didn't they come after us until now?"

He sighed. His jaw flexed. Finally he said, "They

had a colleague a long time ago who went rogue. He was underground for years, and resurfaced a while ago. They kept an eye on him. He had to start over, rebuild everything, and wasn't ready for Kelsey until now."

Kelsey watched her mother working that around in her head. It was too much for her to wrap her own brain around.

"Who is he? Why does he want Kelsey?"

"He apparently wants both of you."

"How do you know that?" her mother asked.

Tyler shook his head.

"Who is he?"

He shook his head again. Regan took a deep breath and clenched her fist, but held tight to her calm. "Don't hold things back, Tyler."

He didn't say anything.

"Please," she whispered, and he closed his eyes.

"I don't know everything. Just that a project Ben and Jeanne were working on had something to do with Scott, which is the reason he died."

"The reason someone killed him," Kelsey ground out.

"No, I don't think they wanted him dead. They needed him, and when he was gone, they needed you. But not for the project itself. The person after you—" he looked directly at Kelsey now, "—wanted to change whatever they were doing and turn it into a weapon."

Kelsey's mind raced, tension shifting into appalled shock. "A weapon? Like, for the military?" All of a sudden she wanted to jump back to when she had no answers. "I'm a tool for murder?"

Her mother started toward her, probably to offer comfort, but Kelsey shook her head once, hard. "How? What did they do to me?"

"I don't think they did anything to you. It was what they did to your father. You share his blood."

She jerked to her feet, the urge to burst outside and take off running almost overwhelming her. "That's like science fiction."

"No, just science."

"What did they do to my father, then?" Her voice had gone shrill. She pulled her sleeves down over her palms and hugged herself. "Did what they did to him kill him?" *Stupid question*. He'd been shot. And she'd been fine for eighteen years. Just because she found out now that something had been done to her dad didn't mean an alien was going to bust out of her chest.

The extreme notion pricked her bubble of panic and almost made her laugh. She took a deep breath, aware of her mother's concerned gaze on her. *First things first*, she thought.

"How do you know this stuff?" she asked Tyler.

"I picked it up in bits and pieces," he said quietly. "I wish I could tell you more."

"This information is necessary," Regan broke in, "but not immediately helpful." She paused. "How much have you told them, Tyler?"

When Kelsey turned back to Tyler, he looked as if he was sitting on a bed of nails. Shit.

"Just about everything."

Yeah. Shit.

"List it for me."

"I had a secure phone, and they double secured the call from their end. No one could listen in, even on an in-house extension."

"Obviously, it didn't matter. What did you tell them?"

He ran his hand through his hair and winced, touching the butterfly bandages holding his cut closed. "That you were safe, and Tom and Van were with us but we were taking them to rent a car to go back to school. That you were researching their son's death." He lifted his hands. "As I said, everything."

Regan slumped onto the second bed, her head down, her back curved. Kelsey hated it. Hated she looked so defeated. So small and hurt. There'd only been one other time she'd seen her mother like this— the day she dropped Kelsey at Whetstone. And even then, she put up a strong front. At the time, Kelsey had felt impatient with her. Her mother couldn't protect her forever, she couldn't keep her a child. She'd dismissed her mother's fear as paranoia, maybe psychological illness.

Now, all she felt was regret and fear.

And she didn't know what to do about it.

TWELVE

REGAN NEEDED TO be alone. Since that wasn't possible in a thirteen-by-thirteen room with four other people, she escaped to the bathroom, locking the door and stripping off her clothes to take a shower.

A long, hot, plan-inducing shower.

She already knew what she wanted to do. She just had to figure out how to pull it off without harming anyone, least of all Van and Tom. But right now, she couldn't think. The rage was gone, leaving her completely drained.

She left her clothes in a heap on the floor. There was a laundry room somewhere in this motel. She'd go launder them after she was clean. Wearing a towel if she had to.

She was just stepping into the hot, gloriously pounding water when someone knocked on the door.

"Mom, give me your clothes. Tom and I are going to the laundry room."

Regan smiled at the mirroring of her thoughts. She cracked the door and peeked through. "What are you planning to wear while you wash the clothes?"

Kelsey should have looked sheepish or cagey, but she met her mother's stare head-on. "I'm going to wear his T-shirt and he's going to wear his boxers."

"And what will he wear for underwear later?"

"He'll go commando."

Kelsey tried a cheeky grin, but it didn't fool Regan.

"He'll wash them in the sink later," Kelsey relented.

"All right. Be very careful. They're still out there." She didn't want to let her out of her sight, but it wasn't practical to tie a rope around her waist. She wasn't willing to sacrifice Van any more than Kelsey, and the three had held their own the first time they confronted these jokers. The second time, too.

Besides, Kelsey wanted time alone with Tom and she deserved some. Much as Regan didn't want to think about what would be going on in that laundry room.

"Just remember you're in public." She handed over her clothes. "Stay alert."

Kelsey rolled her eyes and took the bundle. "Yes, Mother."

Regan didn't let go. "Wait."

Kelsey paused, wary, and Regan hesitated. "About what Tyler said."

"Which part?" Her voice came out clipped.

"About the reason they want you."

"Doesn't change anything. We're still trying to get away from them, right? The reason they're doing it doesn't matter."

There was pain behind the logic, Regan could hear it, but she didn't know how to address it. And she was too emotionally weary to try right now.

"I suppose."

Kelsey tugged the clothes from her hands and walked away, leaving Regan feeling like she'd failed. For now.

She closed and locked the door again and this time made it all the way into the shower. It felt cooler and she hoped it wasn't running out of hot water already. She adjusted the temperature and ducked under the spray, and every muscle relaxed.

Something outside the curtain clicked. She froze, then tipped her head out of the water to listen. Someone was in the bathroom. That was the door she'd heard.

She blew out a sigh. "Tyler, I don't want to talk to you anymore."

"Too bad." The toilet clinked. She stuck her head around the curtain to see him wrapped in a towel, sitting on the closed lid of the toilet.

"What the hell are you doing?" Besides showing off that he was in very good shape. She kept her eyes on his face.

"They took my clothes. I already go commando." His grin tried to be unapologetic, but sadness weakened it. "You're a captive audience. I have more to say."

Regan yanked the curtain closed and backed under the water again, the thought of him naked under his jeans floating through her head next to the image she'd just captured. "Does it involve my daughter's safety?"

"Not directly."

"Then I'm not in the mood to hear it."

"There are reasons I didn't question my employer."

"Tyler—"

"Just listen, Regan. I know you don't owe me any-thing, but I'm asking you to listen anyway."

He was wrong. She did owe him. He'd found her in his yard, taken her to the hospital, chased all over Ohio with her, and got beaten not once, but twice. He'd done everything in his power to prove she could trust him. She was too broken to give that trust, and had almost killed him because of that. So, yeah. She owed him.

"All right." She poured shampoo into her palm. "I'm listening."

He didn't talk right away. The silence grew as she lathered and rinsed her hair and put conditioner in it. Half her body had been soaped by the time he spoke again.

"I come from a world of dark things," he finally said. "I've had lots of exposure to the ways people hurt other people."

"I imagine you have." She bent to wash her legs and feet.

"Most of the work I've done for Ben and Jeanne has dealt in some way with that darkness."

Regan jerked a little at the casualness with which he referred to them. She'd barely known their names, never mind used them so easily.

"Are they dark people?" she asked, thinking of Kelsey.

"No. They fight it."

"Ah." Of course, fighting the darkness meant touching it. Sometimes worse. "I understand."

"When I got this assignment, I couldn't believe it. You and Kelsey were so fresh and innocent and light."

She laughed. "No way."

But his serious tone didn't change. "It's true. You were very different from what I was used to."

She heard the toilet seat clink again and assumed he'd gotten to his feet. She rinsed her body quickly and ducked her head back to rinse the conditioner, keeping her ears free of the water so she could hear him.

"I liked being around you. You may have noticed."

Something buzzed low and deep inside her. "The garbage can thing?"

"Yeah." There was a smile in his voice now. "The garbage can thing. I talked to Kelsey a lot, about school and soccer. Gave her some advice on boys."

Regan hadn't known about that. She'd seen Kelsey talking to him occasionally and hadn't liked it, but it was suspicious not to be friendly with the neighbor and, at the time, she hadn't thought any harm would come of it.

Maybe she wasn't wrong. Maybe if she'd followed her instincts and kept Kelsey away from him, he wouldn't have been so quick to help them. To put himself in danger.

She started to turn off the water. At the squeak of the faucet Tyler said, "Leave it on."

"It's getting cold."

"I'll be quick. I don't want anyone to listen in."

She turned the temperature all the way to hot and leaned against the wall. "Okay."

"Under normal circumstances, I would have tried to learn more about what I was doing there. Two years is a long time, and Ben told me at the beginning it might be a few months. But it only took a few weeks for me to realize I didn't want to know if the darkness had touched you. So I never asked for details. Not until this week."

Regan watched his shadow through the curtain. He'd moved closer. "Why was it so important to you?" But she knew why. He'd started to tell her, in the bathroom at McDonald's when she'd tried to kill him with her bare hands. Nausea flared at the memory and she squeezed her eyes closed. She couldn't face what she'd become, even temporarily. Even if she hadn't succeeded in what she'd attempted.

"Regan."

It was low, almost pleading. The curtain moved slightly. Regan pulled away from the wall and slid it sideways enough to see his face, and the pain and hope there almost undid her.

"Tyler," she whispered, and then there was no space to say more. He caught her against him, his towel falling to the floor, his mouth capturing hers in a desperate, plunging kiss. One hand braced on the back of her neck and the other just above her hips, he stepped over the edge of the tub and crowded her against the wall.

Regan fell. Not physically, because she held him as tightly as he held her, and neither one was letting go.

But she fell just the same, into a swirling maelstrom of desire and fear and need. She met him more than halfway, pushing her body closer to his until even the water wouldn't fit between them anymore.

"Your ribs," she murmured against his mouth, but he only kissed her harder. She kept her touch careful, somehow maintaining awareness of his injuries even while the rest of her brain misfired.

Tyler broke away and cupped her head in his hands. "Regan?" It was a question this time, and she nodded. He took her mouth again, running his hands over every part of her body he could reach. She moaned, and he answered it with a growl deep in his throat. The ache his kiss had brought earlier returned, throbbing. She pushed forward and pinned his erection between them, but that wasn't where she wanted it to be.

"God, Regan." He gasped in her ear before biting down on the lobe. She shivered, her elbow thumping against the plastic wall of the shower, and she froze.

"The kids," she whispered.

Tyler chuckled. "They're adults, all of them. And you can't be naive enough to think Kelsey and Tom aren't—"

"I'm not," she murmured. "But that doesn't mean I want them to know what I'm doing."

"They're in the laundry room."

"Van?"

"Asleep."

This was as close as they were going to get to privacy, and if they waited until they were completely alone, it might never happen.

Right now, she desperately needed it to happen.

Making love with Alan had been gentle, quiet. Fucking Tyler Sloane in the shower blew that experience away. His mouth and hands were everywhere, hot and slick and touching her with the perfect amount of pressure no matter where they landed. She clutched at his head when he took her nipple into his mouth and dug her fingernails into his shoulders when he went lower. She stopped him before he went past her belly, tugging him to his feet.

"No time," she murmured. His neck was next to her mouth so she latched on and sucked, hard, closing her hand over his erection. He slammed a hand on the wall and held her up with one arm around her back.

"I don't have anything," he warned her. "I haven't had sex with anyone in two years, and I never intended for this to happen."

She laughed against the skin of his shoulder. Such a difference from Alan's earnest need to protect her. "It's been just a few times in nineteen years for me." She hesitated, then made the second-most-foolish decision of her life. "I don't care, Tyler." She stroked him and raised her leg, trying to lift herself to the proper position. He shifted his grip under her buttocks, moving her almost against his own will, judging by the tightness of all his muscles.

"You have to care."

"I don't." STDs and pregnancy seemed distant, ridiculous specters. Long before either became reality, she'd either have resolved their situation, or she'd be dead.

Tyler might have a problem with that, a little voice of reason said. She tugged his head back by the hair so she could see his eyes. "I could get pregnant. That doesn't bother me."

Tyler stared at her, his expression tight and hard to read. Then his features softened, a new light in his eyes glowing even deeper than it had a few minutes ago.

"No," he whispered roughly. "It doesn't bother me, either."

He shifted her again, letting the wall do most of the work to hold her up, and drove deep and true on the first thrust. For a moment they held still, both arched, savoring the feel of him inside her. Then Regan clenched around him, and it was almost over before it began. He thrust half a dozen times, sliding against her clit and driving her up until pleasure burst. She bit his shoulder so she wouldn't scream. She couldn't process all the sensations filling her, from the heat of his own release deep in her body, to his almost inaudible moans in her ear and the tenderness of his open lips on her cheek.

It seemed to take forever for her to recover. Tyler held her there, against the wall and surrounded by his body. She felt sheltered and cherished but also splintered and raw. Aftershocks swept over her each time they breathed, and when Tyler pressed his face to her neck and she felt wetness that she wasn't sure came from the shower, a tear slid down her own cheek.

A minute later she realized the moisture on her neck felt different because it was warm, whereas the shower was approaching icy. She shivered and Tyler slowly released her, letting her get her balance and pull away from him to turn it off.

"I—"

He stopped whatever she was about to say—she didn't even know what it was—with another kiss. His lips clung to hers and his hand caressed her face, and she knew no words were needed. Not for now.

REGAN ENVISIONED THE two of them emerging wet from the bathroom and being chastised by her daughter, leered at by Tom and laughed at by Van. But all was silent in the room outside as they dried off and wrapped towels around themselves. Tyler rubbed a hand towel over his hair until it was mostly dry while Regan used the motel's blow dryer on hers. She was almost done when Kelsey knocked on the door.

"Here are your clothes." She pushed them through the crack Regan had allowed. "Where's Tyler?"

"He's in here. Brushing his teeth."

Kelsey's lips twitched. "We don't have toothbrushes."

Of course they didn't. They'd dumped just about everything when they left the packs in the elevator.

"He's using his finger and water."

"So…should I hand his clothes through, or leave them out here?"

Regan hesitated a stupid second, making Kelsey laugh.

"Oh, for God's sake. Give them." She grabbed the jeans and shirt and yanked them through, shutting the door harder than necessary on her daughter's self-satisfied face.

"So I guess we don't need to worry about them finding out." Tyler picked up his jeans from where Regan tossed them on the tiny sink and pulled them over his long legs.

"I guess not." She chuckled, letting go of the tension and fretfulness she'd built up over the last few minutes. There was no sense getting worked up. It was done.

"Are you okay?" She eyed his bruises and cuts before he pulled his shirt over his head, but he just shrugged her off.

"I'm fine if you are."

Their eyes locked. Neither of them was close to fine, but she nodded anyway. She stood behind the door while Tyler went out, then dressed quickly. When she came out of the bathroom herself, it was to applause. She could tell Tyler was trying not to smirk and threw a pencil from the desk at him. But the laughter felt good.

"I'm going to the vending machine," Tyler announced, taking orders. When he left, Kelsey cornered Regan by the desk.

"I don't even want to know what happened in there," she said, holding up a hand. But she bent closer and murmured, "You deserve a little happiness. Good for you."

"There's nothing to be happy about, Kels." But she couldn't lie and say nothing had actually *happened*.

"He's a good guy."

A while later, after they'd eaten their snacks and played charades and pretended there wasn't a Big Ugly Something hanging over them, Regan lay awake on the floor between beds. Tyler and Tom shared one bed, and Kelsey and Van the other, but both were too narrow for three. Since there was no way Regan was letting Tom and Kelsey sleep together and she wasn't sleeping next to Tyler with her daughter three feet away, she'd insisted on taking the spare blanket and pillows and finding the most stain-free area of rug to sleep on. No one had dared argue.

Kelsey was right. Tyler was a good guy. And that made what she had to do infinitely harder.

THIRTEEN

KELSEY WOKE SUDDENLY with her mother's hand over her mouth and the room pitch dark save for the faint glow of neon between the opaque curtains. She didn't move until she'd processed everything around her. They'd played this game when she was little, and practiced it when she was older. Both ways, so if anyone invaded their home while they were asleep, one could alert the other without alerting the bad guys.

Tonight, though, there didn't seem to be any. Van dozed back-to-back with Kelsey, and she could see two big lumps in the other bed that had to be Tom and Tyler. She shifted her focal point so her peripheral vision took over. Both men were breathing. She couldn't see or sense anyone else in the room.

She gave a tiny nod, and her mother removed her hand and bent over her ear. "Get your shoes on and come outside with me."

As silently as possible, Kelsey slipped her feet into her untied shoes—she'd been sleeping in her clothes, as they all had for the past couple of days—and followed her mother out the door. They moved away from the building, but when they didn't stop in the shadows at the end as Kelsey expected, she grabbed her mother's arm.

"What's going on?"

"I'll tell you in a minute." She continued across the parking lot and onto the street, walking in the silent darkness along the edge of the curb.

Realizing they weren't staying close, Kelsey called softly, "Hang on!" and bent to tie her sneakers. Her mother waited, her weight shifting back and forth, betraying her impatience.

Irritation surged. If her mother couldn't be bothered to tell her what was going on—

As soon as she straightened, her mother started walking again, going in the direction of the highway.

"Mom! Come on! Tell me where we're going!"

"In a minute," she said over her shoulder. "Wait until we get further away. I don't want them to wake up and come after us."

Kelsey's breath caught, and she understood. Argument and reason had gotten them nowhere, so they were just sneaking off in the dark.

Part of her was relieved. Maybe now Tom and Van would be safe. But what if they were wrong, and the bad guys punished her friends? Unless…

"Are we going to the airport?"

Her mother hesitated fractionally, then nodded. Kelsey held her tongue with difficulty. If they were doing what the guy on the phone had told them to do, everything would be okay. Her friends wouldn't be hurt, and she and her mother could handle whatever came next.

She only wished she could believe that.

REGAN HURRIED, MOST of her senses tuned to her daughter's presence behind her. The rest listened and watched for people or vehicles. She hoped to God she was doing the right thing.

Half an hour later, after leaving the commercial strip and crossing through three residential neighborhoods before returning to a business district, she found what she was looking for. It was almost two in the morning, when the bars all closed down. This street held a couple, and several cabs idled in front. Regan caught Kelsey's arm and rushed her to one, shoving her into the back seat and sliding in behind her.

"Airport, please."

The cabbie hit some buttons and pulled out, humming softly. Only then did the relentless pressure at the back of Regan's throat ease. They rode in silence back to the airport, which was surprisingly busy for the middle of the night.

"Arrivals or departures?" the driver asked.

"Arrivals," Regan said. He took the ramp down to the lower level of the terminal and braked in front of the Delta sign. She paid him with a good tip and got out of the cab. Kelsey frowned next to her while Regan scanned the crowd for signs of the people who'd attacked them earlier. They hadn't been on the flight the caller wanted them on, so he might have people looking for them in case they took another flight, or one to somewhere else.

Kelsey's thoughts must have run in the same direction. "They're probably looking for us. Why haven't they called?"

"I turned all the phones off."

"He's going to be pissed."

Regan motioned for them to cross the now-empty drive. "Who? The caller or Tyler? Or Tom?"

Kelsey laughed, though there was little humor in the sound. "All of the above. I meant Tyler, though." Once they were in the dimness of the garage, she moved closer to her mother. "Will you please tell me what we're doing?"

"Looking for Tyler's truck." She led the way to the long-term garage and walked up the main aisle, scanning the crowded structure for the big white pickup. "We're going to take the truck to California."

"How are we going to do that?"

Regan pulled Tyler's keys out of her pocket and hit the remote button. No beep sounded. She kept hitting it as they walked, but there was nothing.

"You lifted his keys?" Kelsey sounded so incredulous, Regan stared at her.

"Why are you so shocked?"

Kelsey shrugged. "It's just, you—you know, you guys—in the shower."

Regan's face heated and she avoided her daughter's eyes. "Up one level. And we're not talking about that."

"But, I mean, don't you care about him?" Kelsey's breath came faster as they jogged up the stairs in the corner of the garage. "Why would you betray him?"

She couldn't help it. She whirled on her daughter,

startling her so she fell back a couple of steps. "I'm *not* betraying him," she insisted. "I'm trying to protect him. He's in more danger with us. They all are."

"Okay, okay, geez. I just thought…" Kelsey trailed off, a sad note in her voice that echoed the ache in Regan's heart.

Even if the Harrisons were behind everything, she didn't think Tyler believed it. He knew she couldn't trust them, couldn't take his word that they weren't the enemy, and that was why he'd resisted telling her for so long. But whether they were the enemy or not didn't matter. Being caught in the middle could be deadly for him, and she couldn't allow that.

They searched three more levels before they found the vehicle. Regan unlocked it and climbed in while Kelsey went around to the passenger side. She lowered the visor and plucked the parking ticket from the strap holding it, then took a moment to familiarize herself with the controls. After adjusting the seat and mirrors, she started the truck with a roar that subsided immediately to a comforting rumble.

"Can you drive this?" Kelsey asked.

"Of course." She backed slowly out of the tight spot and headed for the exit. "Look in the glove compartment."

"For what?"

"Anything."

Kelsey popped the handle and started rummaging through the items inside. "So, when did you learn to drive a giant pickup truck?"

"I didn't. I drove a forklift and a dump truck."

Feeling her daughter's surprise, she added, "When you were little."

"The things I don't know about you."

Regan paid the fee at the gate and made it to the highway without mishap. "Okay, what have we got?"

"Tissues, napkins and three packs of gum," Kelsey inventoried. "The registration—"

"What's it say? Address?"

Kelsey used two fingers to hold open the envelope and read the paper inside. "Tyler Sloane, and his address next to us in Ohio."

She'd hoped it had a corporate registration or something, but after two years undercover, it was logical all the bases would be covered. "Okay, what else?"

"A surprisingly compact national road atlas." She waved the thick book. "His phone."

"Ditch it." She'd almost forgotten about the phone and its GPS signal.

"It's off."

"Doesn't matter. It might have been modified to transmit his position anyway."

Kelsey rolled down her window and tossed the phone out. "GPS destroyed. Check." She reached back into the glove compartment. "There are a couple of repair orders for the truck, an old stick of lip protectant, a receipt for McDonald's, and this." She pulled out a pistol in a pancake holster, her hand wrapped over the side of it.

"Give me that." Regan snatched it out of her hand.

"I know how to handle a gun," Kelsey protested.

"I know you do. But I don't want you to have to."
Keeping her left hand partly on the wheel, Regan
checked the safety, chamber and clip before secur-
ing the gun and tucking it into her rear waistband. It
made driving uncomfortable, but it was safe.

Awfully cavalier, the way she was tossing that
word around. It was starting to lose its meaning.

Kelsey replaced everything in the glove compartment and leaned back, bracing her feet on the dash.
"What now?"

"Now, we drive. We've got a full tank and a lot of
distance to cover." She glanced at her daughter. "And
we talk about the new information Tyler gave us."

Her daughter sighed and folded her arms. "This
is going to be fun."

REGAN DROVE UNTIL she couldn't keep her eyes open.
Then she gave Kelsey a crash course in controlling
a rear-wheel-drive diesel and let her drive for a few
more hours.

Off and on, she tried to draw Kelsey into conversation about why Tyler had said they wanted her. It
usually spun off into speculation on the science of it,
matter-of-fact suggestions on why Kelsey was important to them. Regan kept dragging it back to emotions,
but Kelsey resisted talking about it. She contended
that it didn't matter.

Around noon, both too tired to continue—either
driving or talking—they checked into a cheap motel
outside Des Moines, Iowa. Regan paid cash and used
the new names, though the clerk didn't ask for ID.

"We should call them," Kelsey said for the ninth time. "They might think we were taken."

"The call could be traced," Regan repeated wearily.

"We'll keep it short. Use the pay phone out front."

Her daughter looked so hopeful Regan couldn't resist her anymore.

"All right, but I'll do the calling."

Kelsey jumped to her feet. Her eyes sparkled despite her obvious fatigue. Tom had put that life into her, Regan realized. Just the thought of talking to him gave her daughter a lift. Her heart throbbed once, twice, with regret. Motherly sorrow, of course, the kind all mothers have when their children become adults. But also regret that she had to interfere in their happiness.

Kelsey skipped down the sidewalk to the phone. She jingled a handful of quarters and reached for the receiver, but Regan gently removed it from her hand.

"Let me." If the bad guys had gotten to the kids and Tyler, she didn't want Kelsey to be the one making the call. She dialed Van's phone number and deposited the coins requested. It rang only once before Van's anxious, high-pitched voice answered.

"Hello? Who the hell is this? If you bastards have her, I'll—"

"Van, it's me. Regan." Apparently, Kelsey had been right to insist they call. "We're fine."

"Thank God." She didn't pause before launching into her. "Do you have any idea what we're goin' through?" Her accent thickened as she went on, but

Regan cut her off again. They didn't have time to be yelled at.

"Are you all okay?"

Van shifted gears without a stutter. "Tom is goin' apeshit. He upchucked when he woke up and Kelsey was gone, and Tyler is so furious, he's rigid. He can't talk without shattering his jaw. I figured you'd skipped on us, but we didn't *know*, because no one left us a frickin' *note*."

"I'm sorry, Van. We had to. Let me talk to Tyler." Regan ignored Kelsey's frantic motions to hand her the phone. "We have to be quick so no one traces the call."

Van handed off the phone without another word.

"Where the hell are you?" Tyler's voice was so tight Regan realized Van hadn't been exaggerating. "Don't answer that," he contradicted himself.

"I wasn't going to. Anything happen?"

"Besides the wham-bam-thank-you-Tyler-now-I'm-ditching-you? No."

"You haven't heard from him?"

"No. And I haven't talked to the Harrisons, either."

"Where are you? Don't answer that."

Tyler didn't laugh. "We left the motel. We're behind you."

Unease flitted through her. "What do you mean, you're behind us?"

"I mean we rented a car at the airport—three of those guys were still there, but they didn't see us—and are on our way to your destination."

"Are you sure they didn't see you?"

"Positive."

"How do you know where we're going?"

He sighed. "Let's just say I've figured out how you think. Let Kelsey talk to Tom, will you? I think he's going to throw up again."

Regan handed the phone to her daughter, who stopped clawing at her hand and snatched it away.

"Tom?"

Regan stepped a few feet away to give her privacy, and distance herself from the cooing. Amazingly, it didn't frighten her to know Tyler was on her tail—assuming he really was. She wasn't sure how he knew what she was thinking when she didn't know herself. But if he had figured out more than she had, and was following them…dammit, she found it comforting. Despite the danger he could be driving right back into.

Why did he still have Van and Tom, anyway? She turned to take the phone from Kelsey but found her hanging up. She cursed, making her daughter's eyebrows go up.

"What?"

"I thought he was mad at you," Regan said.

"Nope. Scared." Kelsey started back to the motel room, covering a huge yawn with the back of her hand. "He thought we'd been taken. But he's cool now."

"Why didn't Tyler send them back to school?"

She shrugged and held out a hand for the key card, which Regan handed her. "I dunno. I think 'cause if he did, they wouldn't know how we were."

There was nothing she could do about it now, so Regan locked the room tight behind them, pulled the drapes, and kicked off her shoes.

"Four hours," she said. "Then we hit the road again."

"What's with you and four hours, anyway?" Kelsey grumbled. She automatically took the bed farthest from the door and dropped face-first onto it, snuggling into the pillow she pulled out from under the garish comforter.

"It's optimum—" She stopped. Kelsey was already asleep. She slid the gun under her own pillow, then lay down and closed her eyes.

She knew when she woke they'd far exceeded her time limit. Between the drapes showed a dim red and blue glow, not the bright sunshine there'd been when they came inside. She started to lift herself off the pillow, then froze.

There was someone else in the room.

FOURTEEN

NOT AGAIN, SHE moaned silently. This was getting old.

She murmured as if in her sleep and rolled her head to the other side, slitting her eyes to try to see who was there and what they were doing. She could barely make out the outline of someone standing between the beds, unmoving. The person was tall and wide, probably male by the shape, and dressed in dark clothes.

Sleep held her body in enough grip to let her analytical mind continue processing. The figure was too far away for her to hit, even if she rolled across the bed. She couldn't tell if he held anything in his hands. She chanced a glance at Kelsey, who was now partly under the covers and seemed to still be deeply asleep, lying on her side with her back to the room. Regan's muscles tensed, ready to spring into action, but even the slight movement caused twinges all over her body, from her weak shoulder to her lower back and all the cuts in between.

"I know you're awake." The voice was low and strangely unmenacing. She didn't recognize it as belonging to any of the men they'd confronted so far.

She didn't bother trying to pretend she was asleep

anymore. She just waited. Thirty seconds. A minute. The man didn't move, and neither did Kelsey.

Was Kelsey even breathing? Had they succeeded in killing her? It took every ounce of willpower Regan had built over the years not to leap up and check.

"She's okay," the man finally said, and Regan wondered how the hell he was reading her mind. "She's sedated."

No. Her heart rate picked up and energy flooded her muscles, preparing her for action. "What do you want?" she asked, keeping her eyes just to the left of him so her peripheral vision would tell her if he moved.

He didn't. "I want to take you to my employer. No one is going to be hurt. Trust me."

Regan snorted despite her tension. "Yeah, right. You killed my boyfriend and left me for dead, beat up one of your own, chased and attacked us more than once—lots of basis for trust there."

"You've got it wrong." He took a couple of steps up the narrow space between beds and lifted his arms a little. She could now see a syringe in his right hand, and for the first time since she'd woken up, she tasted fear. She couldn't let him sedate her, too, and drag them both to whomever he worked for.

The fool bent over her, and now she tasted satisfaction. Hadn't he been told about their first attempt? Regan twisted at the waist and scissored her legs across the bed and up around his forearms, one under them, one over, hoping to knock the syringe from his hands without getting stuck. On the way by, her top foot glanced off his cheek, the impact reverberating up her leg. He grunted and spun away, but in the confined space his feet got tangled and he went down.

With a short burst of elation, Regan dropped to the floor and landed in a crouch, straddling his legs. She flattened her right hand and slammed it into his nose. He howled, his hands flying to his face, leaving his abdomen exposed. *Kick him*, her brain urged, but she didn't have the leverage and since he was on his side, she couldn't drive her knee into his solar plexus. Where the hell was a weapon when she needed one?

Knock him out.

She searched frantically for the syringe, barely avoiding his weak grabs for her. The pain blinding him wouldn't last long. Her heart jumped when his left hand latched on to her wrist. Her breath now coming in sharp pants, she jerked her right foot out from under his hip and slammed it down on his biceps, dragging his arm to the floor.

There. The syringe had fallen onto Kelsey's bed. She grabbed it and shoved the needle through his sleeve and into his upper arm, pressing the plunger down as quickly as it would go. He struggled wildly at the first sting of the needle. Regan fell sideways onto her bed, where she could use her feet to keep him at bay. Within a few moments he slumped back to the floor, his eyes rolling back in his head, the whites looking purple in the glow from the neon sign outside.

Regan didn't waste any time on relief or recovery. She didn't know if he'd come alone or if he had

a partner—or partners—waiting outside. She slid off
the foot of the bed and grabbed the man by his wrists,
dragging him around the end of Kelsey's bed and into
the bathroom. There wasn't enough room to pull him
all the way in without a lot of effort. His feet would
be visible from the doorway, but she didn't have time
to worry about it.

She hurried to Kelsey's bed and shook her shoulder, not having much hope for a response. She hadn't
moved during the entire scuffle.

"Kelsey."

Nothing. Even though she'd expected it, it still
made her stomach roll. She checked her daughter's
pulse and timed her breathing, both of which seemed
fine. Then there was nothing to do but carry her out.

The clock on the table between the beds said it was
eight-thirty, over two hours later than she'd intended
to sleep. Again. It was dark outside, though well lit by
the neon that not only illuminated the motel's name
and "vacancy" sign, but also lined the roof over the
room entrances.

Moving as fast as she could, the specter of Seda-
tion Man's partners on her tail, she gathered the few
things they'd brought into the room and carried the
backpack out to Tyler's truck, which she'd parked
several spots away from her door. There was a couple nuzzling each other several doors away and a car
parked in front of the office, as well as one pulling
into the lot. Nerves jittered up Regan's spine when she
spotted the new one. She watched the nuzzly couple
disappear into their room, then went back into hers

and peered through the window. The new car bypassed the office and pulled down to the far end of the lot before reversing into a space on the other side of the U-shaped building. No one got out.

"Shit." The nerves buzzed harder. The car might be unconnected, but the timing and actions were too coincidental. How was she going to get Kelsey out of here? Especially if they'd spotted her by Tyler's truck when they pulled in.

Abandoning the supplies again to go out the back chafed, but she didn't have much choice. Newer motels didn't have bathroom windows, but this one, being very old and very unremodeled, did. Part of the reason she'd chosen it, of course, besides its seediness making it more likely the staff would bypass usual ID protocols.

Don't rush it. She drew a few deep, calming breaths while she watched a moment longer. A man came out of the office and climbed into the car in front. His tread was heavy, as if he was a weary traveler, and he pulled around to park next to her truck. Regan couldn't see him now, but heard thuds like the car door and trunk, and then the unmistakable bang of a room door slamming closed. Immediately, three doors of the other car across the way opened.

Regan exploded into action. She rushed back to Kelsey and hauled her out of the bed, dragging her limp form with Kelsey's right arm draped around her neck and her own left arm around her daughter's waist. It was the wrong way to do it and sent her shoulder screaming, but she didn't have time to change position. She dragged her into the bathroom and over the body of their latest attacker, then propped her against the tub while she opened the window over the toilet and poked her head out to assess the area.

There was a narrow alley between the motel and the restaurant next door, not wide enough for most cars. A motorcycle was parked on the right, near a door into the restaurant, probably the kitchen or storeroom. She needed a vehicle but that wouldn't do, obviously, with Kelsey unable to hold on.

Traffic drove by without ceasing on her left, far enough away she didn't think anyone would see her climbing out the window. The window itself was plenty big enough to get through, but it was high on the wall, leaving a drop of a good seven or eight feet to the alley below.

Kelsey would hate her if she knew what her mother was about to do.

Steeling herself, Regan reached down and hauled Kelsey's limp form off the floor and onto the toilet seat. Using one arm to hold her in place against the tank, she climbed up onto it and put her right leg through the window. Pressing her leg to the outside wall for leverage, she pulled Kelsey up higher, then grabbed her T-shirt, bunched at her shoulder blades, in her left fist.

Kelsey sagged and slid over the side of the seat, but Regan's grip was firm. Kelsey's weight served as ballast as Regan maneuvered her left leg through the window and backed out, balancing on her chest, her toes braced against the wall but providing no lever-age. The ridges of the windowsill dug into her and she gritted her teeth against the pain. A few more bruises were nothing when compared to her daughter's life.

But now she had a problem. She had at least two feet before she hit the ground. She'd be unable to reach the window, but could hardly pull Kelsey through while she herself hung one-handed from the sill. If she pulled her through on her back, she'd scrape her up and bruise her delicate skin. She hung there, cursing herself for doing something so stupid and wishing she'd never tried this.

Then she heard a knock on the door.

Panic shot through her. She stuck her wrists under Kelsey's armpits, lifted her, and let the weight of her own body pull her back and through the window, Kelsey slithering over the edge like a giant squid, arms and legs dangling like tentacles. When Regan's feet hit the ground she fell backward, holding tightly to her daughter so her head didn't hit anything and most of her body landed on Regan.

She allowed herself to lie panting for five sec-onds, then struggled to her feet, this time supporting Kelsey on her right side to give her moaning shoulder a break. She hesitated one more moment, thinking which way to go. Dragging an unconscious person would definitely call attention to herself, so the main street was out. She headed for the dark, motorcycle end of the alley. There was a copse of trees back there, with a cluster of bushes she might be able to hide in until the sedative wore off.

She'd only gone three steps when the end of the alley was blocked.

For two seconds, Regan almost gave in to the fatigue and pain and overwhelming aloneness and sank down into a heap on the broken macadam.

Then, somehow, she got a whiff of her daughter's familiar scent and determination came back. She carefully lowered Kelsey to the ground as the shadowed figures at the end of the alley approached. She didn't take time to evaluate anything, just started running full-speed toward them, a roar building in her chest. She was *not* going to let them take her daughter.

She recognized the tallest man a second before her shoulder plowed into his midsection, knocking him back into the other man, who made a grab for the woman's arm and missed. The three of them fell to the ground, Van yelling her name as they went.

"What the hell are you doing?" Regan punched Tyler's shoulder before she could stop herself. The poor guy had been beaten twice already, and her considerable weight on top of him couldn't be comfortable, especially with Tom under him. She scrambled to her feet with Van's help. "Do you know what you just did?"

"Punished myself." Tyler grimaced and held his ribs in the now-familiar protective pose as he reached for Regan's outstretched hand and let her pull him to his feet. "If your phone was on, you would have known we were almost here."

"I didn't trust it."

"Yeah. You don't trust much, do you?"

She felt his eyes on her but didn't look up. Tears welled, pissing her off. She was tired and overwhelmed, but that was no excuse for weakness.

Tom had spotted Kelsey on the ground behind her, dragged himself from under Tyler, and dashed down the dirty alley to his girlfriend.

"What's wrong with Kelsey?" Van demanded, starting to head her way, too.

"She's okay, I think. She was sedated."

"You sedated her?" Tom demanded, carrying her back to them cradled against his chest.

"By who?" Van asked at the same time, sounding just as angry and protective.

"By some guy who managed to find us and break into the room. He almost got me, too. I was so tired, he was in the room for a while before I woke up. I was about to carry Kels out the front when you guys showed up." She knew she sounded accusatory but couldn't help it. "How did you find us, anyway?"

Tyler turned her and started moving them all to the far end of the alley where they could go around the building. "Same way he did, probably. The GPS on the truck."

"We threw the phone away," she said inanely. He hadn't said the GPS in the phone.

"My employer has a GPS installed in all his employee vehicles. It's hidden and not easily disabled." Tyler stopped them and peered around the corner, then motioned them all forward. "You need me to take her a bit?" he asked Tom, who shook his head. He didn't show any sign Kelsey was at all heavy.

They swiftly got to the next corner and moved on around the rear of the far side of the building, this one backing up to an even narrower alley. They had to walk single file. She let Tyler go ahead, with Tom behind her and Van bringing up the rear.

"We'll leave the truck here and take the rental," Tyler said.

Regan wanted to cry. "And go where? Besides, doesn't the rental have a GPS and a tracker, too? So the agency can keep track of its location?"

Tyler flashed her a grin over his shoulder. "That one I disabled. Piece of cake. They're trying to keep renters from violating their terms. They don't expect people like us to be renting their property."

People like us. What was that, Regan wondered? Crooks? Ex-military? Mothers on the run? Illicit lovers? She banished the last thought, both in regard to herself and to her daughter and Tom. Ugh.

"Where are we going?" she asked again. Complete and utter weariness made her feet heavy and her back bow as they got to the other end of the building and stopped.

"I'll tell you later. Let me bring the car over and get us away from here." Tyler disappeared toward the center of the lot where he'd parked. Regan waited with the others, grateful when Van leaned against her side, holding her up.

"I'm sorry we left you," she said. "I was trying—"

"I know. Just remember how we saved your ass tonight, 'kay?"

Regan smirked. "If you don't lord it over me forever."

She didn't know what was going to happen next, but she finally accepted that whatever it was would include the entire group. Which made it all the more important to come up with a plan.

One putting them in control.

Tyler pulled up with the car and they all hurried into it. Regan got into the front seat, the déjà vu so strong she knelt on the edge of despair. Nothing was going to change. They were going to keep running and being attacked and running again, until they couldn't run anymore. Or couldn't fight. Either way, it would lead to failure.

"Don't worry," Tyler said. "I figured something out."

"What?"

"When I realized you'd stopped here I remembered it." He slowed for the red light and glanced at her. His lopsided smile reminded her of a little boy who'd made his mother a clay pencil holder. "My stepfather's mother left me a house in Minnesota. I haven't been there in years. A property management firm rents it for me, but no one is there right now."

"Sounds convenient," Regan retorted.

"It is." Either oblivious to or ignoring her sarcasm, he explained, "I lived with my father growing up and saw my mother once a month. Dad hated my stepfather and was very resentful of my grandmother—step-grandmother, though I thought of her as blood—so I never told him when she left me the house. No one knows about it."

"What about your stepfather?"

He went quiet even before he spoke. "He and my mother died in a plane crash when I was nineteen, four years before my grandmother passed away."

"And the Harrisons don't know about this place, either?"

"Nope."

Regan was skeptical. What little she knew about the Harrisons pointed to their being the kind of people who learned every possible tidbit about those who worked for them.

But they needed a place.

"Did you see the guy in the bathroom?" she asked him.

"Just his feet."

"Didn't happen to recognize his feet, did you?"

Tyler chuckled. "No. Should I have?"

"He said his employer sent him."

"Doesn't mean his employer and mine are the same." He glanced at her. "Really, Regan, I don't think the Harrisons would have killed Alan the same night they sent me to protect you."

Unless they'd recognized Tyler's growing feelings for her and couldn't trust him anymore.

It was the first time she'd thought of his feelings since she'd left the last hotel. It unlocked a floodgate of its own, and suddenly she was glad he'd found her. She rested her hand on the console between them and Tyler immediately took it in his, raising it to his lips and pressing a tender kiss to her knuckles. His fingers trembled as he lowered their hands to his thigh, and this time he stared straight ahead, obviously avoiding looking at her.

For the first time, Regan believed he cared about her. She'd scared him when she left. Her inner cynic reminded her he could have been scared about what the Harrisons would do when they realized he'd lost them, but she didn't think, despite the performance he'd put on for the last two years, he was that good an actor.

Or maybe she just needed to believe in something new.

She looked over her shoulder. Tom cradled Kelsey on his lap, and Regan didn't have the heart to tell him to put her in a seatbelt. His face was taut, his hands clutching her against him, and he even rocked forward and back as he watched the side mirror through his window.

"She'll be okay, Tom," she told him. "It's just a sedative." She hoped. There was no reason to believe otherwise, at least, not at this point. Kelsey's breathing was still steady, and when she reached back to check the pulse in her wrist, it was strong.

Van, who held Kelsey's lower legs on her lap, sighed. "Too bad I wasn't there to help kick his butt."

Regan turned around so Van didn't see her smile. The girl was tough-minded and fearless, no doubt, but Regan didn't think she had the kind of background that led to a lot of butt-kicking.

Then again, neither did she or Kelsey. Not in actuality.

"So what happens after we get to this house?" she asked Tyler. "We can't just keep running. We have to go on the offensive or this will be a very short game. One we'll lose."

Tyler squeezed her hand. "We're going to try, *again*, to rest and get clean and up to full power. Then we'll figure it out."

Regan didn't say so, but she planned to have something figured out long before then.

FIFTEEN

THREE DAYS PASSED before they had a workable set of plans in place.

They'd arrived at the house, Kelsey awake and fine, if groggy, and once Regan discovered how truly isolated they were—the bungalow was a mile up a private dirt lane twenty miles from the nearest town with no TV, phone, internet access, or cell signal—she finally relaxed.

The kids didn't, of course. After the first day, which they spent sleeping and chopping wood and preparing meals and discussing the little they knew of their situation, all three were going stir crazy. The one saving grace was the stereo system and collection of CDs in the master bedroom upstairs, and on the second day the kids remained up there, listening to music, dancing, and hopefully nothing else. In the meantime, Tyler insisted Regan rest until the dark circles disappeared. He prescribed soaks in the hot tub—alone—a novel, and more sleep than she'd managed since Kelsey left for school. When she stopped fighting him and succumbed, she found her injuries finally began to heal, aches and pains faded, and her mind cleared.

On the third day, she and Tyler schemed. By dinnertime, they had a plan Regan was okay with and Tyler was certain would lead to the solutions they sought.

The kids didn't agree.

"What's the goal here?" Kelsey scooped mashed potatoes onto her plate and traded them with Van for the meatloaf. "You're walking right into the lion's den."

"But the enemy is the crocodile," Tyler said. Something in his voice made Regan turn sharply, but he didn't *look* like he'd said anything significant. He spooned peas onto his plate and handed the bowl to Regan, stopping in midair when he found her staring at him. "What?"

"What do you mean, crocodile?"

He smirked. "I mean the lion isn't the enemy, the crocodile is. So walking into the lion's den isn't unsafe."

"Hmm." She studied him for another few seconds, sure there'd been a hard undercurrent in his tone.

"Mom." Kelsey waved her fork. "Goal? Den? What's the point of going out there?"

"I need to talk to the Harrisons and find out what's going on," she explained. "If they are the ones after us, I want to find a way to stop them. Running from state to state won't get us anywhere, and I can't keep Van and Tom out here any longer. Him missing tonight's game is already going to send up red flags." He'd notified his coach he was sick, but this had already gone on too long. Regan couldn't think about how their parents would feel if they knew their kids were missing. "If they aren't the ones after us, they can tell us who is, and fill in the blanks on their plans."

"But we won't have any way to contact you, or know if you're okay," Kelsey argued.

Regan swallowed against the terror her daughter's what-if mentality stirred up. Leaving Kelsey went against every instinct she'd developed for eighteen years. "I'll check in," she tried to say casually. If Kelsey balked too hard at this, Regan wasn't sure she could go through with it.

"How? We have no phone and no service here."

"I have a way." Tyler outlined his plan to send a telegram to the office in the nearest town and have it delivered. "The courier service here is very well known and has distinctive uniforms."

"Doesn't sound very secure to me." Tom set down his fork. "Sorry, but that could be easily compromised."

Tyler nodded. "It's unlikely but not impossible. So we have a code word to legitimize it for you. We'll only be gone three days, four maximum," he assured them. "This is a recon mission, and I trust the Harrisons."

"But not completely." Kelsey twirled her fork in her potatoes, making a hole. "If you trusted them completely, you'd take me with you."

Tyler didn't answer, and to Regan that was tantamount to agreement.

"So what happens after you go there?" Van asked. "Good meatloaf, Ms. Miller."

"Thank you, Van, but call me Regan. After all this…" She sipped her milk and took a bite of a dinner roll before answering. "I guess it depends on what we find out."

Van eyed her roommate and Tom with slight disgust. "You're leaving me with these two lovebirds?"

"You can go back—"

"No. Thanks. I'll endure it." She stabbed at her meat, the scowl still on her face. "Rather go to California with you."

"Well, so would we!" Kelsey snapped. "We don't want to be stuck here any more than you do."

"What's that supposed to mean?"

"Come on, chill out." Tom tried to soothe them, but the two girls switched from glaring at each other to glaring at him.

Tyler looked at Regan, who shrugged. "They've been stuck in close proximity too long." She waved her fork at them. "After dinner, separate rooms. You need to get over it because I'm not leaving unless I can trust the three of you to watch each other's backs."

"How can you say that?" Kelsey shot at her, in time with Van's "She's my best friend!" They gave each other sheepish grins. "We'll be okay, Mom."

"I hope so. I'm afraid you'll fight and one of you will go off, believing everything will be fine because it has been for two days, and that's when something will happen."

Kelsey rolled her eyes. "This isn't the movies, Mom. Don't worry. We'll be fine."

Regan had doubts about that, but she was also aware she could be looking for reasons not to leave her daughter.

After dinner she stood on the porch, leaning against the rail and looking out across the pitch-black space surrounding the house, trying to convince herself she was doing the right thing.

"You are."

She turned her head enough to see Tyler leaning against the doorjamb inside the screen, the light inside casting him in shadow.

"I am what?"

He came out and leaned on the rail next to her. "Doing the right thing."

She shook her head but couldn't help the tiny smile. "You think you know me."

"Tell me I'm wrong, and you weren't fretting about the danger you're putting Kelsey in by leaving her without your protection."

She didn't answer, because of course she couldn't deny it. "I know she'd be in more danger if she went with us."

"I don't know that." His voice had hardened a bit. "I keep telling you—"

"The Harrisons are saints."

"No, far from it. But they aren't the ones trying to hurt you."

"You don't know for sure."

He hesitated before saying, "No."

The soft admission was one he'd never made before, and Regan twisted to look at him, her mouth open slightly. "What?"

"No, I don't know for sure. Not well enough to put Kelsey's life on the line."

"Tyler." Something swelled in her chest and started to close her throat.

He put a finger against her lips. "Besides, the threat is there whether it comes from the Harrisons or not. They might get more determined to stop us when we get close to safety."

It would be petty arguing to say she doubted the Harrisons' would be safe, so she turned away to face out into the fields again. "It's so dark," she commented. She didn't live in the city, was used to farmland surrounding her, but even then there were highway lights or street lamps or the ambient glow from downtown. Here it was dark black as far as she could see, with only a faint difference on the far horizon between the slope of land and the sky. It was also overcast, so no stars sparkled overhead.

"That's a good thing. It would be difficult for anyone to get here without being spotted."

"Not at night," Regan countered. "If they have NVGs and the kids aren't watching—and face it, they won't be watching. They're kids." She waved a hand at the six-foot circle of light the windows cast into the front yard. "Someone could be feet away from us right now and we wouldn't know it."

He looked out for a minute, then back at her. "You're right. There's risk. I think it's a small one, but you're already shouldering too much and I wanted to lessen your worries."

Regan's shoulders slumped, and Tyler slid a hand across them and tugged her against his chest. "Come here. I promise you, I won't do anything to endanger Kelsey any more than she already is."

She sighed and turned her face into him, letting him wrap his arms around her and rub his hand up and down her back for just a few seconds. She'd been without this for so long, it didn't bother her that she craved it so much. That she was so tempted to give in to the need to be comforted and protected.

But she couldn't let it go on. Not until she had answers. So she pulled back too soon, and Tyler let her.

"You don't know what they did to him? To Scott?"

He shook his head slowly. "I wish I did. But I don't think it was anything that would have caused harm to Kelsey. I mean—"

"She's been fine for eighteen years, I know. She's pointed that out several times. Enough that I know it scares her."

"That's understandable."

Regan sighed and stared out into the darkness again. She still felt impotent, unable to soothe Kelsey's fears or fix whatever was wrong. But the only way to make it right was to do what they were about to do. So she turned her attention to the plan.

"How long will it take us to get there?"

"Not long. We're chartering a flight out of Fairmont Municipal. Flight will be about four hours."

"What?" She'd assumed they were going to drive,

because by the time they got to Minneapolis and took a connecting flight to Sacramento, got a vehicle, and drove to the Harrisons' secure property, they could almost have driven there for a lot less money. "I can't afford a chartered flight, Tyler."

"The Harrisons are paying."

Her whole body tightened. "They know we're coming?"

"Nope. But they're paying nonetheless."

"Hell of an expense account you've got."

She sounded bitter, but didn't care. These people were her daughter's grandparents. If they had nothing to do with Scott's death, she'd cheated her daughter out of a connection with the other half of her family. In the meantime, they had resources she couldn't even imagine. Resources she could have used to protect Kelsey, if they *weren't* the ones after them.

In other words, she might have completely and unnecessarily fucked up her daughter's life.

"Stop it." Tyler lifted her chin. His eyes looked almost black in the dim light, but she couldn't miss the intensity in them. "You've done the best you can, Regan, and it's been an incredible job. Look at the girl you've raised."

She nodded slightly, his hold on her chin restricting her movement. "You're right. Thanks."

But his attention had shifted away from her neuroses. His head tilted slightly as his eyelids went to half-mast, and slowly his mouth descended. Slowly enough so she could stop him. Slowly enough for her mind to list all the reasons she *should* stop him.

Slowly enough to build her anticipation and need exponentially for every inch he crept nearer.

When his mouth touched hers it was hot and hungry, despite the excruciatingly slow pace he maintained even after contact. His hand slid from her chin and up to the side of her head, where his fingers cradled her skull and his palm cupped her jaw. His mouth opened and hers followed, letting him in, deeper than he'd been in the shower. His other hand came up to mirror the first and she felt cherished, desired.

Her fists wrapped around the loose fabric of the untucked polo shirt at his waist so they wouldn't wander. Her knuckles brushed bare skin and he jerked before angling his body closer to hers. He loomed over her, yet instead of making her feel threatened, it turned her on.

She heard the scrape of a foot on wood floor before she heard her daughter's voice at the open doorway.

"You guys can go upstairs if you want to. We won't bother you."

Kelsey sounded matter-of-fact and encouraging instead of teasing or annoyed. Regan watched Tyler back away, still slowly, and a rush of air cooled her cheeks as he let her go.

"Thanks, but no." He never looked away from Regan as he backed across the porch and started down the steps. "I'm going to walk the perimeter. I'll be back in a bit."

As Tyler disappeared in the darkness, Kelsey came out and took up his position against the rail.

"So you haven't shut him down yet," she observed.

Regan studied her, expecting resentment or disgust, but Kelsey still showed nothing but mild interest.

"No, I guess I haven't."

"But you're not letting it go anywhere."

"How can it? There's too much unknown. Once I can prove he's not part of—"

"Come on, Mom, it's pretty obvious he's on our side." Using her fingers to tick off her points, Kelsey listed all the reasons Tyler could be trusted. Each one resonated in Regan, but her mind also had a counterpoint for each. She'd conditioned herself not to trust for so many years it had become reflex, unconnected to her true feelings. Add the image of Alan with the knife in his chest, the consequences of trying to change, and she was left tangled and uncertain, and hating it. In the end, she could only err on the side of caution, and tried to explain to her daughter.

"Trust isn't always about measurable factors, Kels. There are intangibles at play I can't ignore."

"Like what?"

She raised her hands, palm up. "I don't know yet. That's why they're intangible."

Kelsey blew out an exasperated breath. "Just take a chance for once, will you?"

"I did. With Alan."

The silence that followed rang with Kelsey's shocked chagrin. She didn't need to voice it; Regan felt it as much as saw it in her daughter. She let their mutual grief and regret flare and fade.

"Tyler's not Alan, though," Kelsey finally said softly. "He's not defenseless."

"No," Regan agreed. "But I'm surprised you're in favor of it. Most kids in your position—"

"There are no other kids in my position."

"—would resent the idea of me moving on, especially with all this about your father being dredged up."

"I didn't know my father. And I think Tyler's good for you, and you've lived for me for far too long. Maybe there's no—" she lifted her hands in the air to indicate something big, "—*grand passion* here, like you had before, but a little nookie ain't gonna kill ya."

"Are you just saying that so you don't feel guilty for the nookie you're getting?"

Her daughter's skin darkened with a blush and she stared at the darkness instead of at her mother. "No-oo."

"What if this *is* a grand passion? What if all the rest of it is over and I still want to be with Tyler?"

Kelsey's smile was genuine. "Then I'd ask to be your maid of honor at the wedding."

The most startling part was that Regan didn't find anything wrong with the notion.

"Triple word score makes it…sixty-three points." Tom scribbled Van's score as she crowed and turned the board toward Kelsey. "Beat that."

"Okay." She had been ready since her last turn, and luckily no one had taken her spot. She slipped her three tiles into place and smiled serenely at Van.

"Seventy-three. And I'm out of tiles." She shook the empty bag. "We're done."

"Crap!" Van pounded both fists lightly on the table and stared at the board. "I was going there! Crap-crapcrapcrap."

"Doesn't matter." Tom scribbled the final math. "I beat you both." He straightened with a grin. Van picked up his pencil and threw it at him. He tossed one of his tiles back at her, and in seconds it was a three-way tile fight. A few minutes later they'd run out of steam, and a few minutes after that they had the game all cleaned up, every letter accounted for.

And they were still only halfway through the first day.

"Where do you think they are now?" Van asked from where she'd slumped on the couch.

"Somewhere in the air." Tom slid the game box back onto its shelf and turned. "Too early for them to know anything yet." He stood there a moment, thinking. "I wonder if the school notified our parents we're missing."

"I don't know, but even if they didn't notice, I'm gonna miss my call tomorrow, and they'll totally freak out." Van flipped open her phone and sighed at the "no signal" message. "I wish we had a TV and could watch the news or whatever."

Kelsey didn't know what to say. Guilt was starting to overwhelm everything else she was feeling, *had* been feeling, since they'd insisted on coming with her. "I'm sorry, you guys. You didn't sign on for this."

Van shrugged and Tom grabbed his button-down

shirt off the back of a chair, shrugging it over his T-shirt. "I'm going out to get some air. Anyone want to come?"

Kelsey could tell he wanted her to and hoped Van wouldn't join them. Luckily, her friend was on board. She waved a lazy hand in the air and played with her cell phone.

They went out the back door, joined hands, and started strolling. Kelsey examined the landscape around them, but there wasn't much to see. Farmland, mostly, with a few trees and bushes on the property and a couple of silos in the distance.

"Let's check out the shed." Tom raised their hands to point at the graying, rough-boarded building at the back of the yard. A wide gravel path led from the driveway at the side of the house to the crooked double doors.

"Looks more like an old garage," Kelsey said. The big doors looked heavy despite their dry condition, and as they got closer she could see a rusted metal latch holding them together. "Is it locked?" She tried not to be disappointed. It was probably empty or filled with junk anyway, but exploring it would have been something to do.

Tom let go of her hand. She wrapped her sweater more tightly around her and tucked her hands under her arms while he wedged his fingers in the crack between doors and pulled one open a few inches. They creaked.

"See anything?"

"Too dark." Tom let them go and examined the

padlock on the latch. It looked as old as the building. "I bet I could break this."

"Tyler might get pissed if you do."

Tom shot her a look.

"Well, it's his property! And he's been helping us."

"He also dumped us here with nothing to do and no way to contact them." He ran his hand lightly up the side of the door and tugged on the hinges. "I'm bored as hell."

"We could find another way to occupy ourselves," she said hopefully. Tom peered under his upraised arm at her, and she moved closer to press her body up against his. "It's been forever."

He took the bait, bending to kiss her, wrapping his arms around her, and trapping her against the wall. Their mouths had barely met when pain erupted in the back of her head.

"Ouch!" She jerked away from the wall and touched her scalp, which seemed okay. A huge splinter of wood stuck out of the wall behind her. "Okay, maybe out here isn't such a good idea. But Van's inside."

"Don't worry." Tom caught her hips and spun to put his own back against the wall. His jeans protected him, and since he was taller than her he leaned forward to kiss her, anyway. He pulled back slightly. "Better?"

She nodded so their noses rubbed. "Better." She pressed her lips to his, licking them once before backing off an inch again. "Much better."

She didn't know how long they stood there making out. A while later, when parts of her were achy and damp and she was barely aware of where they were, the door to the house slammed and Van shouted to them.

"I'm bored out of my fricking skull in there!"

Kelsey turned a little—Tom didn't let go of her—and watched Van trip lightly across the grass. "What do you want us to do about it?"

Van grinned. "Let me in on the action." She playfully shoved Kelsey aside and jumped up to kiss Tom. "Let's do a threesome. I'll even go for some girl-on-girl for ya, Tommy-boy."

"Ugh! No way!" Kelsey pushed her back and plastered herself against Tom so Van couldn't get close again. "That's so gross."

"No, it's not!" Tom laughed. He pulled Van in to his side and pretended he was going to kiss her for real. Kelsey slugged him and he laughed again. "Okay, fine. One at a time then."

"In your dreams," she snapped, only partly joking now. What if Tom really did want Van? What if Van's boredom got out of hand and she started playing with him? Kelsey didn't think she'd really try to steal him from her, but she did like to say outrageous things and had acted on them once or twice.

Luckily, her friend dropped the game and turned to look at the lock on the door. "So what's inside here?" She peered through the crack. "Too dark. Any other way in?"

"Didn't look yet." Tom held Kelsey against him, his hands roaming over her even though his attention was on Van and the building. "Can't be windows or there'd be some light in there."

"I'm checking." Van tromped down to the end and disappeared around the corner.

Tom attacked Kelsey's mouth again. She thought maybe they should go inside and hide in one of the bedrooms, but then Van appeared on their left.

"Nope. Nothing." She passed them and yanked on the doors. "I bet if we pulled hard enough these screws would come out." She fingered the rusted metal. "It's totally ancient."

Tom heaved a put-upon sigh and let Kelsey go. "Fine, whatever, let's try it."

Van shot him a dirty look, but together they started pulling on the right door while Kelsey watched, feeling bad for fooling around in front of Van and ignoring her friend, but resenting her for being there and getting in the way. Couldn't she just hang out for a while? Read a book or something? After all, if the people after Kelsey got her, she might never see Tom again. She should get everything she could before that happened, so they both at least had good memories and no regrets.

A loud *crack* echoed in the still air, and Van and Tom fell back a step. The door sagged, held up by the lock in the front, but the top hinge had broken.

"Whoops." Van giggled.

"Come on, guys, this isn't our property." Kelsey moved forward, anxious. "You're going to destroy it."

"I can fix it, if there are tools inside," Tom said. "But now we have to see if there are." He smiled, looking carefree and charming, and her heart melted. Unfortunately, her heart didn't overrule her brain, so the whole thing just pissed her off.

"Just stop. We don't need to get in there. Leave it alone, and we'll go back inside."

"Aw, come on, Kels!" Van cajoled as she tried to see inside from the opening by the hinge. "It'll be cool." She gripped the side of the door in both hands, braced her foot on the wall of the garage, and pulled. With a loud shriek, the screws holding the bottom hinge pulled out of the wood and the whole door jumped outward a few feet.

"Sweetness!" Van disappeared inside and Tom followed, pausing to hold his hand out for Kelsey. Feeling like the doomed goody-goody character in every teen horror film, she shoved his hand aside and pushed past him into the dark interior.

"Whoa."

"Yeah, that's what I said," Van agreed.

Kelsey moved away from the opening so she didn't block the light. Far from matching the exterior of the barn-garage, the inside was in perfect shape. Dusty and rife with spiders, but otherwise amazingly clean and well organized. Shelves lined two walls. On the left were the usual things you found in a shed: paint cans and supplies, rolled or folded drop cloths, jars of screws and nails and drill and driver bits, cases looking like they contained power tools. The back wall had car parts. Kelsey saw a carburetor and boxes of filters and spark plugs as well as containers of oil and transmission fluid. Bags held various belts and things her car repair classes hadn't covered. A radiator leaned against the wall under the bottom shelf, next to four pristine tires. The right-hand wall was pegboard, and rakes and other yard things hung on it.

"Awesome." Tom wandered over and fingered a chainsaw, which hung next to an axe and a pair of pruners. "Some cool stuff in here."

But Van had glommed on to the tarp in the center of the building. It wasn't deep enough front to back, so somehow Tyler or someone had maneuvered a car so it was sideways, the nose aimed at the right-hand wall.

"What do you think it is?" Van asked.

"Well, look," said Tom.

"I like to savor things." She bent and lifted the edge of the tarp. "It's red."

"It can't be anything special or he wouldn't have left it here untouched all this time," Kelsey said. "He hasn't left Ohio in two years, remember?"

Van lifted the tarp higher. "It looks pretty clean. Shiny." She moved to the front and loosened the drawstring holding the tarp tight around the vehicle, then did the same at the back. "Ready? Back up, Kels."

Kelsey did, and a second later Van whipped the canvas into the air and yanked so most of it flew off the car without touching it.

"Whoa." This time all three of them said it at once. Kelsey'd been wrong. What they saw *was* special.

"It's a sixty-four Corvette," Tom said in the kind of voice usually reserved for stuff like Superman stopping a plane crash.

"It's cherry," breathed Van, running her hand along the rear of it.

"Not quite." Tom couldn't stop touching it, either, as he circled around to the driver's side. "Looks like the upholstery needs some repair, and the steering wheel isn't the original." He bent to look through the window. "God, I want to drive this."

"How do you know so much?" Kelsey drifted closer, unable to help herself despite her lack of interest in cars. This one had such gorgeous lines. She traced the ridge along the side, and marveled at how shiny the chrome on the windows was. She glanced up just in time to see Tom's frown of incredulity.

"I'm a guy. We know cars. It's, like, wired into us."

"Do you think it runs?" she asked him.

He tried the door, but it was locked. He peered through the window again. "I can't believe the body would be in such good shape if the engine wasn't, too." He straightened and looked around. "There's gas up there." He pointed to the can on the top shelf behind him. "I bet we could take it out."

"No way." Kelsey picked up the tarp and started to pull it back over the car. Tom rushed to help her, lifting the canvas so it didn't touch the paint but settled gently over it from the top. "It's not our car, we don't have permission, and we're supposed to stay here." She tightened the drawstring. "Come on. Let's go back to the house."

Van went willingly, chattering about their find, but

Kelsey had to push Tom out the door while he looked longingly over his shoulder.

This was going to be a problem.

SIXTEEN

"REGAN, can you come back here a minute?"

They'd been in the air nearly two hours, and she couldn't sit still. She'd paced the tiny aisle a dozen times, changed seats until she'd sat in every one and deemed them all equally uncomfortable—ridiculous in a jet, but of course it was her, not the seats—and quizzed Tyler on Ben and Jeanne Harrison until he'd gone to the bathroom just to escape her.

He'd known surprisingly few answers for someone who had worked for them for so long. He explained that security staff were not friends, so it wasn't odd he didn't know about the family or which of their friends they were close to, or what they'd done in the service and what they were doing now. He had managed to distract her for about twenty minutes while he described the layout of the house and grounds and the security they had in place.

"We won't have to worry about the security, though," he'd said confidently. "The guys at the gate will let us through and I'm sure Ben and Jeanne will be eager to see you."

Regan had trouble focusing after that. Her imagination ran amok, spinning scenarios in which Tyler got let in and she got shot, or someone opened fire on both of them or dragged them to the pool and threw them in to drown, or locked them in a metal box with no light or air source. She kept seeing Tyler moving from her side to the Harrisons' and changing into someone she didn't know. Which reminded her she didn't know him very well, anyway, and what if someone was on the way to Kelsey right now?

"God, stop," she murmured, pressing against her aching temples. She had to shut off her fricking brain.

"Regan," Tyler said again, and she reluctantly stood. He waited at the back of the plane, in front of the tiny sleeping area.

"I can't sleep," she told him. "I tried."

"I know." He put his hand on her shoulder and coaxed her through the door and onto the narrow bed. "I want to help you relax." Regan let him stretch her out face down, realizing that a week ago, she'd have demanded to know what he was doing before she gave an inch. She'd changed, and wasn't sure it was a good thing. Dependency wouldn't protect her or her daughter.

For cripe's sake... She was so tired of herself.

Tyler straddled her thighs at the same time his thumbs dug into her back, right at the sore spot at the base of her spine. She moaned without realizing she was going to. Her eyes drifted closed as Tyler massaged her lower back and hips, then up along her spine to her shoulders and neck. He applied the perfect amount of pressure, and when he was done her entire body felt looser than it had in nearly two decades.

She was about to thank him when he braced his

hands next to her head and lowered himself to kiss her neck. He moved her hair aside with his nose, then brushed his lips up the side of her neck to the spot behind her ear and pressed. His mouth was hot and his teeth sharp when they nipped her earlobe.

His body sank onto hers and she felt a brief moment of panic, of feeling trapped, before he eased to the side and rolled her against him, her back to his front. Did he know, or was it coincidence? In the next instant it no longer mattered. His hand slid under her long-sleeved T-shirt and splayed across her belly while his mouth continued working its magic on her neck.

"Tyler?" she whispered, not sure she wanted to do this.

He uncurled his other hand, which was in front of her face now, his arm supporting her head. He held a condom in his fingers. She smiled, pleased he'd thought of it even after they'd taken a chance in the shower, but that wasn't what made her hesitate.

"Don't worry," he murmured. The hand on her belly glided up to trace the underside of her breasts. "We'll do this slow and easy, take the edge off. It'll pass the time, and you'll be more alert when we get there than you will be if you keep stressing out."

It might have been the most creative reason to get laid she'd ever heard, but she decided he was right and turned to face him.

"I'm not sure I can do slow and easy with you," she admitted, unbuttoning his shirt. Her blood quickened when she touched his warm skin.

"Then I guess I'd better take over." He pressed her onto her back and pulled her arms over her head. When she dropped them down to his shoulders, again he put them back up. "I mean it, Regan. You just lie there and take it for once."

She chuckled, not believing him, but he was deadly serious as he loomed over her.

"Don't move." She stilled and he gave a short, satisfied nod. "Good."

At first he just touched her, mostly while taking off her shirt and jeans. His big hands smoothed up her legs, across her ribs, down her arms. Then his mouth took up the journey, traveling from her collarbone to the valley between her breasts to her belly button, then between her legs to her knees and ankles and back. She was humming head to toe by the time he stopped.

She opened her eyes to see him looking at her with a hunger that did more to arouse her than his hands had so far. She moved her fingers to the front closure of her black satin bra, but he caught them before she opened it.

"Leave it on. It's hot." One side of his mouth quirked and this time, when he replaced her hand over her head, he leaned down to kiss her. Slowly, languidly, devouring her mouth as if she were a decadent dessert he wanted to savor but couldn't. He traced the edge of her bra, which felt too tight now, and his bare chest brushed her skin. She arched but he pushed her back down.

His mouth left hers and went straight to her breast.

He pulled down the right cup and caught her nipple, tugging until she gasped. He reached between her legs, stroking across the damp satin again and again. She shuddered, already on the edge.

"Tyler."

"Not yet, love."

When his hand moved away a kind of desperation rose up unlike anything she'd felt before. As if she'd truly explode if he wasn't inside her. But again, when she reached for him he avoided her hands. He gave attention to her other breast and this time slipped his hand inside her panties, stroking her so lightly she could barely feel it, yet so powerfully she thought she'd come if he breathed on her right.

"Tyler!" This time it was a plea more than a sigh. But a moment later her ears popped and the constant whine of the plane's engines changed pitch.

"Dammit." Tyler shifted to her other side. "We're descending."

"Don't stop!" Regan protested.

"I don't intend to. But I think slow and easy is over." He undid his jeans and rolled the condom on quickly, then stripped off her underwear and positioned himself over her. "Are you ready?"

"God, yes." She grabbed his ass with her hands and wrapped her ankles around his legs to lever her hips upward. He thrust smoothly inside her and immediately took up the perfect rhythm. She threw her head back, already approaching orgasm, and clenched around him trying to stave it off. He grunted and plunged harder, faster.

"Tyler!" She couldn't help crying his name over and over again as she climbed, then exploded, her entire body bursting into flames that died into sparkles. He pounded into her a few more times, then buried his face in her neck and clutched her to him as he came. The new angle pressed him against her clitoris and she shuddered into another, smaller orgasm. Her eyes prickled and, shocked, she opened them to stare hard at the molded plastic ceiling.

Sex couldn't make her cry.

Loss could. In the past week she'd cried for Alan, and for Scott, and for Kelsey. But that was different.

Wasn't it?

WHY THE HELL hadn't her mother taught her how to cook?

Kelsey banged the pot on the stove, sloshing water across its surface, and glared at the reflection in the dark kitchen window over the sink. She could clearly see the well-lit room behind her, where Van was back on the couch, napping, and Tom prowled in his second search for the fricking keys to the fricking Corvette. Neither of them seemed to care about making dinner.

And she, apparently, couldn't even boil water.

"What's the matter, Kels?" Tom stood behind her and rubbed her arms. Her temper tantrum must have drawn him over.

"I'm trying to make dinner, but it turns out my mother put weapon handling and offensive driving way above food preparation on the lesson list. I should be able to handle mac and cheese, but the fricking…

water…won't…*boil!*" She slammed her hands on the stove.

Tom turned her and wrapped her up in his arms, rocking and shushing her until she relaxed. "We don't need to eat mac and cheese," he soothed. "Sandwiches are fine."

"I'm tired of sandwiches," she whined into his chest. Then she pulled back, calmer, and bent to look at the flame of the stove. This was stupid. She'd helped her mother cook hundreds of times. "It's because it's a gas stove. I've never used one before. I don't want to get the flame too high."

Tom made a weird noise. She turned her head to look up at him. His mouth twisted and she knew he was trying not to laugh.

She narrowed her eyes. "Do not let that out."

He shook his head and pressed his lips together. "It's just…maybe that's why the water won't heat up."

"Screw it." She jerked the dial around to "off" and went to the cupboard where the bread was. "Knock yourself out." She tossed it on the table and dropped into a kitchen chair, bracing her chin on both hands.

Tom folded himself into the chair next to her, rubbing a hand across her back. "What's going on, Kels?"

She shrugged.

"Seriously, I know it's not just boiling water. Is it your mom and Tyler? You know." He made a face.

Kelsey shook her head. "No. I mean, ick, but no, that doesn't bother me. It's—" She sighed and sat up. "It's what he said. About what they did to my father, that probably affected me. My blood, or whatever."

"What about it?"

She stared at him. "What do you mean, what about it? I'm a tool for murder."

He made another face, this one telegraphing how stupid he thought that idea was. "No, you're not. That's like saying it's metal's fault they make bullets out of it."

"I didn't say it was my fault," she protested.

"But that's what you mean, right?" He closed his hand over the top of her shoulder. "You feel guilty. Or responsible."

That clicked. "Yes. Responsible. I mean, before, it was just me. Even with you and Van, it's just two more people. Important people, but just two. Now, the fate of the whole world might rest on my shoulders."

"Nah, just enemies of America." Kelsey glared. "Sorry. But like you kept saying, it doesn't change anything. They'll stop the guy who wants you, and then the past won't matter. Once you're safe, everything will be okay. And we'll go back to school, and I'll pretend to help you study for tests." He grinned wolfishly.

It shouldn't have made her feel better. But the fact that Tom didn't seem to care that she could be some kind of freak eased the pressure and made her believe him—that everything would be not only okay, but normal, once this was all over.

"I hope Mom and Tyler are okay."

Tom leaned over to kiss her. "I'm sure they're fine." He straightened and opened one of the drawers. "Did we look in here?"

Kelsey rolled her eyes. "You did. Twice. Why are you so obsessed with finding these keys, anyway?"

He shrugged. "I just want to get the car unlocked. Look inside. Sit in it."

"But we can't get back into the barn." Tom had found a manual screwdriver in the house—none of the power tools were charged—and Kelsey and Van had held the door in place while he worked to replace the rusty screws of the hinges. The broken hinge, luckily, had snapped back together. Kelsey wasn't sure either one would hold under pressure, but if they tried to open it again, they'd do damage they couldn't repair. She wouldn't want to face Tyler then.

"I'm hoping the key to the padlock is on the same ring as the car keys," Tom said.

Van sat up and stretched. "You're still on about that car?"

"He never stopped," Kelsey complained. "It's getting old."

"It'd be cool to get inside, though." Blinking heavy lids, Van slumped in the chair next to Kelsey and laid her head sideways on her folded arm. "Too bad it's a two-seater."

"It doesn't matter if it's a two-seater. We're not going anywhere in it."

Van reached into her pocket and removed her cell phone. She fingered the buttons while she sighed at the screen. "Still no signal."

"It's not gonna change, Van," Tom said from under the sink. He'd stuck his head and half his torso in there.

"I know. I'm just worried about my parents, you know? I've missed a week's worth of classes. What if they find out? Plus, it's Sunday. I'm supposed to be calling them today."

"Too bad we don't have a working TV here," Kelsey moped. She ignored Tom's continued prowling. "We could see if the news has anything about three missing college kids."

"Hey."

They looked up at Tom, who stood on the counter, holding baskets that had been stuffed into the space above the cabinets. He grinned the grin that had made her fall in love with him, and some of her worry and annoyance faded.

"What are you doing up there?" she asked.

"Look what I found." He pulled his arm out, now covered with dust.

Dangling from his forefinger was a set of three shiny silver keys.

ALMOST NOTHING ABOUT her current situation made Regan happy.

The plane they'd arrived in had been refueled and was on its way back to Minnesota. When she'd complained, Tyler explained it had been chartered by someone else for the next day and would never get back in time if it waited for them. So she had no easy way to get back to Kelsey.

She was currently a passenger in a car she was not driving, in a part of California she was unfamiliar with, heading for an unknown destination. The only way she could be less in control was if she was in shackles.

A baggage truck accident at the airport had held their plane away from the terminal for two hours. Tyler said the Harrisons no longer lived in Sacramento, but had a home two and a half hours away, beyond Clear Lake. He wanted to get a room overnight at Lakeport and arrive at the Harrisons' well rested and in daylight. The delay completely erased the calm his massage and lovemaking had given her.

"Did you call them?"

He shook his head. "When could I have without you knowing?"

"You went to the bathroom in the plane and in the terminal."

"So did you."

She laughed. "That's not the point. The point is we were away from each other then and you could have called them to say we were coming."

"I could have, yes. But that would risk alerting someone on the inside of our location. Someone we don't want to alert."

"You said we'd get in with no problem," she accused. He shrugged. "You think the mole will stop us."

"Maybe. Depending on who it is, they could order the rest of security to stop us, without Ben and Jeanne even knowing."

"Great."

"Don't worry. We'll handle it. Then once we're there, everything will be fine."

Regan wished he hadn't said that. Someone always said it just before everything went FUBAR.

Tom HAD BEEN right. The key ring he found did have a key for the lock on the barn. But since it was already dark and they hadn't found any flashlights in the house—Kelsey was totally going to ream Tyler out for leaving them without flashlights—she convinced him and Van to wait until morning to explore.

They slept late the next day, partly because they could, and partly because she and Tom and been awake until three, having sex. Kind of having sex. They didn't have any condoms and she wasn't going to risk getting pregnant now. Not only because of what a screw-up that would be, but because she didn't want to repeat her mother's history and negate everything she'd sacrificed for Kelsey.

Still, you didn't need to have sex to have sex.

They were all in much better moods by the time they traipsed out to the barn. Kelsey wondered what had cheered Van up so much, but decided she didn't want to know.

Once the barn doors were unlocked they opened wide, plenty far enough to let in tons of sunshine and let out the car, if it had been necessary to drive it. Which it wasn't.

Tom and Van made beelines for the vehicle, carefully removing the tarp and unlocking the door. Kelsey wasn't really interested, so she let Tom be macho about engine size and performance and Van get all squealy about seats and dials. She moved deeper into the barn and started exploring the stuff stored there.

She was wondering if the white things on the back of a workbench were bones, pieces of antlers, or very old wood when she heard the whirr of the car's starter behind her.

She whirled. "Tom!"

"Don't worry!" He stuck his head out the window, his expression rapturous. "I'm just putting the top down."

"I'm surprised the battery still has a charge," Kelsey said. Tom was too engrossed in the instruments to respond.

Once the top was all the way back Van stuck her arms in the air and "woo hooed" a few times. "Can you imagine taking this baby on the road?" She clicked on the radio and tried to tune it, but all she got was static.

Kelsey shook her head and walked along the back wall, identifying car parts and wondering if they were all for the Corvette or if Tyler liked working on cars in general. Some of this stuff looked too modern.

Her toe stubbed against something and she looked down. There was something metal on the floor. She kicked at it, but it didn't move. That was weird. The floor was dirt. What was buried here?

She crouched and brushed away some leaves and dried grass that must have blown in under the door, and stared at what she'd uncovered.

"Guys! Look at this!"

"What?" Tom craned his neck to see over the side of the car.

"Come here." Kelsey pried the iron ring away from the dirt and lifted it. It was attached to another iron piece she could only see the top of. "You know what this is?"

"What?" Van repeated, looking over her shoulder. "Another rusty piece of metal? Big deal."

"It's not rusty." She pulled, but knew right away she wouldn't be strong enough. She shifted to one side and motioned to Tom. "Help me."

He braced his feet and stuck two fingers into the ring, then pulled hard. A crack appeared in the dirt, like three sides of a square. Kelsey brushed away more leaves and saw where the back of the trap door had to be. Tom shifted position to stand behind the hinges and heaved.

A wooden trap door slowly rotated open, exposing a large opening in the floor of the barn. Tom released it and it fell back onto the floor, showering their feet and jeans with dirt.

"Awesome," breathed Van. "Let's go down."

"Wait." Kelsey held her away from the opening. "We have no idea how deep it is, whether there's a ladder to get out, or what's in there. We need light." She stood and went back to the tool shelves, where there was a spotlight-sized flash. She worried it wouldn't work, but when she flipped the switch, it shone brightly.

"Damned good battery," Van said. "Let's go."

They lay flat around the opening and stuck their

heads into it. Kelsey shone the light around, first at the floor, then the sides. The floor was about eight feet down, the room probably the same size square. More of a chamber than a room. Off to one side, flat on the floor, was a wooden ladder. There didn't seem to be anything else in there, but they couldn't see all of the walls from where they lay.

"Look." Tom fingered a couple of grooves worn into the wood forming the frame of the opening. "I bet this is where the ladder rests. When they come up they drop it back down inside."

"I'm goin' in." Van swung her legs around and into the hole, then turned to balance on her stomach, grabbed the side, and dropped to the floor. "Give me the flashlight!" she called up. Kelsey held it over her friend's hands and let it go. Van caught it deftly and shone it around. "Coooool," she breathed. "You guys have got to see this."

Kelsey used the same move Van had and landed lightly on the floor. "Wait!" she called up to Tom. "Let me make sure the ladder works before you come down, or we'll be trapped down here." She raised the wooden ladder and braced it against the opening. It extended a mere three inches above the lip, but when she tested the rungs, they seemed solid. "Okay."

Tom ignored the ladder and swung down beside them.

Van ran the light over the walls. "Look!"

Tom let out a whistle Kelsey would have echoed if she'd known how. The bottom halves of the walls, the parts they could see from up top, were smooth dirt peppered with stones. But above the halfway point they were much more.

Racks and racks of weapons, at least a dozen guns, were sealed in clear plastic cases to protect them from the dirt. Goggles, sensors, trackers, and tons of gadgets Kelsey had never seen before lay on neighboring shelves. A doorless cabinet was full of canned foods. She pulled down a small box from next to a row of beans and tuna and opened it. Silverware, two can openers and a stack of napkins.

"It's a panic room," she said. "An old-fashioned one. But look." She showed them the box. "Enough food to last a good long while."

"And water." Van pointed up at the corner behind Kelsey. A dozen gallon jugs hung from the ceiling.

Kelsey breathed the crisp, clean air smelling only of fresh earth and not of the musty staleness she would have expected. "Why does it feel like we're outside?" she wondered. Her friends looked at her like she was insane.

"We're in a box, Kels. Underground."

"I know, Van. I mean, the air is fresh." She took the flashlight from Van and aimed it at the upper corners. The rear corners on the left and right both looked darker than the rest of the walls. She moved closer, and discovered a tube embedded in the spot where two walls and ceiling met. "Circulation."

"So no one would suffocate," Tom figured. "And maybe to keep the other stuff from getting too damp or whatever?"

"Why didn't Tyler tell us about this?" she wondered. "It's the perfect place if someone finds us."

"Because of the guns." Tom was still studying them. "He probably thought it was a bad idea to let us know there were guns here."

"I know how to handle a gun," Kelsey protested.

"You do. But we don't. My family doesn't hunt or anything. And they could easily be turned against us."

He was right. But it didn't stop her from selecting a small pistol and a box of ammo before she went back up.

SEVENTEEN

THE RAIN POUNDING on the roof of the car was so loud Regan and Tyler couldn't talk. So much for going in daylight—the storm clouds and sheets of water reduced visibility to "don't be stupid enough to drive" levels.

They were going anyway. Regan didn't think Tyler even considered suggesting otherwise. He knew she wouldn't bother to argue; she'd just leave him behind.

Not that she knew where they were going.

Regan was glad for the noisy rain, at least for now. The upcoming confrontation and all the possible scenarios tied her stomach in knots until she had to put a halt to it, breathe deeply, and think about something totally innocuous. The difficulty of finding a topic like that distracted her enough to ease the tension until she realized it had eased, and the whole cycle started up again.

After far too long, yet oddly way too soon, Tyler pulled the car over and turned off the engine. The trees overhead muted the rain somewhat.

"We're a mile away from the access road." He half turned and stretched his arm across the gap between the seats. "There's no security posted at the end of the road, but there is a trip sensor so they'll know we're coming and will have visual of both sides of the car."

"I know this, Tyler. We went over the plan and layout last night."

"I'm repeating it anyway. Protocol."

Again, arguing was pointless, so she took up the recital from there.

"The access road ends at the main gate, where there's a guard house with one guard. He's likely to be one of your colleagues and should let you by fine. But—"

"Yeah, but." He looked grim. "There's a chance they're not happy I went off the grid. Or they might have concerns about why I did. So we might have difficulty getting through. Follow my lead."

"Inside the main gate we've got another quarter mile of driveway to another gate, where they'll search the car and us."

"Whatever happens, follow my lead," Tyler repeated. "I know these people and how to handle them."

"Let's go. I'm tired of wasting time."

"Regan." He waited until she met his eyes. "Follow my lead."

She sighed. "Fine. As long as it seems to be working."

His jaw flexed. "Fine."

"And Tyler?" She put her hand on his arm before he started the ignition. "Thank you. For everything so far. No matter what happens, I do appreciate your help."

He scowled. "You sound like you expect me to betray you."

She dropped her hand and looked away so he wouldn't see the truth of her feelings for him, which by now were the opposite of what he thought. "I have no expectations. I'm keeping open to all possibilities."

"Great," he grumbled as he started the ignition. "Perfect."

He pulled back onto the main road behind a tractor-trailer that seemed out of place way out here, then made a left turn onto a road she could barely see until the nose of the car entered it. She imagined this was beautiful countryside when it was visible. She had an impression of mountains, evergreens, and a variety of oaks. It was also likely inhospitable to someone on the run, on foot. Something she hoped to avoid.

Regan leaned toward the center of the car, unsure where the cameras would be mounted. She hoped they'd been mounted above the top of the vehicle so they'd be harder to locate and sabotage, and not at window level, which would give viewers a clearer shot at her face. She didn't know why, but she wanted to have the element of surprise about her presence. Nothing else was in her favor.

A couple of minutes after turning onto the road, the white-sided, black-roofed guard shack came into view. It looked the same as the guard house of any resort or time-share community, and too innocuous for its purpose. A red-striped gate blocked the road.

Tyler slowed the vehicle as they approached, his ID

out and friendly greeting already in place. Then, suddenly, he slammed on the brakes and lost the smile.

The guard came out of the shack and stood in front of them, gun drawn and aimed directly at the car.

IF VAN HAD ever stopped fretting about her mother's infuriating tendency toward the dramatic, and if Tom hadn't been staring morosely at the keys on the table for three hours, Kelsey never would have given in.

She also blamed exhaustion, worry, boredom, and the infuriating status of not knowing anything happening anywhere.

Tom started with a reasonable suggestion in a reasonable tone. "I can drive to town and get a paper, so we can at least see if anything's happening. I can probably do it without being seen. It'll take me an hour and if our parents have been talking to the media, we'll know."

Reasonable was easy to shoot down, but Van didn't give her a chance. She pounced on the idea.

"I can go with him and call my folks! Then they'll know everything's fine."

"What would you tell them about missing class, if they know?"

"I've been sick all week!" She gave a fake cough. "You know I had that terrible cold."

"Yeah, weeks ago. What if Mom and Tyler get back before you do? They'd be furious."

"They won't," Tom assured her, his attitude perking up now that she hadn't said a flat-out no. He laid his hand over hers. "There's no way they could get there and back so soon, even if they didn't see your grandparents. Tyler told me how far they are from the airport and stuff. They won't be here until tomorrow."

"Someone will recognize the car. There can't be any others like it out there."

"They might, but they won't think anything of it. None of them know what Tyler does or who we are."

"C'mon, Kelsey, it'll be fun. We can get out of this house and cure ourselves of the godawful monotony of this place. And then we'll be in better moods and won't fight." Van folded her hands under her chin. "Please, please, pleasepleasepleaseplease let's do this."

Kelsey looked out the window toward the barn. All of her other arguments stalled in her brain. She knew Tom could get the car out of the barn and drive it without damage. She knew they'd be better off if Van could call her parents, and if they had some outside information. And the chances of any of them getting caught by someone who knew what was going on were very slim. If their enemy knew about this place, something would have happened by now.

"All right," she finally said. Van cheered and Tom beamed, and they rushed around getting their things. Kelsey stayed where she was until Van skidded to a stop at the front door.

"You're not coming?"

Kelsey shook her head. "It's a two-seater. I can't go with Tom because I can't call your folks. If anyone is watching the town because they know this house is somewhere around here but not exactly where, they'll

be looking for me. So I'm safer actually being here."
She stood and walked over to them, realizing she
couldn't just let them go. They didn't have the training she did.

"Watch cars to be sure you're not followed, especially coming back. They might trade off two or more
vehicles so it looks like different people are behind
you. Try not to be seen together outside of the car.
Keep the top up in town, don't go anywhere except
to get the paper, and come right back." For a second
she wished she was the one going, but strengthened
her resolve and hugged them both. "Be careful."

Tom held her tight and kissed the top of her head.
"You, too. Here." He twisted the key to the barn off
the ring and handed it to her. "Get to the trap room
if you get scared about anything."

"I'm fine. I'm better equipped for this than you
are." She followed them outside to open the barn and
watched while Tom expertly maneuvered the little
car onto the gravel drive, then locked the barn before
watching them go slowly up the driveway. She knew
the slow speed was for her benefit and he'd open her
up on the main road. She'd have done the same.

She stood on the porch for a while, the car getting
smaller and smaller until she could only see it from
its movement rather than its shape. Birds twittered,
and a confused cicada buzzed once. Those were reassuring sounds, because they meant no one was hanging around out here who shouldn't be.

But even more reassuring was the weight of the

gun in the small of her back, and that wasn't something she'd ever thought she'd say.

"So MUCH for plan A," Regan said wryly, watching the guard step slowly toward them, his aggressive posture muted a bit by the black slicker he wore over his head and body. "Take the lead, boss."

"Shush." He shoved the car into park and slowly opened his door, keeping his hands up so the guard could see them. He held his ID up between two fingers. Water poured into the car and plastered Tyler's longish hair and loose oxford shirt to his body. He kept one foot in the car and stayed in the crook of the door.

"That you, Dyson?"

Regan couldn't hear what the guard shouted. He didn't change his stance, though, and her heart rate slowly increased. She schooled her breathing, trying to stay focused and ready to act. Adrenaline seemed to seep through her body.

"It's me, Tyler Sloane."

More shouting. The guard stopped about ten feet away, gun aimed at Tyler but his eyes on the windshield like he was trying to see who else was inside the car. Regan held still, letting the rain on the window obscure her features.

"Dyson, I need to see the Harrisons. Let me through."

Feeling helpless only hearing one side of the conversation, Regan rolled down her window. Of course, a gust of wind blew water through the three-inch gap. So she was wet—at least she could hear.

"I've got orders to detain you, Sloane!"

"For what?"

"Not my job to know."

"Who gave the order?"

"McCormick."

Regan knew McCormick was head of security here. Tyler's boss, though he'd said he reported directly to Ben Harrison while in Ohio. So was McCormick the leak? Or was Ben Harrison the bad guy?

Tyler kept his body loose and unthreatening while he pressed Dyson for information. Regan knew it was a mask, knew how fast he could move if attacked, but that wasn't faster than a bullet. She tried to think rationally, to hold down the growing need to slam her foot on the accelerator and get past Dyson.

Being detained didn't bode well for anything. They could turn around and regroup, but it wouldn't do them any good. Harrison's team would just come after them. They'd be back on the defensive, exactly where she didn't want to be.

She reached for her door handle. Her presence might alter things, push through this standoff.

"Stay in the car."

Tyler's voice was low but reached her anyway, his urgency clear. Dyson edged closer, coming around the front of the car toward Tyler, who still stood casual and unthreatening behind his door. Regan squinted through the rain, trying to see if anyone was approaching from a different direction, but if they were, they were well hidden by the sheets of gray. She carefully opened the glove compartment and lifted the top tray, beneath which Tyler had stashed two pistols. She didn't know where he'd gotten them, but relaxed as soon as the cold grip was in her hand. She shifted her weight away from the driver's side and pulled her legs up so she could jump into the other seat and take off with the car, if necessary.

It wasn't.

Dyson reached for Tyler's upraised left hand. Tyler jerked it down and around, latching on to Dyson's forearm and pulling him off balance as he shoved the door forward. Dyson's forehead hit the edge of the door and he fell back onto the ground. Tyler grabbed his gun as he did, then jumped into the car and slammed the door. The car was moving before Dyson had rolled to his knees, never mind gotten to his feet. A moment later, they smashed through the wooden gate.

"I think they're gonna know we're here now," Regan quipped.

"I think they already did."

Tyler raced the car about halfway up the quarter mile between the first gate and the second. Then he whipped it around to a skidding stop, blocking the road, and turned it off.

"Forget Plan A completely," he said, pulling the other gun out of the glove compartment, hesitating a second when he realized Regan already had one. "We need to be armed, we need to be ready, and we're probably going to have to fight."

Regan checked her clip and chamber and nodded.

He did the check routine of both guns in his hands. "There's a curve up ahead, then a straight shot to the gate. If we approach by road, car or not, they'll plow us down."

"So we're going through the woods."

"Yep." He grabbed her chin and kissed her hard. "Ready?"

If I die, there's no one to protect Kelsey.

So don't die then, idiot.

"Ready."

They shot out opposite sides of the car and split the road, Tyler to one side, Regan to the other, without having planned it. For a second she panicked, but kept going. Hesitation was fatal. Then she decided it was better this way. Splitting up gave them two targets, potential confusion, and double the opportunity to get through.

Regan ran easily through the mature forest bordering the drive. The ground, shadowed by the tall, old trees, was clear of small plants and debris, and the trunks were spaced far enough apart so she could move at near-top speed. It also meant tripwires and other alerting devices or traps were more difficult to hide. She spotted and avoided two motion sensors but didn't know how many more she'd set off. Not that it mattered. They knew they were coming.

As she ran, a calm she'd never felt before filled her. Finally, she was doing something real. She wasn't a victim, or trying to prevent becoming one. She was going to put a stop to whatever was happening. She was going to get answers. And—

The epiphany blasted through her, a jolt to her system. Euphoria. She was going to get a life. It faded quickly—after all, she didn't have it yet—but it left behind a conviction and sense of purpose that made her positive everything was going to work out.

A few minutes later she slowed. Several dark shapes moved around another white-painted guard enclosure, this one much less friendly looking. Instead of a bar gate, ten-foot-tall chain link topped with barbed wire blocked the entrance. Regan crouched just inside the tree line and studied the group. Five figures. In the rain she couldn't tell if they were men or women. She also couldn't see how they were armed, though she knew they had to be.

She looked across the glistening blacktop and saw Tyler crouched opposite, watching her. As soon as she spotted him he nodded once, raised his weapon slightly in a two-fisted grip, and tilted his head at the gate.

Dear lord, he wants us to rush it. She didn't see how that would work, but nodded anyway. He knew the property. If there was a better way in, they'd be taking it now.

She stood and started running again. She kept to the tree line, hoping her dark, wet sweatshirt and jeans would blend against the as-wet tree bark. Sure enough, Tyler's light blue, flapping shirt drew their attention, and all five of the bodies aimed their weapons his way as they shouted. Three of them moved toward him while the other two stayed near the gate. But they were angled away from Regan, watching Tyler, and she darted behind them and headed for the gate.

As soon as she touched it, she realized she'd made a mistake. It was clearly a motorized unit, unmovable by hand, and latched to boot.

And alarmed.

A klaxon-like whoop started above her. The two guards in front of her—one woman, one man—whirled. She had her weapon up before they finished their movement, but they had theirs on her, too. They shouted something she couldn't hear, probably "drop your weapon," so she shouted it back. Out of the corner of her eye she could see Tyler advancing slowly across the macadam, his gun aiming alternately at the other three guards, all of whom kept theirs trained firmly on him, even as they slowly moved backward.

The woman guard shouted again. The alarm was driving Regan insane. The shut-off must be in the guard house to her right, so she feinted left, like she was going to run around them and join Tyler, and then dove right, twisting the door handle and knocking the door open all in one move. She landed on her right hip on the cement floor, kicked the door closed, and reached up to lock it before she lay panting on her back, her right hip screaming.

Shit. Her left one had just healed enough so she didn't feel the sting or pull of the knife wound anymore, and here she went, messing up the other one.

The klaxon wasn't as loud in here, but a flashing red light on a console, timed to a beeping sound, looked like it might be the right signal for the alarm. She dragged herself to her feet and hit a button below the light. The alarm stopped.

Outside, four guards now had Tyler surrounded while the fifth one aimed her pistol through the window, straight at Regan's head.

KELSEY CALCULATED THAT if Tom satisfied his need for speed over the first five miles or so, it would take him half an hour to get to town and at least that back. Depending how quickly they found a newspaper box, and how long Van had to talk to her mother, it might be another half hour in town. By the time they got back, it would be dark.

She tried reading a book but couldn't process any of the words. She listened to music and managed to kill about half an hour, but got tired of that quickly, too. Finally, she decided to cook dinner to have waiting when they got back. She could stretch it to take all the time they'd be gone, and have something to show for her time alone.

Calmer and more focused than before, she decided to try making spaghetti. She pulled a package of ground meat from the freezer, unwrapped it, and stuck it in the microwave to thaw. Then she found two jars of sauce and a pound of pasta in the pantry. Would be kind of boring, though. Had they bought peppers and onions on their way here?

As she pulled open the crisper drawer, she found herself missing her mother. It was weird. She hadn't missed her much when she'd gone to Whetstone. There had been too much going on, and she was making new friends and was pretty wrapped up in Tom. She turned on the stove and adjusted the flame a bit higher than the last time she tried, then filled a pot with water and set it to boil while she chopped the veggies.

So did she miss her only because she was bored here? Or because of all the crap going on? She didn't have a clue if her mother was even alive at the moment, never mind getting the answers she was determined to get. And even though Tom made her feel better about the becoming-a-weapon thing, it was still there, in her head. Without her mother here, she felt more alone in this than she had even when they were separated.

The microwave beeped. She hit the start button again and watched the bright red meat revolve. No, she didn't think the boredom or the danger was the reason she missed her. It was the domesticity. She could ignore it when she was with Van and Tom, but making a whole meal by herself was too much like being at home. So she was a little homesick.

She had to get over that. Not only had she grown up and left home, Tyler had entered their world. Even if things went back to "normal," or better than normal, and even if her mother and Tyler didn't work out, things would never be like they were before.

The microwave beeped again and she removed the meat and dumped it in a frying pan. While she browned it—adjusting and readjusting the flame until it seemed the right height—she wondered what it would be like to have a father type around the house. Would Tyler try to impose curfews and stuff when she was home on break? Probably not. But the idea made her smile.

Until she thought about her real father—and how he'd never had a chance to set a curfew, or say she couldn't date until she was thirty. Who had robbed him of all that? Robbed her of even more? What about them was so important, or so frightening, it had been worth killing an eighteen-year-old boy, and kidnapping a baby?

That was another thing. Those people had found her and her mother after she was born. And in the last week, they'd found them over and over again. So how come they hadn't found them in the years in between?

Or had they? Tyler'd been around for two years. Maybe they'd always known where she was but didn't want her, as he'd said, until now.

Damn, it made her head hurt.

She poured the pasta into the boiling water and stirred it, then turned down the heat under the meat sauce and put the cover on, pleased with herself. It should be about done by the time—

A click at the front door made her freeze. But she hadn't heard the car or seen lights, so it wasn't Van and Tom. Carefully she turned off the burners and took stock. The lights were all on, so she could be seen from the front windows and the back yard through the kitchen window. She couldn't act like she'd heard anything.

If she had.

As the pasta water slowed and silence filled the little house, she heard the click again. Then a creak. The floorboards on the porch. There was definitely someone out there.

Pretending to have forgotten something, she snapped her fingers, half turned away from the stove, and mimicked turning the dials, her body in front of them so no one could see they were already off. Then she jogged across the living room and lightly up the stairs, hoping she looked unconcerned and teenager-y.

She hit the light switch to off at the top of the stairs and turned left into the bathroom. It was the only door up here with a lock, and was weirdly constructed. The window was over the tub, but was set low, the windowsill at the edge of the porcelain and the top of the window reaching nearly to the ceiling. Tyler said it had something to do with conversion in the fifties from the original farmhouse, but the end result was a shorter drop to the ground than any of the other windows.

Kelsey stepped into the tub and stood to the side of the window, looking out onto the back yard and listening hard behind her. The moon was bright, thankfully, and the yard fairly free of shadows. And bodies, as far as she could tell.

A dull thud from below could have been the front door opening. She didn't have any more time. She unlocked and slid the window up until it was fully open. They'd soaped the edges so it moved with almost no sound. She grabbed a folded towel from the back of the toilet, dropped it onto the edge of the window to cushion her stomach, and maneuvered herself out. Using her stomach muscles and arm strength, she slowly lowered herself until she hung full length. Then she let go.

Her feet landed with surprisingly little impact and she dropped immediately to a crouch. She could hear footsteps now, moving around inside. They weren't trying to be quiet—idiots or overconfident?

She grinned. She should be terrified, but she was... exhilarated. After all those years of being prepared, of training and having nothing come of it. She didn't want this to get so exciting she died, but it was kind of fun avoiding these guys. Professionals. Trained in huge facilities and stuff. She was a kid trained by a teen mom.

"So there," she whispered. She saw no shadows cast from the windows and gambled that no one was looking out. She tugged the key to the barn door from her pocket, inhaled, and took off across the grass.

She was halfway to the barn when she heard the distinctive growl of the Corvette coming up the road. *Shit!* She changed direction and headed for the trees to her left instead. She had to get to Van and Tom before the guys inside the house did. She pushed the key back into her pocket and made a beeline for the front yard, pulling the gun from the small of her back as she ran.

And dammit, the car passed her on its way to the back yard. She reversed yet again and sped past the slow-moving vehicle to unlock and open the barn door. She shoved it open and motioned frantically to Tom to get his ass inside. He couldn't have been watching her; he positioned the car carefully, aiming it at the corner of the house so he could back it into the barn exactly as it had been.

The back door opened and a figure appeared, a semi-automatic rifle clearly outlined in his hand. There was a second, a heartbeat, when Kelsey watched from the shadows, not breathing, certain she was about to see the end of her true love and her best friend. And in that instant, everything inside her changed.

The man shouted instead of raising his weapon. Tom must have seen him right away, because he reversed so fast he nearly took off Kelsey's right leg before she could get out of the way. She slammed the doors behind them and slid a piece of wood into the inside handles, suddenly understanding why they were there.

Van was out of the car already, running around to help Tom open the trap door. None of them wasted time with questions or exclamations or stating the obvious—that they knew they were in here now. The little room would be a trap.

Kelsey thumbed the safety and shoved the gun back in her jeans, then helped haul the trap door back.

"Get down there," she said. Van obeyed immediately and caught the flashlight Tom dropped to her. Tom looked for an instant like he was going to argue, but he must have seen the look in Kelsey's eyes.

"Did you get a paper?" she asked.

"Yeah. Nothing. And Van's parents were fine."

"Good. Go."

Tom dropped onto the dirt floor below and looked up.

"I love you," she said.

His expression changed from concerned urgency to furious horror when he realized what she'd said. She knew he would have shouted if it wouldn't give their position away. She lowered the door and quickly scooped dirt onto it, packing it down and blending the seam lines. But Tom had the ladder, and he'd be up it in an instant if she didn't do something. She stood on the door and wrapped her fingers around the end of the radiator sitting against the wall, gritting her teeth against the pull in her back when she tried to drag the heavy thing. It moved an inch. She widened her stance and pulled again. This time it moved more easily. She only needed to cover the corner of the door and the handle.

The tarp usually covering the car was in a heap on the floor. She flung it across the back of the car so it spilled over the radiator, further disguising the door and disturbed earth.

Then she drew the gun again, thumbed off the safety, positioned herself next to the main doors.

And waited.

EIGHTEEN

REGAN AND THE guard eyed each other for a moment. Regan knew they were trained to expect a fight, but there was no way she and Tyler would win two against five without someone getting seriously hurt. So she didn't hide, she didn't raise her gun, and she didn't leave the building.

She picked up the phone.

The guard frowned but her weapon didn't waver. Regan looked briefly at the face of the phone unit, then back up at the unchanging view outside, then back down. She spotted the tiny black label with white type reading "Mn Hse" and pressed it.

It was answered immediately. "Report."

"Is this McCormick?"

There was a second while he adjusted to the un-expected voice. "Yes. Who is this?"

Lord, she hoped she was doing the right thing. "This is Regan Miller. Formerly known as Chelsea Conrad. I want to speak to Ben Harrison."

She could almost hear flesh tearing as the phone was ripped from McCormick's hand.

"This is Ben Harrison." His voice was booming and arrogant, as she'd expect from a military officer. But then it was tempered by something else—something sounding suspiciously like relief and pleasure when he said, "Is this really Regan Miller?"

"Yes, sir." She grimaced at the automatic address. "I want to talk to you and your wife, but for some reason your staff is harassing my escort."

Away from the phone she heard Ben give the order for the guards to stand down. Another voice repeated it, and a few beats later the guards outside lowered their weapons. Tyler looked wary, squinting through the rain and the guard house window to her. Regan nodded, and he put away his gun.

"Thank you. Can we come up to the house now, or shall we play war games a bit longer?"

"A car is on its way down. I didn't realize you were with Sloane." A touch of gruffness was the only hint of apology in his voice. "He hasn't reported in for several days. We didn't know—"

"Yeah, we figured." She stretched to unlock the door, and a moment later the room filled with dripping rain slickers and squeaky shoes. "We're going to need some towels and dry clothes, Colonel."

"Call me Ben, please. And of course you'll receive our full hospitality. We'll see you in a moment."

Regan replaced the receiver and quirked her mouth at Tyler, who leaned against the wall watching her.

"We'll receive their full hospitality," she said wryly. Tyler didn't smile. Instead he gazed at her a moment more, as if to be sure she was okay, before turning to the woman who'd covered Regan.

"What reason were you given for bringing me in?" he asked softly.

She didn't blink or move a muscle. "We weren't told."

"Liar."

A younger-looking man with flaming red hair and more freckles than Regan had ever seen on a man said, "She's not lying. They just said we were to consider you dangerous and of unknown loyalties."

Tyler rolled his eyes. "That's a reason, you dipshits. I've worked with you for ten years, you can't—"

The woman interrupted him. "We haven't seen you in two, Sloane. We didn't even know if you were still working for the Harrisons."

"I was just here!"

"How are we supposed to know that? None of us saw you!"

A black car pulled up very close to the door and honked, interrupting the escalating argument. Tyler swept the room with a disgusted look, then held the doors of both building and car for Regan before sliding into the back seat with her.

Regan sighed and let her muscles go limp for a moment, to give them a respite. "That could have gone worse," she murmured, surprised to see Tyler's jaw clench. He didn't look at her.

"It will."

"What—"

But Tyler shook his head once, still not meeting her gaze. A new unease spread through her. There was something wrong, something beyond the "wrong" they'd prepared for.

There wasn't time to get any information from

him. The car glided to a stop next to a large white mansion fronted by pillars and a tall, wide stairway. Regan had the impression of waterlogged bushes, climbing vines and hanging plants from the second-floor porch before she and Tyler were hustled out of the car.

She didn't like being hustled. The guy who opened her door and pulled her out by the arm held tight to her as they hurried up the steps and across the wide-planked porch floor. Two other men cuffed Tyler and jerked him around. When they cleared the double doorway into the foyer, more black-clad security surrounded them, most standing at ready with their hands on their weapons. Any tension she'd shed in the car snapped back into every muscle. The room practically hummed with it.

So when a tall, silver-haired, mean-looking man came toward her with his arms out, her brain screamed *threat* and she drew the pistol from her waistband and aimed it at his face. Her stance went wide, her left hand came up to support her hold on the weapon, and she sent him a glare that made no doubt she meant business.

Ben Harrison halted, his hands half raised, but at the same time the clicks of a dozen weapons echoed in the high-ceilinged foyer. Regan didn't care. She'd take him out before they took her, and they knew it.

Her moment of panic faded into cool calm. She'd regained a measure of control, and they could move on. She glared at the man she recognized as Scott's father, though he'd aged more than she would have expected in the time since she saw him at Blaydes Academy.

"Nice greeting," she said.

Harrison inclined his head. "A bit aggressive, I admit. I apologize. I was simply about to give you a hug."

Regan snorted. "Sure. People with guns always hug first, shoot later."

"He means it," said an elegantly feminine voice from behind him. A woman stepped around his up-raised arm. She looked so much like an older version of Kelsey, Regan's arms dropped a few inches before she recovered and jerked them back up.

"Major Harrison." She, too, looked much different from Regan's vague memory. Back then she'd been polished and regal but also very feminine, despite her military occupation.

"Please, call me Jeanne." She smiled, and Regan couldn't quite connect the smooth voice and manners with her current appearance. She wore her dark red hair close-cropped, almost spiky, and she was dressed in black like the security team—cargo pants, a long-sleeved T-shirt, and a weapons belt.

She saw Regan studying her and glanced down at herself. "Forgive me, I was training with the team. If we'd known you were coming I'd have worn some-thing more appropriate for company." She snapped her fingers and the security team immediately low-ered their weapons, except for one man who kept his about a foot from Regan's right temple. She guessed he was McCormick, the head of security, overcompensating for his staff not taking her gun at the guard house.

"As I was saying," Jeanne continued, "my husband is an effusive man. He's been very worried about you and Kelsey and considers you family. You and Scott may not have been married, but we've always thought of you as our daughter-in-law." Sadness crossed her face, and Regan was so surprised she lowered her gun completely. After a second, she made it safe and stuck it back in her jeans. McCormick relaxed, too.

Jeanne's words and the emotions behind them didn't fit the scene in the foyer at all, so all Regan could come up with to say was, "That's not what I expected to hear."

"I'm sure it's not," Ben finally spoke again. He nodded to the stoic-faced men around him and they dispersed, all except McCormick and the two hold-ing Tyler. Another man, this one wearing dress pants and a button-down shirt, approached her with a towel. Regan had forgotten she was wet. She dried off as best she could and handed the towel back to the man. She noticed he didn't offer one to Tyler.

"I apologize for alarming you," Ben continued. "I didn't think—a rare and deadly thing. I was under the influence of relief and joy." He held out an arm toward Regan and another toward one of four arch-ways leading out of the foyer. "Shall we go sit down? We have plenty to discuss, I know."

Regan didn't move. "Not until you release Tyler."

The steel behind the soft emotions showed itself. "No. His loyalties are unknown."

"Not to me, they aren't."

During the short conversation, Tyler hadn't moved. His expression matched those of the security people, except she'd come to know him well enough to see the pain behind his eyes. Though he'd expected treatment like this, it hurt him that they didn't trust him.

"Where's Kelsey?" Jeanne sounded as if she'd just realized the girl wasn't there.

"I'm not telling anyone that." Regan's anger grew.

"She's not with you?"

She raised her eyebrows. "You really thought I'd bring her here? To the home of the people who might have killed her father?"

The shock sweeping through the room was almost visible. Jeanne looked stricken and even teary, something Regan wouldn't have expected from an Air Force major.

Ben nodded, though his shoulders slumped. "We can hardly blame her for thinking that, Jeanne." He sighed. "There's obviously a lot to discuss. Please, come in and sit down. Tyler will remain with us, but I'm fully aware of his capabilities and I won't authorize removal of the restraints until I'm certain he's not working for our enemy."

Regan considered. Tyler's proclamations, her growing feelings for him, put her on his side. She'd been suspicious long enough that she couldn't blame the Harrisons for their caution. But… "If he was compromised, or bought, he wouldn't have brought me here."

"Not an invalid point, but there is a great deal at stake. You'll understand in time."

Obviously considering the debate settled, Ben turned and went through the archway into a comfortable-looking living room furnished in rich earth tones and decorated with items collected from all over the world. The front and back walls were both mostly tall, cathedral-style windows.

Jeanne waited patiently, her eyes on Regan, who finally followed and sat, as indicated, in a plush armchair. The gun dug into her back so she removed it and rested it on the arm of the chair. The Harrisons settled on the matching loveseat, Jeanne sitting on the edge but Ben relaxing against the cushions. They all watched as Tyler was walked into the room and pushed into a straight-back chair, his handcuffs removed and replaced in front of him. The two men stood behind him, each with a hand on his shoulder.

"You are dismissed," Ben told them. "But he's as effective with his hands cuffed as he is with them not. Better secure him to the chair."

One of the men bent and shook out another pair of cuffs. He wrapped one around Tyler's ankle, making it so tight Regan winced, and the other half to the rung of the chair. Tyler's expression slipped into a glower before he smoothed it out again.

Silence reigned until the men had left. Then Ben looked at Tyler. "Explain yourself."

"No."

Three sets of eyebrows went up.

"I beg your pardon?" The steel was back in Ben's voice.

"I have nothing to explain."

"Tyler," Jeanne started in a softer tone, but Regan cut her off. She understood what Tyler was doing.

"When did you last speak with Tyler?" she asked Ben.

"A week ago."

"Since then we were attacked at the airport, received a phone call from our attackers' leader—at least, to the best of my understanding—on a phone no one should have been able to call, and attacked again in a motel room no one should have known we were in. There's someone on the inside here."

"Impossible."

Jeanne touched her husband's knee. "Not impossible, and you know it. Do you have any idea who?" she asked Tyler.

"It's more logical Tyler was the one conveying information to Archie," Ben protested.

Excitement rushed through Regan. Archie. Who was Archie?

But Tyler's stoicism had gone. When he spoke, his voice icy with rage, his face darkening. "After ten years, you know better than to say that to me." He started to rise, but the chain holding his leg to the chair clanked and he sat again, jerking his foot against the restraint. "I kept them safe for two. Why would I suddenly turn?"

"*You* kept her safe?" Ben barked. "You were a watchdog, yes, but hobbled. I was the one who kept them safe, at huge costs. You let them kill her lover, almost kill her!"

"Wait." Regan shook her head against her confusion. "Back up. What—" She stopped herself and took her own advice. "Five people pounded on Tyler at the airport. Were those your men?"

Ben's eyes narrowed, but he admitted, "No. They weren't."

"Then Tyler's on your side." She didn't say "our" side and wondered if they noticed. "Now can we please start at the beginning? With Scott's murder?"

Jeanne gasped softly at the word. "What happened?" she asked. Despite her appearance as a kick-ass military officer, she sounded like a grieving mother. "We never knew…the details."

The telling had become easier now that Regan had done it once. She finished with, "He died in my arms."

"Did he—" Jeanne pressed her hand to her mouth. Ben rubbed her back gently while she regained her composure. "Did he say anything?"

Regan's eyes stung in response. "He said 'they' wanted the baby, and I needed to run. That 'they'd' tried to kill him. And he said he loved me. Loved us."

Jeanne sobbed into her hands, and Ben's eyes shimmered.

"He did love you," he said, his voice rough. "It was obvious long before he came home and told us he was going to be a father. But he almost burned with it that weekend."

"What did you say to him?" Regan pleaded. "What scared him so much we were going to run?"

Ben sat forward and rested his elbows on his knees. He stared at his hands, which he rubbed together, slowly, back and forth. He didn't address her question directly, but Regan remained silent, listening.

"Scott arrived home Friday evening, about to burst with happiness. He couldn't even wait until dinner, or until he unpacked. He sat us down. And he told us he was going to be a father."

"As his mother, I was devastated, of course," said Jeanne, who'd plucked a tissue from the box on the table next to her and now looked like she hadn't been crying at all. "But there were so many other…factors."

"We had nothing against you," Ben assured Regan. "We always liked you. But no parent wants their son to be a teenage father."

"So what did you tell him?"

"We made…suggestions."

Regan didn't need him to spell out what those were. She would have done the same had Kelsey come to her with similar news. She couldn't blame him, though knowing what it would have meant to her life, to her daughter, made her sick to her stomach.

"I was afraid he was going to hate us by the time it was over," Jeanne said. "So we told him the truth. He was furious with us. I didn't want to let him go, but we couldn't exactly lock him up. And we didn't understand what the truth really meant."

"He missed his call-in," Ben continued before Regan could ask what truth. "He was supposed to call when he got back to school. He didn't answer his phone in the dorm, and you didn't answer yours. So we called campus security—"

"They'd just found him."

Regan cringed inside, waiting for Jeanne to lay into her for leaving her son lying in his own blood, but she didn't.

"You know who killed him," Regan accused.

They both nodded.

"Who?"

"We have to back up again," Ben said. "The information is still classified—"

"Screw classified!" Regan clenched her fists and forced herself to remain still. "You're not going to hide behind that." Her hand tightened on the pistol.

"No, of course we're not," Ben scoffed. "I'm simply trying to impress upon you the need for secrecy."

Regan rolled her eyes. "Okay, I'll scrap my plan to run out to the media."

"Twenty years ago Jeanne and I worked on a project. Despite appearances—" Ben motioned to his wife's attire, "—we are less fighting soldiers than scientific explorers. The program was benign. We were seeking a way to boost soldiers' immunity without requiring complicated immunization plans or forced exposure to dangerous illnesses. Increased immunity would allow the body to fight a wide range of pathogens, including those we had no immunization for. It would make our military less vulnerable."

"And like any such program," Jeanne took up, her eyes sparking with obvious passion for the subject, "it had vast non-military applications, as well. Decreasing frequency of illness in a population would also decrease health care costs and pressure on the medical system, as well as increasing productivity and competitiveness in business and other arenas."

Despite herself, Regan was fascinated with the idea. "Did it work?"

"We'd succeeded in developing a compound that had promise, but its duration was too limited. We believed a second-generation product could provide near-immediate and lasting effect."

"How do you develop a second-generation product?" Regan wasn't surprised to see guilt color both the Harrisons' faces. She hadn't finished high school or gone on to college, so the science of such a thing was well beyond her. But with what she did know, horror began to fill her before Ben made his admission.

"It varies, but in this case you use the first generation product on a live subject. His offspring's blood should contain the elements needed to process the new compound."

"Oh my God." Regan stared at him. It was worse than she'd ever expected. "You *planned* all this?"

"No!" Jeanne burst out. "No, none of it! Scott was given the compound simply to keep him healthy. Schools are always so full of pathogens," she explained weakly, as if knowing how ridiculous she sounded. "I know it sounds stupid to use something so new on your child, but we wanted what was best for him."

"But when he got me pregnant, you decided it was the perfect time to try phase two," Regan said bitterly. She realized she'd wrapped her finger around the trigger of the pistol and eased it out to rest along the guard.

"No, that's not it at all." But Jeanne's guilty expression deepened. She glanced at her husband, who nodded.

"We didn't have time to decide anything, Regan," he said. "But there was a lot more going on. Just days before Scott arrived home, we'd learned some disturbing news about our partner on this project. He believed he could reverse the effect of the compound to create an undetectable killer. The implications of such a thing were against everything Jeanne and I believe in—"

"You were working for the military!" Regan cried. "That's what the military does! It kills!"

"We worked for the military," Jeanne informed her, "because they have the resources to do the research and development that was so important to us. We never worked on weapons."

"It didn't matter, because your research could be used to create them, anyway. Especially if Archie had no such principles." She looked from one to the other. "Am I right? This Archie you mentioned earlier? He was your partner?"

"Yes," Ben said. "And yes, he could have gone on

to develop the weapon under the Air Force's aegis. But he wanted more."

Jeanne went on, "He tried to convince us we could all be hugely rich if we developed the reverse compound independently of the government and sold it commercially."

"You mean, to terrorists and opposing governments," Regan said.

Ben nodded. "We would have no part of it and reported him. He was removed from our project. I thought the Air Force was detaining him, but at some point he escaped custody. He had to have someone inside. Here. And we think that person intercepted our son." His voice cracked, and they sat in silence for a minute.

It was a fantastic tale, but Regan couldn't disbelieve any of it. The worst part was…it had worked. She had always thought it beyond lucky Kelsey never got sick. As a baby she escaped the usual ear infections, colds, fevers and flus that plagued other families. Even when she started kindergarten and was exposed to so many more germs, she never got sick. She had perfect attendance all through school, and if she hadn't been so normal in her development and everything else, Regan would have worried.

It had never occurred to her it might have been deliberate.

She swallowed against an increasingly dry throat. She'd expected to feel different after learning the truth. As if understanding why Scott died, why someone tried to take her baby, would fill some hole inside her, one carved by the years of fear and precaution. But she felt as empty as ever, and realized that no words, no intentions, could ever make up for the lives they'd been forced to live. Bitter as it was, it was more important to accept it and move on.

"What happened after Scott died?"

Suddenly, Jeanne seemed unable to look at Regan. Ben didn't avoid her gaze, but did appear more discomfited than before.

"We assumed Archie had something to do with Scott's death, but he disappeared. We knew he'd go after the baby."

"I disappeared, too." Regan knew it was stupid as soon as she said it. "Those were your men? Who came for Kelsey?"

Ben shook his head. "We tracked you down and as soon as the baby was born, sent someone to protect you. But we were too late. They got to you first."

"Too late!" Regan couldn't believe it. "Why the hell didn't you just *call* me?" Except she hadn't been able to afford a phone back then. And the hovel she lived in, at the back of a house not designed for its one-room "apartments," wasn't conducive to reliable mail delivery.

"Look," Ben said defensively, "I'm a scientist. This entire situation was out of my realm. The government wasn't going to help us, and I was afraid if we tried to get them to, it would lead Archie to you more easily. When we found out those men had tried to take Kelsey, we decided it was safer for you if we didn't contact you directly."

"It doesn't seem out of your realm now." Regan looked at Tyler, then up at the cameras she'd identified in the corners of the room. "In fact, you seem very well-equipped and well-staffed."

"For the same reason you are so well-trained and knowledgeable."

Regan gave him points for that. "Reactive security?"

Ben nodded. "You kept running, of course, and we couldn't find you immediately. Archie went underground, as far as we could tell. He had no equipment or samples, no facilities or staff, so we let it go. We focused on building our defenses and protecting you."

"How?"

"The key to disappearing, we learned, is misinformation. The more false leads the searcher has to track down, the more time and money they waste. So we laid trails, updating them over the years, giving your enemy enough false information to keep his investigators busy for years."

"But if he wasn't looking…"

"We didn't know he wasn't," Jeanne said. "There was no evidence he was working on his project, but we couldn't be sure. And if he didn't have the resources to develop the compound, he had no need for you or Kelsey. So we set up utilities and leases and video rental accounts in your name, all over the country, at different times and far away from where you really were."

"You knew? The whole time?" She didn't know what to think. It had been bad enough to fear she might have kept Kelsey from her family needlessly, but to know they could have made contact at any time and hadn't? Hadn't they wanted to know their granddaughter?

"Most of the time, we knew," Ben confirmed. "We lost you several times. Most recently about ten years ago."

Regan reflexively looked at Tyler. That was how long he said he'd been working for the Harrisons. He sat ramrod straight on his chair and looked at no one, but again she could see behind the mask. He looked—afraid.

And that made Regan afraid.

"Unfortunately, we lost you at the same time we got intelligence that Archie had resurfaced."

"How did you manage to do all this?" Regan asked. "It had to be outrageously expensive."

"We sold the patent for one of our creations, which allowed all this—" Jeanne waved a hand to indicate the house, "—and the development of a security team and the resources to track and protect you. When we retired from the Air Force and went private sector, our finances were well secured."

She smiled, but Regan could tell she wasn't sure how her next words would be received.

"It allowed us to finance a scholarship for Kelsey's education."

"You—" It was all she could manage, with her jaw hanging halfway to her chest. The scholarship was from them? Gratitude twisted around resentment, but the huge unimportance of it—at least for now—

let her shove it aside. Still, curiosity had her asking, "What was it? The patent?"

Ben smiled proudly. "A treatment for erectile dysfunction."

Her mouth dropped again. They'd sent their granddaughter to college on… "Viagra?"

"No, but a similar idea. And many other things since. But it's not really relevant." He looked at Tyler. "Perhaps you'd like to take up the tale."

Tyler's jaw flexed. He turned to Regan, who felt pressure in her chest she recognized as apprehension. She trusted him. Had put herself and her daughter fully in his hands. If he hadn't been straight with her, she didn't want to know any more.

"I came to the Harrisons deliberately," he admitted. "They didn't simply hire me."

"What do you mean?"

"I mean, I told them about Archie."

She couldn't catch a breath. Her body knew what her brain didn't want to grasp. "What about him?"

"He'd reached a point in his research where he was ready for the next stage. The stage where he—"

"Needed Kelsey." Regan got that part, it fit with the rest. But what she didn't get was, "How did you know?"

Before Tyler could answer, the room exploded in showers of glass.

NINETEEN

KELSEY NEVER STOPPED fighting.

She'd learned from pretty much every instructor she'd ever had, from her mother to her teachers to her soccer coach, the only way to get anywhere in life was to set goals.

Her first goal was to get the people in the house away from her friends without them being discovered or hurt. She assumed they only wanted her, and if she could lead them away, she'd meet her goal.

She crouched behind the barn door, focusing intently on keeping her breathing inaudible and listening to her pursuer. Her hand cramped around the barrel of the gun and she carefully loosened it. The brush of footstep on dirt. A shadow. And then...

The first guy crept around the edge of the barn door. Kelsey pounced, clocking him hard across the face with her gun, gritting her teeth against the impact that reverberated up her arm. Exhilarated when he rocked back, his hand automatically going to his jaw, she shoved him backwards and stepped on him. He'd be down for at least a few minutes. She thought. But hot fingers closed around her ankle and she crashed to the ground. She sucked back a scream, her mind on Van and Tom. The impact knocked the air from her lungs and the gun from her hand, but she scrambled to recover both quickly. He hung on to her leg, his grip sending snakes of disgust and panic writhing through her belly. She *had* to get away, get them away from her friends! Bending her knee hard to pull her foot out of his grasp, she immediately drove her toe downward into his stomach again. This time he didn't grab her.

But he'd slowed her down. Two more men ran out of the house and across the lawn by the time she got to her feet. Her heart went into overdrive. She started to run to her right, but another guy came around the side of the house. Shit, how many had they brought?

Now she was trapped with the barn behind her, one recovering attacker on her left, and three spreading in a semicircle to cut off her options as they approached her.

"She's got a gun," one of them said.

Kelsey waved it, grinning. "I do. And I know how to use it. Wanna see?" She squeezed off a shot, aiming high but sweeping the gun so they'd all duck. She darted around behind the barn and took off across the field, cursing the turned soil that made running difficult. Assuming they were behind her, she zig-zagged across the field. On one zig she glanced back, dismayed to see only two pursuing her. The others were probably looking for her friends, hoping to use them to lure her back. Well, screw that. She reversed direction and angled for the far corner of the field, arcing her way back to the house.

She widened her stride, but her right foot landed on

a clod and twisted, sending her stumbling and a zing of panic into her brain. A few steps proved there was no damage to her ankle, thank God, but she took a hit on her speed. The gap between her and her pursuers closed quickly, forcing her to fire another shot over their heads. This trigger pull was easier, and her aim better. They hit the dirt and she sped on. They shouted for their companions, who emerged from the barn, spotted her, and joined the chase. She went around the house to the open front door, darted through, and crouch-walked to the back door to watch what happened next.

"Yesss!" she hissed when all four shapes converged, then parted to go around both sides of the house and meet in the front. She went out the back door into the center of the yard, and…crap. She'd underestimated them—only two guys had gone around to the front. The other two hovered in the shadows, watching. She'd barely registered this when the one on her right raised his gun and fired.

The bullet snagged her hair, then went through the door of the barn. Kelsey froze in shock, practically departing from her body for an instant while her brain processed what had just happened. One second later, every nerve ending screamed *move!* and she reversed back to the house, ducking inside.

"What the hell are you doing?" the other guy screamed. "You can't hurt her, asshole!"

"Good to know," she muttered, heart pounding, brain scrambling. Coming back was a foolish move, since it trapped her again. But her mother's training triumphed. When guy number one came in the front and number two in the back, she rolled over the back of the couch and let them collide where she'd been standing, giving her enough space to get out the front. Three and four were on either side of the porch, but she was too fast for them and flew up the driveway before they could reach her.

Score one for soccer. Playing intramural at school this year was paying off in speed and stamina.

When she was a hundred yards up the drive she looked back. All four were chasing her now, her friends apparently forgotten.

Goal one accomplished.

Goal two immediately became evasion, which failed because she somehow passed their car without seeing it. When they reached it, their horsepower trumped her soccer-built running skills. When the car neared her she took off cross country, but all-wheel-drive was better than two feet and they caught up to her easily, passing her and disgorging Number Three to tackle her and press her into the dirt.

Winded and with a couple hundred pounds on her back, Kelsey could do nothing. Instinct and helplessness drove her struggle to get free, but didn't totally kill the exhilaration of the chase. Her friends were still safe, and these guys had orders not to hurt her. There'd be an opportunity to get away, probably more than one. She just had to be smarter than these guys… and keep setting goals.

One of the other guys tied her hands behind her back and a third roped her feet together. They hauled her up, tossed her into the car, and bounced back to the road, where they took off away from the house.

Kelsey closed her eyes and prayed. *Please let Van and Tom be okay.* She focused on the fact that she'd protected them, kept them safe, until her body adjusted to her circumstances and she could keep the anxiety from turning into full-bore panic. *Fear gives you the means to save yourself, panic takes it away.* Another lesson of her mother's, and so far, it was working.

Goal Three. Escape. Big goal. How? Listen. Plan. She lay across the laps of the two jerks in the back seat, tuning in to their conversation. Big goals should be broken down into smaller ones, but she needed information before she could set them.

"Did you call it in?" the guy in the passenger seat asked the guy driving once they were on the main road and their teeth were no longer clacking together from the bouncing.

"Not yet. No signal out here."

There was a beep. First guy said, "Shit, you're right."

"I told you. You never listen to me."

Kelsey was facing forward so she could see the driver, the second guy, yank the phone out of the first guy's hands.

"We'll call when we get to the airport."

Okay, so they planned to fly her out. To where? California? Didn't matter. She couldn't let them load her on the plane. If she managed to get out of the car now, though, she would just be running across empty farmland again. Her best bet would be to get out while they were in town, before they got to the airport. It left her a small window, but with town traffic she might be able to do it.

Of course, being tied up presented a bit of a problem. She'd held her hands so the rope around her wrists was pretty loose, but she couldn't slip it with her hands up against the third guy's abdomen. The fourth guy's hand rested on the rope around her legs, so she couldn't work at that, either.

You're pretty screwed, Miller. But wait. She held herself still when she really, really wanted to squirm away from their smelly bodies and icky hands.

"Why is everyone starin' at us?" One wondered as they did a rolling stop at a stop sign.

"Dunno," Two answered, sounding wary. "That guy's pointing at us."

"Shit, he's a cop! Step on it!"

"I knew we shouldn't have stolen this friggin' thing!" Four shouted from Kelsey's feet. "It's red! They always pay attention to red cars!"

She couldn't stifle a laugh. Driving back through the town you stole a car in, especially a tiny, isolated town with a matching grapevine, was very stupid. She felt a little less okay with letting these idiots get the better of her, but determined to best them first chance she got.

Two squealed around a corner. Three and Four lost their grips and Kelsey rolled to the floor. This was her chance! She wiggled and writhed against their hands, and when they dragged her back up, this time facing them, her feet were loosened and hands free, masked by the rope still hanging around her wrists. So when they slammed to a stop at the airport and Kelsey toppled off their laps again, she had the element of surprise. She thrashed her feet until one came out of the binding, kicking Four multiple times, once in the face.

"Ow! Goddamn it! Help me!"

Two opened Four's door. But young athletic soccer stars with paranoid mothers were excellent fighters with their feet. Kelsey nailed both of them good before she dragged herself across Three's lap, kneeing him in the groin in the process, and scrambled out his door.

She got halfway to the little terminal—almost far enough to feel a hint of relief—before, out of the blue, two men in black jackets and cargo pants caught her arms and lifted her right off her feet. "Oh, come *on!*" More furious than scared, she twisted and screamed and yanked, but they stood solidly, holding tightly but not actively fighting her. She knew they were letting her tire herself out.

It didn't matter. They didn't know how fierce she was, how much she needed to keep her friends safe. She wasn't going to tire. She wrenched her right arm free and landed on her feet in a half-crouch, but then there was a sting in her left arm. She looked, and saw a needle sticking out of her skin.

"Oh, shit."

REGAN HIT THE floor automatically. Despite the size of the room, the force of the explosions from both sides sent shards flying in all directions. Pieces landed on her back. Her hands, covering her head, stung with cuts. Sound had disappeared, and her breathing came with such a gaspy quality she thought she'd die.

The explosions were immediately followed by the thuds of booted feet and chatter of automatic weapons fire. Regan could hear them through the cotton in her ears enough to recognize them, but could see nothing. She had no idea who wielded the weapons, where the bullets were coming from—and where they were aimed.

She hadn't even had time to lift her head when someone hauled her roughly to her feet. At first she thought it was one of the Harrisons' security team, he was dressed so much like them. But he wore a ski-style mask and instead of a gun, he held a wicked-looking knife.

A knife she'd seen before, or at least one like it. Adrenaline kicked in.

She fell toward the man, surprising him enough to release her arm. But not enough for him to forget what he was doing. He drew back the knife, aimed at her gut. She scrambled back a few steps and kicked. Her foot missed his wrist, but her heel glanced the knife blade. It got caught in the hard rubber just long enough to pull it partway out of his hand. While he struggled to secure it, she slammed her elbow into his nose.

He went down without a sound. She stood over him, waiting, but the blow had been hard enough to splinter the cartilage. He was unconscious.

She snatched up his knife and her gun from where it had been knocked to the floor and huddled beside the chair, taking stock.

Black-dressed figures were everywhere, fighting, firing guns, jumping in and out of the blasted windows. She couldn't tell who was friend and who was foe without scrutiny, and taking the time to do that would be deadly.

Jeanne Harrison was nowhere in sight. Ben fought fiercely with two men, one of whom drove him backward into the wall. His head hit the stone around the fireplace and he fell, his eyes rolling. He was too far away for her to help him.

Other figures converged on Regan, half a room away but obviously coming toward her. She rose to a crouch, trying to keep all three of them in view. She spared a quick glance behind her and was surprised to see Tyler standing, untouched save for some glass cuts on his face, the toppled chair still attached to his leg. No one went near him, and the occasional bullets remained near the back windows where the fiercest fighting was going on. As she watched, one of the men in a ski mask ran past Tyler without even looking at him. The man barked something at the men descending on her, and they leaped into action.

Slipping into a cold warrior mode of which she'd never expected herself capable, Regan raised both knife and gun. She fired, hitting one man in the leg. He yelled, took a step on the injured leg, and collapsed, clutching it. Her knife swipe missed the guy on the left, who dodged, and the guy in the middle came too fast for her to react. His fist was heading for her face when out of nowhere a chair flew at his head. Regan fell back over a small table, barely registering the chair was still attached to Tyler's leg. He'd done a spin kick, flinging the chair into the guy. Regan's fall kept her from getting caught on the follow-through.

She fired the pistol again, fear and chaotic confusion making her hand shake a little. The bullet grazed the upper arm of the guy on her left. He didn't stop coming. She rolled right and onto her feet, but he hit her wrist with the side of his hand. The nerve vibrated, numbness taking over. Her fingers went limp and the gun clattered to the floor.

But she still had the knife. She swept it at his face, but he easily caught her wrist and held the knife away, baring his teeth in a feral growl as he bore down. Rage boiled, flooded her. No way was she letting one of these guys keep her from Kelsey. She didn't stop fighting before, and she wouldn't now. She moved her right foot behind her to brace and slammed her right forearm against his throat. She didn't have the strength to really hurt him, but it held him away and kept the knife aimed at him. He gurgled a little, the grin dropping, but twisted her left arm downward, centimeter by centimeter. Her muscles burned, the knife trembling. He was stronger, and if he kept turning her hand, all it would take would be one shove to plunge the knife into her heart.

Time slowed. She pushed with her back leg, but her forward leg began to give way. The knife continued to rotate. She jerked, trying to cut him, but he had her too tightly. His face turned red but he grinned again, knowing he was winning.

With a surge of desperation, Regan drove her right knee upward. It connected solidly with his balls. His eyes bulged, and his breath came out in a high, almost inaudible scream. His grip loosened and his legs sagged, though he struggled to stay up. Regan shoved against his neck and he held on as he fell backward. She released the knife as they landed in a heap, terrified it would gut her.

Someone caught her by the shoulders and pulled her away from the goon, who rolled onto his stomach, now gasping. Regan spun, her vision blurring, her determination to keep fighting outstripping her ability as she nearly knocked herself over. But Tyler held her shoulders, keeping her on her feet. The cuffs dangled from his ankle, the smashed chair a few feet away.

She was about to thank him when someone shouted his name. They turned to the man striding toward them, his hat pulled back, his face furious.

"Your father's going to be pissed," he called. "What the hell are you doing?"

His father? Regan looked at Ben, who was lying ignored at the base of the fireplace wall. She looked back at Tyler, who scowled.

"Shut up!" he yelled and made a motion to wave the man away.

Confused, Regan scanned the room and the much-reduced activity. Bodies lay everywhere, some moving, some still, all in black. She spotted Jeanne through the archway into the foyer. The woman stood with her back to a wall, pistols in both hands. As Regan watched, she fired one. A body fell into view. Jeanne spun as another person rushed her.

The man yelling at Tyler had reached them now. Tyler released Regan and stepped in front of her. She slowly backed away. The man got in Tyler's face, roaring something about loyalty and following orders. Regan barely processed it until he said Archie Sloane. Then it all clicked.

Archie was Tyler's father.

She stood in shock for one precious second before her mind began to race. Ben was hurt, but now ignored. Jeanne fought, but most of the activity was centered here in this room. Near Regan. If the security team hadn't been close, she knew most of the attackers would have been on her, and she'd be dead—or taken? But during the fighting, they'd left Tyler alone.

Tyler's father had killed Scott. Had killed Alan. Tried to kill her, abduct Kelsey, use her as a weapon. Tyler had known all this and hadn't told her.

Betrayal poured through her, the pain enough to make her collapse if another, simultaneous thought hadn't immediately countered it.

Archie had known where she was, had come after her with a full force. Even if his intent was to capture her, he didn't seem too concerned about her getting killed in crossfire. Which meant he didn't need her to get to Kelsey.

Which meant they knew where Kelsey was.

Later, Regan would not have been able to explain

how she got out of the house. Slices in her jeans and cuts on her side and arm indicated she'd gone through the broken window. She didn't really remember fighting, but she had to have. There was a bruise on her cheek as if she'd been punched, and another on her left ribs.

But it was all a blur until she came to awareness, speeding down the road in the black car that had delivered them to the house. One hand clutched her pistol and the steering wheel, while the other lay pressed flat against the knife on her thigh. She was cold, a block of ice from deep inside all the way to her fingertips.

And she was being followed.

The car was luxuriously appointed, with walnut trim and leather upholstery. Regan set the gun on the console and found the controls for the heat, pressing a button for the seat warmer, too. It made her slightly more comfortable, though nothing touched the cold at her core.

She was at least a day's drive from Tyler's house. She couldn't fly back, having little money, no safe ID, no vehicle on the other end, and people chasing her.

Seated in a custom holder at the base of the console was a walkie-talkie. It kept squawking, the voices giving her notice that Tyler, with a couple of Harrison's men, was chasing bad guys who were chasing her. She must have gotten a head start on them because it sounded as if they were a few miles back. She was doing eighty now, though she suspected she'd been going faster when she'd been in the fugue state, or whatever it was.

Darkness had fallen early because of the rain, which had lightened. The wipers flashed across the windshield intermittently, the headlights on automatically in the dark, and the steering wheel responded to the tiniest correction. It felt a bit like flying.

She glanced at the gas tank. Nearly full. Where the hell was she? She paid attention until she passed a sign for CA-20. A mile later she approached one for I-5. Shit. She'd been on the road nearly an hour. She'd blacked out that long? What else had she done?

She took the ramp for I-5, mercifully as empty as 20 had been. She stretched to open the glove compartment, but all it held was a packet with the car's registration and some maintenance paperwork. The center console held an unopened bag of cashews, a pack of gum, a spare set of car keys—where had she gotten the ones in the ignition?—and what appeared to be a second battery for the walkie-talkie. There was no GPS in the console, but she was certain the car was marked with it. So she had to stay ahead of them, and not backtracking would be a damned good way to do it. She hit the map light above her and looked around, spotting an elasticized leather pocket in the door. She slid a hand into it. Bingo. A U.S. road atlas.

A short distance later she pulled off the highway at a wide spot in the shoulder, hoping the others weren't very close. The radio had gone silent. Maybe she was out of range, or maybe they realized she had one and switched channels.

She took a few minutes to plot a route. I-80 would take her all the way through Nebraska. She weighed the pros and cons of staying on such a direct route. Pro was getting to Kelsey fastest, which won out over losing the people behind her. She could head north at Omaha instead of Des Moines, where Tyler would expect her to go because of familiarity.

The word brought forth a flood of recent memory and the realization of just how close she'd let Tyler get. Pain burst from her chest, blinding her for precious seconds. She didn't want this. There was no time for loss and betrayal and hatred. She had to get to Kelsey.

As always, her focus sharpened and cleared away the rest when she thought of her daughter. She took a deep breath, turned off the heater, and got back on the road.

AVERAGING EIGHTY MILES an hour and stopping for no more than five minutes at a time to fuel the car, go to the bathroom, and buy snacks and caffeinated gum, drinks and mints, Regan made the final approach to the house just over twenty-four hours after she'd regained awareness. She'd fought to stay awake at times, blasting the radio, driving with the window down, pinching herself, and sucking down so much caffeine and energy shots she'd vomited about five hours ago.

Now, she couldn't have dozed off if someone hit her on the head. Her foot pressed harder and harder on the accelerator, the car speeding up to match her racing heart, until the tires caught dirt at one point and she almost spun out. She took a few deep breaths and slowed down, regained control, and counted the last five minutes by seconds.

There were tire tracks at the side of the house. Her heart stopped racing. Stopped beating entirely for two counts before thudding back so hard it cramped. Someone had been here. Might still be here. After a brief debate whether to go to the back or inside, she shoved the car into park and grabbed the keys before racing in through the unlocked front door.

"Kelsey!" she shouted into the cavernous silence. She knew before she finished the word that no one was in here. "Van! Tom!"

Nothing.

"Be methodical," she muttered. *Don't run off half-cocked.* She searched the downstairs, checking the bathroom and the closet before rushing upstairs and doing the same. No one was in the bedrooms, under the beds, in the upstairs closets. She yanked on the rope pull for the attic access, but when paint cracked and dust showered onto the clean floor below it, she knew no one had gone up there.

She checked the bathroom last and found the window open and footprints in the tub. She leaned out and looked down. A white towel was on the ground directly below. The yard, oddly lit by the late twilight, appeared deserted. But—

Regan's heart skipped again. The doors to the run-down barn out back were hanging open.

She raced back downstairs and outside, her feet

flying as she crossed the lawn, shouting her daughter's name. She stopped dead when she reached the edge of the barn entrance. Momentarily surprised to see a vintage Corvette gleaming beneath a coating of dust, she hovered there. The driver's door was open, the keys in the ignition. What the hell...?

Slow down, look at everything. The dirt just inside the door was marked up. Not just footprints but marks that could have been made by sliding feet, a fallen body. She put her hand on the door for balance as she started to move inside and edge by the car. Her ring finger went through the wood. She stopped and looked. It was a clean hole, recently made. A bullet hole?

"Fuck." She couldn't help herself. The barn was only one room, no loft, but she called Kelsey's name again, anyway, then Van's and Tom's for good measure. Then she listened.

And heard them.

Shouts, muffled and incoherent, but nearby. She circled the car, pausing every few feet to listen, and the voices grew slightly louder. She looked to the right and saw a canvas tarp lying bunched, half on the car, half on the ground. She pulled it away and found a radiator sticking out onto the floor, obviously awry when compared to the neat shelves surrounding her.

Exhaustion took that moment to descend on her. When she shoved at the unit, it didn't move. Her feet did, sliding out from under her and hitting the car, which knocked her onto her knees. She barely avoided smacking her chin on the metal. When she got back to her feet her legs shook, joined by her arms when she tried to push the thing again.

Dammit. This wasn't going to work. She checked the shelves and found a rope, tying one end to the radiator and threading it through a support brace under the nearest shelf. The angle wasn't right to drag the unit across the dirt, but when she braced her back on the car and her foot on the radiator and heaved, the radiator lifted just enough for a shove with her foot to move it several inches before it thudded to the floor. The voices underneath her went quiet. She could see a metal ring now, embedded into the dirt from the weight of the radiator, and guessed where the lines of the trap door might be. Two more heave-shoves later, she was able, with difficulty, to pry the wooden door out of the dirt.

She leaned over the entrance, knowing how foolish it was to present such an easy target but too sluggish and eager to find her daughter to care. She stuck her hand in front of her face to block the bright beam of light hitting her.

"Thank God," breathed Van when she saw Regan. A second later Regan flinched out of the way when a ladder poked up through the opening. Van climbed up first, throwing herself into Regan's arms and hugging her so tight she couldn't draw breath.

"Are you okay?" The girl vibrated with tension under Regan's hands, but wouldn't let go when Regan tried to shift her away. She looked at Tom when he emerged from the hole in the ground, his face smudged with dirt and despair. An answering echo pierced Regan's already-damaged heart.

Kelsey hadn't come out of the hole.

"Where is she?" She went for calm, but the words came out shrill. "Where is my daughter?"

She realized Van was endlessly whispering. "I'msosorry I'msosorry I'msosorry."

Tom shook his head. "We don't know."

TWENTY

WHEN KELSEY CAME to, everything was dark. She lay on a bare mattress, untied, and tried not to moan at the pain in her head and the dryness of her mouth. A flash of memory brought back the sting of a needle in her arm. They'd caught her, and she didn't know where she was. But she felt too crappy to be scared.

Moving might alert someone she was awake, but she couldn't help herself. Nausea welled up and she rolled, waving her arm around next to the bed automatically, not really expecting to find anything. But her hand collided with a plastic trashcan and she grabbed it just in time to empty her stomach.

She groaned, rolling back onto the bed and wishing she had a pillow. "Never eat bananas again." She rested and let her head clear a bit. Maybe vomiting had been a good thing, because it seemed to push along whatever they'd put in her system. Slowly she regained her ability to think, the surest antidote to fear. She vowed not to entertain even an ounce of it. She was getting out of here. Period.

No one had come, so they either weren't monitoring her or didn't care she was awake. She got to her feet by degrees, then turned and knelt on the bed to feel the wall next to it. It was smooth, like painted drywall, and warm. In fact, the whole room was warm, and the image in her head of a dank cement cell disappeared.

She felt the entire wall above the bed, but there were no windows or anything hanging that might help her. She climbed off the bed and shuffled around the room, one hand on the wall, the other waving in front of her so she wouldn't hit anything. She'd only gone a few feet when she bumped into a piece of furniture. It was varnished and had six drawers—a dresser. The top was clean—not dusty—and clear except for a lamp on the surface. She clicked the button a few times, but the light didn't come on.

The rest of the wall was empty. The next wall had a closet almost in the corner. She opened the door but couldn't find a light switch or dangling string, and feeling around in there didn't seem like a good idea. A few empty wire hangers on the rod were all she touched before she closed the door to check it out later. A few feet beyond the closet she found the main door, which seemed dead-bolted from the outside. Kelsey ran her fingers up and down the wall until she found a switch. She held her breath and flipped it upward.

"Wow."

In the muted glow from the very small, frilly-shaded lamp on the dresser, she looked around a bedroom freakishly like a child's dream room.

The walls were painted lavender, a color echoed in the little lamp, the carpet, and flowers painted on the white dresser as well as a desk and armoire on the last wall. Purple kittens and puppies pranced along a wallpaper border near the ceiling. At the head of the bed was a tall bookcase filled with what looked like children's books. The bed itself was white metal tubing, the head and footboards simple arcs, and an eyelet dust ruffle hung below the bare, thin mattress. She went to the closet and opened it, finding the rod empty of clothes but the shelf filled with a little girl's toys: ponies and a Barbie head for hairstyling, pink and white Legos—she didn't know they made such a thing—and baby dolls and stuffed animals.

"What the hell is this place?"

"It's your room."

Kelsey jumped a mile at the voice behind her. She hadn't heard the door open or the man behind her come in. She spun and started to pull back her fist, but lost the advantage when she froze at what she saw.

Part of her registered the sterile, white, glow-bright hallway like the science labs in action flicks. But the rest of her goggled at how much the man in front of her looked like Tyler Sloane.

He smiled, then wrinkled his nose. "The sedative *did* make you a bit woozy, then?" He came into the room to retrieve the trashcan. Kelsey started to bolt, but the open doorway was blocked by a totally new goon. He literally filled the space, his shoulders wedging against the sides and his head brushing the top. She decided to call him Bulldozer.

The Tyler clone handed Bulldozer the trashcan. "Dispose of this, please. Then come back." He closed the door in the man's face and locked the deadbolt with a key, which he pocketed. He left his hand in the pocket, which made picking it impossible even if he let her get close enough.

"Now then, Kelsey Miller, my name is Archie Sloane." He sat on the bed and frowned at the bare mattress. "I can't believe they didn't put sheets on the bed."

"You're Tyler Sloane's…what? Father?" He had more lines around his eyes and mouth, and his hair was a darker shade of blond, surrounding his head more like a lion's mane than the surfer look Tyler had.

He beamed at her as he would a precocious student. "Yes, I am indeed Tyler's father."

Kelsey's heart sank. She'd been so sure her mother had found a perfect match. This betrayal would kill her.

If Tyler hadn't already done the job.

She swallowed hard. "Where's my mother?"

Archie frowned again. "I don't know. We were trying to get her at the Harrison mansion this evening, but she managed to get away. My men lost track of her in Nebraska." He shrugged. "It doesn't matter. We'll catch up to her again. We always do."

Don't bet on it. But Kelsey tried to look despairing instead of fiercely loyal. It wasn't hard. She had to find a way to escape this facility—assuming it was a facility. Which, once again, meant information and maybe a devious strategy.

Much as it renewed her nausea, she crossed the room and sat next to Archie. "Why am I here?" she asked in a deliberately small voice.

He patted her hand. "You're to be part of a very important program, my dear. It's been your destiny since the day you were conceived, believe it or not."

You killed my father didn't you, you bastard? She had to look away so he wouldn't see her hatred. "I don't understand."

He launched into a gleeful tale of discovery and progress, and if he hadn't peppered it with casual mentions of murder and deception and a cavalier disregard for her mother and his own son, it would have been a good story. Kelsey now understood why she never got sick, why her father had made her mother run, and even why Archie hadn't found them for so many years. She kept her face averted toward the rug because revulsion and hate had set themselves up permanently behind her eyes—she could feel it, a burning fire he might not even notice, he was so wrapped up in his tale.

Strangely, despite her awareness that he'd killed, she wasn't afraid of him. He needed her alive, which gave her a lot of power. She didn't think he realized that. Plus, he wasn't exactly imposing. The Bulldozer, he was another story, but even he was still harnessed by the whole "keep her alive" thing.

Since Archie was being so chatty, she decided to pump him for more answers.

"Did you set up Tyler next door to us, or did my grandparents?"

Archie's face fell. "It was not me. I've been estranged from my son for ten years."

"Why?"

He didn't answer for a long time, and Kelsey wondered if she dared ask another question. But she decided to be patient, and finally he said, "We didn't see eye to eye on my work."

She just bet. "And how do I…fit in with your work?"

"You'll understand in good time." He tilted his head to look down at her, and a new look came into his eyes, one to make her understand the word *avarice* a little better than high school vocabulary lessons had. "Tell me, Miss Kelsey, when was the last time you had a cold?"

She almost lied automatically and said two weeks ago, but at the last second realized this might be the key to everything. If she gave the wrong answer, he'd probably kill her. "I've never had a cold," she admitted.

"Excellent."

She let out her breath slowly.

He stood and crossed to the door. "You'll have to remain in this room for now. Perhaps when you've been here for a while, you'll be allowed supervised strolls around the facility."

So she'd been right. "How big is it? Is it underground?"

He merely smiled and began to close the door. She wracked her brain for something to keep him in here, keep him talking.

"Wait! Can I at least get something good to read?" She held up a Little Golden Book. "I outgrew these a decade ago."

Archie blushed. "I'm afraid I wasn't prepared for your age."

"What, eighteen years go by and you don't count them?" she snarked automatically.

His chagrin turned to defensive anger. "There were far more important things to take my attention than updating your reading material every six months. Make do."

Kelsey cursed and kicked the dresser, pleased to see a mark from her sneaker. For a second she thought about letting it all out and destroying the room, but common sense prevailed. She'd create more openings by being agreeable and cooperative.

She returned to the bed and spun, falling on her back and staring up at the ceiling. She'd gotten a few answers today, and Archie would no doubt spill more.

It was a start.

TWENTY-ONE

BY THE TIME Tyler showed up at the house, Regan was running on the residue of fumes. She sat on the couch, propped up by Van on one side and Tom on the other, both as exhausted as she was, if not more. Van had sobbed all through her report to the sheriff's deputies and now clung to Regan's arm, her face buried against her shoulder. She blamed herself, of course, for going to town.

"If Kelsey had been with Tom, they'd be safe," she'd wailed.

"If she'd been with Tom, you'd all be dead or kidnapped," Regan had responded. She'd meant it to be reassuring, but had no energy for tact. It had sent Van into even bigger sobs.

Tom, too, clearly blamed himself. He'd been subdued but detailed in his explanation to the deputies. They'd gone to town, come back, and found men here. They'd barred themselves in the barn and gotten into the hidden room underneath the floor, but Kelsey had tricked them and locked them in. They'd heard scuffling and gunshots and tried to get out, but couldn't. They hadn't slept in over a day.

Over a day. Her body had nearly reached its limit,

but her brain sobbed and wailed and screamed at her to *do something*.

But she couldn't. No one had any idea where to find Kelsey, where to even start. And the authorities were no help. They didn't believe a word she said, not even when they contacted the California State Police and got confirmation of the "incident" at the Harrisons'. Apparently by the time the police got there, all the attackers were gone. Four of Harrison's men had died and several others were in the hospital.

Regan knew because she'd listened to the radio conversation between the sheriff's deputy and his dispatcher, who'd acted as go-between in the absence of a working phone out here.

So she didn't know what her next move was going to be. Her body and brain screamed for sleep, but she couldn't let another minute pass without trying to get her daughter back.

"Sir, you can't come in here."

Regan realized her eyes were closed and forced them open. Tom went stiff beside her. Van didn't move, and Regan thought she might have fallen asleep.

"This is my house," said Tyler, out of sight on the porch.

"Let me see some ID." There was a pause, a brief conference by the deputy standing guard outside and his superior officer, and then Tyler entered looking just as worn out and afraid as she felt. His eyes locked on hers, sorrow and regret and fear and love all conspiring to draw her to him so they could comfort each other.

Then her memory caught up to her emotions. She launched herself at Tyler so abruptly that Van cried out.

"You bastard!" Regan registered shocked faces on the deputies she passed, another cry from Van, and Tom shouting her name. Then she slugged Tyler so hard he went down like a felled tree.

Luckily for him, that was all she had in her. She dropped to her knees beside him, cradling her fingers in her left hand while he rolled to his side and wiggled his jaw.

"I'm sorry," he said.

Regan started to cry. Not Van's sobs, but inevitable, relentless tears. She'd wanted him to have an explanation, not an apology.

"Why, Tyler?"

But he didn't get a chance to respond. A deputy hauled him to his feet, holding him up off the floor by his collar. Tom gently helped Regan up and held her against his chest. She could feel his glare at Tyler even though she couldn't see his face.

"What's happening here, Ms. Miller?" asked the deputy.

"Nothing." She shook her head, defeated. "He's fine. I'm just—overwrought."

"Mr. Sloane, we'll have to ask you some questions." He led Tyler onto the porch.

"About the weapons," Tom guessed. The deputies had been very interested in the hidden room.

The sheriff approached. "Ma'am, we'll take Mr. Johnson and Miss Leigh with us now. Their parents have been contacted and will meet us in town as soon as they can get here."

Regan swiped at the tears drying on her cheeks. "They're going to be furious," she said.

"No," Tom corrected. "They're going to be impressed with you."

Regan snorted. "I almost got you two killed."

"The bad guys did that, and bad guys are everywhere." Van sounded a bit like her normal self, but then slumped. "That won't matter to my parents. They'll take me out of school and try to keep me locked in their house forever. They'll never let Kelsey come see me." She turned her swimming eyes up to Regan. "You'll let me know? When you find her? I need to knock her upside the head for leaving us here."

"I'll call you immediately," Regan assured her. She gave her another hug, rocking her when Van didn't let go. When she finally did, Tom turned her and held her shoulders, looking down at her with such intensity, Regan wanted to weep with joy for her daughter, for finding such love.

And with sorrow for the man who might have lost it.

"Don't," he said, apparently reading her mind. "You'll find her, and she'll have kicked ass. I'm not letting my parents keep me away. You let me know where you're going, and I'm there. Don't start arguing about Kelsey wanting me to be safe," he added when she would have protested. "I just want to be close so I can see her right away."

Regan nodded and managed to smile at his faith in her. "I'll bring her to you. Thank you for everything, Tom." She hugged him, sorry when he let her go. The tears spilled over again when she watched the kids walk away and get into the sheriff's car.

God, she was a mess. She was in no condition to go after Kelsey, even if she knew where to go. She'd be killed in three-point-six seconds.

She managed to get back to the couch and gave in to the need to lie down. All the deputies drifted out except one who remained at the doorway and the one who interviewed Tyler. As Regan faded to sleep, she wondered if they'd arrest him for all the unregistered weapons he had stashed away.

"Babe."

Something soft stroked Regan's cheek, then through her hair. She murmured and turned toward it.

"Regan, sweetheart. Wake up. C'mon, you need to go upstairs to sleep. This sofa is too small."

Don't want to move. But do that again.

Judging by the chuckle vibrating somewhere very close by, she'd said the words out loud. The hand swept through her hair again. The fingers rubbing against her scalp were exquisite. She arched like a cat.

"Regan."

She snapped fully awake, recognizing Tyler's voice and understanding she should not be seduced by it or anything else belonging to him.

"Get away from me." She sat up and shoved him

back but swayed, the room spinning around her.
"Whoa."

"I know. You're beyond exhaustion." Tyler put his
arm around Regan's back and tried to help her up.
"I'll help you upstairs."

"Can't." She couldn't stay here. She needed to be
away from Tyler. Finding Kelsey. "Kelsey. Need—"

"It's okay." He managed to move her toward the
stairs, and she decided to cooperate. He sounded so
certain, and she wanted to believe it would be okay.

"How you know?" she murmured. The stairs were
in front of her, so she put a hand on the banister and
started hauling herself upward.

"I know where to find her. She'll be okay until
we can get there. We can't do anything until we've
both rested."

Regan couldn't argue. After what seemed like
hours, she reached the top of the stairs and made her
way to the bed, not caring if Tyler joined her or not.
She wouldn't even notice.

An instant later, she was out again.

THIS TIME WHEN she woke, she knew much more time
had passed. Hours, though she wasn't sure if it was
four or twelve. She was still groggy. For a moment,
she wished she could feel those first seconds of wake-
fulness when everything was good, normal, routine,
and all she had to do was work out her schedule for
the day. But nothing was all right here. Despair, guilt,
desperation. Rage.

With a moan, she forced herself upright. Her shirt

was twisted all around her torso. When she straightened it, the combined odors of gasoline, fried foods, and too long in the same clothes wafted over her.

O-kay. Shower first. No problem. She searched for the clock and found it on the floor. Nine-fourteen, and since sunshine burned through the thin curtains, she must have slept all night. What little had been left of it by the time the deputies were gone.

She wondered if Tyler was still here. She wanted to kill him, but she wanted to bury herself in his arms and cry, too.

Goddamn it.

When she stepped into the hall carrying a change of clothes from their last Wal-Mart stop, she smelled coffee. And bacon. Normalcy. Routine. She managed a tiny smile before heading to take a quick shower, get dressed, and tie up her hair instead of drying it.

Tyler was putting pancakes and bacon on a plate when she got downstairs. Coffee made the way she liked it already sat steaming on the table. The universe skewed for a second, showing her an alternate reality just long enough to make her crave it. Impatience banished that quickly enough. Tyler knew where her daughter was, he'd said so last night. They had to leave *now*, go get her before it was too late.

But despite the sleep she'd gotten, she was still running on empty, and he probably was, too. He was trying to take care of her.

He *was* taking care of her.

"Thank you," she made herself say.

He didn't look up. "Sounds kinda grudging."

If he could only see the warmth filling her. "It is."

He put her plate in front of her and filled another one for himself at the counter, then joined her. They ate in silence for a while, Regan waiting for Tyler to explain himself, Tyler waiting for God-knew-what. She wanted to push him, demand immediate action, and hated both being at his mercy and loving his care. She didn't believe Tyler was working for Archie. But he had lied to her all along.

"Did you sleep okay?" he finally asked.

She shrugged. "Like I'd expect. Exhaustion makes it difficult not to, though I had some nightmares about halfway through." She sipped her coffee and forced herself to be polite. "You?"

He shook his head. "Not really."

"Guilty conscience?"

"Yes, but not for the reason you think." He pushed the plate away. "I was about to explain when they came through the windows."

The reminder of flying glass had her checking his face. The tiny cuts were starting to heal, and were so many dark lines on his cheeks and forehead. She couldn't see the left side of his face, where she'd punched him.

Her appetite disappeared, but she made herself finish her pancakes. She needed fuel. But she also needed to get to her daughter. She couldn't trust what Tyler had said last night, that she'd be okay until they got there. "There" could be hundreds of miles away, for God's sake!

"Look, Tyler, we need—"

"To know what we're heading into before we do it," he countered firmly. "You need to know the whole story. I need you to know it," he admitted.

"I'm listening," she prompted. "Make it quick. They got what they want."

"They had it by the time they attacked yesterday. I think he still wants you, though I'm not sure why."

"Then why did we stay here last night?"

"His men are tired. He doesn't have many, and he lost six at the Harrisons'. Plus two who went to the hospital and got arrested while they were there. They need to regroup, and he probably figures you're out of it for now, anyway."

"Never."

"Well, last night you definitely were."

"You think I wouldn't have been able to fight if I had to?"

He wisely didn't answer.

She shoved her empty plate across the table. "Stop dicking around, Tyler, and tell me your story."

He drew in a deep breath, then let it out slowly. "I told you I lived with my father growing up. My parents divorced when I was six. Infidelity, I think, though they never really explained. My father was my hero because he worked for the Air Force and created new ways to help people."

Regan wanted to make a gag motion but knew it was childish. Under other circumstances she wouldn't be so uncharitable about his childhood. But the man he had hero-worshipped had kidnapped her daughter, which curbed her sympathies.

"Can you make this a little quicker, please?"

"I went into the service because of him. I found it wasn't exactly what he'd made it out to be, but took my own path. When I was twenty-two, he disappeared."

"From you, too?"

He nodded.

"Did he say goodbye or anything?"

He shook his head. "I didn't hear anything from him for about six years. Then out of the blue he wrote to me. Postcards at first, telling me he was okay and missed me. Then letters talking about his new work, and how revolutionary it would be. Vague stuff, no details. Letters became emails, and about ten years ago he asked me to visit him at his new facility."

"What was he doing?"

"You mean the project, or contacting me?"

"Both."

"Honestly, I think he missed me." He toyed with the spoon next to his coffee. "Or maybe that's just ego talking, or the angry kid he left. Maybe he just wanted someone to brag to."

"And? What did he brag about?"

"Pretty much what Ben and Jeanne told you, except he never mentioned Kelsey. I don't think he fully trusted me. At first he only described the immunity part of the project." He stopped to down the dregs of his coffee. "On the third day, he showed me a 'secret' lab where they were going to weaponize the compound once he retrieved the part the Harrisons had kept. He got kind of manic, very old-school villain-y. It freaked me out."

"Why didn't you go to the military? What reason did he give for disappearing?"

"No one had ever given me any inkling he was doing anything wrong. Neither the Harrisons nor the Air Force ever came to me. Not to ask questions, not to see if I knew where he was, nothing. I wasn't sure what he was doing was wrong. For all I knew, the Air Force was paying for it."

She couldn't fault him. Even the Harrisons hadn't said their project was canceled or the Air Force didn't want the weapon. Just that they didn't want Archie selling it.

"So you went to the Harrisons instead."

"I wanted to warn them he might try to break in. Jeanne was concerned about what my father would do if he knew I'd gone to them, so they hired me. Kept me close."

"Until they found us again."

"Yeah."

"So when were you last in contact with your father?"

"Ten years ago. The day I left the facility." He watched her with anxious eyes. She wanted to tell him she believed him, but…

"They knew you'd be at Harrison's, Tyler. They didn't go after you. The guy who talked to you acted like your father had expectations of you."

"I know. It threw me."

"Oohhhh, Tyler." She propped her forehead on her palms. "I don't know what to do."

"The Harrisons sent their jet back here. We take the Corvette to the airport, fly to Sacramento, and get to the facility. I think my father's people will let us in. We get Kelsey and get out."

She laughed mirthlessly. "That is such a stupid plan."

"I know. Do you have a better idea?"

Of course she didn't. Regan stood and carried her dishes to the sink, thinking while she washed, rinsed, and dried them, then put them away. When she was done she leaned against the sink and folded her arms.

"Why didn't you tell us about the trap door? If they hadn't found it…"

Tyler's face darkened. "I know. I didn't show them the room because of the weapons in there."

"Kelsey can handle a gun."

"But Van and Tom aren't trained. And if they tried to get in there and the enemy did, instead." He held out his hands, palms up. "They'd be trapped and have a lot more weaponry to be used against them."

He could have cleared out the guns, or taken some time to get Van and Tom familiar with them. She supposed his way had been easier, and if he really thought they wouldn't need it, there was no point.

"Everything about you has two possible explanations," she said.

"Like what?"

She didn't believe it, but out of habit, or maybe punishment for lying to her, she heard herself say,

"Like, you could be taking me to your father not to help me, but to help him."

For a moment, Tyler looked completely defeated. Then he stood with his shoulders squared, his spine straightened, and his face cleared.

"I'm tired of struggling over this, Regan. I can't say anything to convince you I'm on your side. I love Kelsey and don't want anything to happen to her. It's up to you now."

He set his plate in the sink and left the room.

SCREAMING AT THE top of her lungs felt so good, Kelsey did it twice.

Which made her desperately need a drink to soothe her now-raw throat, but for thirty seconds it kept her from going insane.

First, she'd explored the room some more, looking for things she could use as weapons or part of an escape plan. Some of the toys in the closet had yielded possibilities. Barbie doll legs would hurt if she jabbed someone, so she ripped them off and kept them handy. She considered making a garrote of tied-together doll clothes, but she didn't have it in her to throttle someone and decided not to bother. Most of the rest of the stuff was too flimsy or light to be any good, but she'd collected the marbles out of a game and the thin plastic sticks out of another, thinking she could make use of them somehow. She gathered her finds into a T-shirt she'd found in the dresser drawer and hid them at the bottom.

The books were mostly very thin paperbacks and

no good as weapons, but they helped stave off boredom for a couple of hours. It was almost cool, reading old favorites and discovering ones she'd never seen before. But kids' stories could only hold her attention for so long.

The Bulldozer delivered a change of sheets and a pillow. She made up her bed, then took a nap, counted everything countable in the room and slept again. They'd fed her twice, but she had no idea how much time had actually passed or what day it was. Eventually, she was so frustrated she wanted to scream, and when she couldn't think of any reason not to, she did.

Interestingly, no one came running. She wondered if Archie was stupid enough not to be monitoring her room. When Bulldozer brought her a sandwich and bowl of soup for her third meal, he didn't bother looking around or removing her toys from the dresser or anything else indicating a hidden camera. And he didn't mention the screams.

When he brought her the fourth meal, she'd been exercising to keep up her strength and work off a little of the excess energy she was building up.

"Good," he said, when he noticed her sweat. It was the first thing he'd said to her. "Exercise will keep you healthy."

"I thought my supergenetics did that." She wandered over to the dresser where he placed the tray and made a face at the sandwich sitting there. "Don't you guys have any imagination? How about a nice lobster or something?"

Bulldozer didn't answer. He removed a plastic

packet from her tray and ripped it open, setting a syringe, vial, rubber strip, cotton ball, and antiseptic wipe on a towel next to the tray.

"What's going on?"

"I'm going to draw the first sample." He lifted her right arm and looked at the inside of her elbow, then compared it to her left.

"Sample of what, blood?"

Again he didn't answer, but he wrapped the rubber tourniquet around her upper left arm and tapped the vein with his meaty finger.

"Okay, I take that as a yes." She watched him insert the needle and push the vial onto it. Dark blood poured into the vial and he snapped the tourniquet off. Then he placed the cotton ball over the puncture, pressed down, and slid the needle out.

"Keep pressure on."

Kelsey bent her arm to hold the cotton in place. Bulldozer gathered up his things and started to leave.

"That's it?"

For some reason, he stopped and nodded at her.

"That's why you're keeping me here? For how long?"

The answer was in his eyes. For as long as it took. She had no doubt when they got what they were looking for, they would no longer need her.

"So I have to stay shut up in this five-year-old's room for God knows how long, waiting to die?"

The door closed, the deadbolt punctuating his silence.

TWENTY-TWO

"THIS IS lovely, Tyler, but not what I was expecting," Regan said dryly. They strolled through a city park, clasped hands swinging between them, Tyler actually ambling and Regan doing her best to look relaxed and happy like most of the other people enjoying the warm fall weather, instead of burning with rage and vengeance and desperation to get to her daughter and make sure she was alive. Whole. Surrounding them were park benches lining meandering jogging-biking-skating paths, open grass, and people playing Frisbee or cuddling on blankets.

Nowhere could Regan see a possible entrance to an underground facility.

Tyler wouldn't be hurried. Every time Regan unconsciously picked up her pace, he tugged her back to slow her down. Once the tug was too obvious, and he covered by catching her mouth in a kiss. She started to shove him away, remembered where they were, and left her hand on his shoulder, her heart aching under the need to push him to *hurry, goddamn it*.

Tyler hovered over her mouth. "We're not getting past this, are we?"

Regan raised her eyes to his and the "no" froze on her tongue. Then she sighed and backed away.

"There's a lot to finish before we can even talk about it."

"Fair enough."

They walked on. Ten minutes later they reached the other side of the park, and Regan was getting angry. How much time had they wasted? Was this much caution really necessary? "Why didn't we just park over here?"

"I wanted to scout the lookouts."

She hadn't seen anyone who looked out of place. "How many?"

"Two. One back in the parking area where we started—he didn't see us. One playing fetch with a dog and a tennis ball. He's still behind us. I don't know if he knows who we are or not."

"When will we get to the entrance?"

"We're here."

They'd just about left the park and were approaching an overpass. The street to their left teemed with cars speeding awfully close to the narrow sidewalk that continued under the bridge. There was a door in the side of the overpass, presumably for maintenance. Regan glanced around, but there was nothing else— no sewer cover, no building or crypt or monument, not even businesses across the street—that could have been what they were looking for.

Tyler moved at a constant pace into the shadow of the road above and pulled open the door. Regan moved inside and he followed, letting it close behind them.

"Light," Tyler said, and a weak fluorescent bulb flickered on overhead.

"Your father's an *Alias* fan, huh?"

"He was here long before that show was on TV."

The room they were in was tiny and bare, painted white so long ago dingy gray chips now littered the floor and water stains striped the walls. Regan couldn't see any wheels or keypads or seams of doorways.

"No lock outside."

"No, too suspicious." He was just standing there.

"What do we do now?"

"We go in." But he looked at her as if trying to decide something.

"How?"

"You'll see."

Exasperated, Regan threw up her hands. "How do you know you'll even be able to get in?"

"He gave me a special code. Even though I left, I don't think he'd have changed it. He has a serious sentimental streak, and I think he always hoped the prodigal son would return." He said it all absently, as if he'd expected her to ask and had prepared his answer, but didn't have his mind on it.

"Tyler, what is going on?"

He seemed to come to a decision. "Look, Regan, I don't like 'if we don't survive' speeches."

"I wasn't going to make one."

His lips quirked upward for half a second. "I didn't expect you to. And I plan for us to come out unscathed."

A tongue of fear stretched inside her, but she smothered it quickly, not willing to be distracted. This was going to be difficult enough without latent insecurities rearing up.

"I plan for the same thing," she said.

"But I have to say it anyway."

She knew what was coming and didn't want to hear it. "You've already said it."

"No. Not like this." He stilled, his eyes locked on hers. "Over the last two years—"

A new fear flared. "I *know*, Tyler. You've watched us, good mother, struggle in the face of unknown danger, blah-dee-blah-blah. You fell in love with me, went against employer orders—"

"Will you shut up and listen!"

Her mouth snapped closed.

"Thank you. Over the last two years I've watched you live the loneliest life I could ever imagine."

Okay. Unexpected. She could have told him she wasn't lonely because she had Kelsey.

"No matter what happens in there," he continued, "your life is about to become even lonelier."

What the hell?

"Kelsey will go back to school, and the center of your life will go away. You'll have to learn a whole new way of living. Of loving."

Now she understood where he was going, and apprehension flared higher. "I don't know if I can make you a part of that, Tyler."

"I know." He took a step toward her. "Like I said, I can't say anything to make you believe. Make you trust me. Maybe the only way I could is to die for you."

She swallowed, hard. "I don't—"

"I'm not going to die for you, Regan."

She stopped talking, her mouth open. "You're—not?" *What a stupid thing to say. You don't want him to die!*

"No. I'm going to live for you." He caught her around the waist and pulled her against him, reached overhead to grab a pipe running the width of the ceiling, and yanked down.

The entire floor started to sink.

KELSEY STARED AT the door in front of her, open a crack, then at the plastic pick-up sticks in her hands.

"Well, that was easy." Too easy, of course. She should never have been able to pick a dead bolt with a couple of plastic sticks. She remembered a TV show she saw once, where a guy was kidnapped and put in a cage. The cage opened suddenly and he ran, with the other caged guy telling him it was a trap. He was right, of course. The smart guy, who stayed put, lived. The dumb guy, who "escaped," was hunted and killed.

She imagined Archie stalking her with a shotgun in the brilliantly lit corridor outside and laughed softly. That wasn't going to happen, she was sure. But she was wary, too. She'd expected him to secure the room better.

The sticks went back into her left rear pocket with the others. The marbles filled both her front pockets, and the Barbie legs stuck out her right rear pocket, toes down, for easy access. She stood against the wall, listening. No footsteps. No voices. No hum of machinery or any other sound.

It was going to be so easy to get caught.

"Oh, well, nothin' to do but to do it!" she murmured in Van's voice, and slipped out into the empty hall.

Her door was near the end of the corridor, so she could only go in one direction. There were about a hundred feet of blank space before a side hall branched off to the left, and no doors in between. Taking careful steps, she went a few feet, checking how loud her shoes were. Luckily, they didn't squeak on the linoleum floor, and she risked going faster.

In the absence of floor plans, she hurried up and down countless passageways, all seeming to intersect and circle back on themselves. They were all identically white and brightly lit, and most contained only one door, unmarked, no windows. There didn't seem to be anyone around, either, which she found as weird as the hallways.

I bet he meant me to get out and see this, she thought. Wear her down, convince her not to try to escape for real. Well, he had seriously underestimated her.

She started trying doors, unsurprised to find them locked. Her sticks wouldn't open them, either, also not a surprise. But she wasn't giving up. Only a few minutes after she started, she found herself back at the open end of the hallway to her room. There was only one direction she hadn't explored: up. Her room's ceiling was solid plaster like the walls, but out here it was acoustical tiles. She jumped up and tipped the one above her enough to glimpse inside. As she'd expected, the lights set into the ceiling illuminated the crawl space above, too. She knew if she spread her weight she could move around up there, but getting up was another story. The metal braces wouldn't hold her.

She quickly did the jumping/tipping thing in all four directions before she found what she was looking for—a wood support beam next to the edge of the metal brace. She jumped harder, moving the tile away from the beam, then again, this time catching hold of the wood.

"Dammit." She hadn't thought it through. The angle was too tight for her to pull herself up. She dropped, toed off her sneakers, and tied the laces together so she could drape them around her neck. Then she peeled off her socks and stuffed them into the shoes.

Better. She turned so she faced the opening, and this time jumped with her hands facing backwards. This was harder, so it took her three tries before she was high enough and timed it well enough to grab the beam again. With her hands twisted, her grip was weaker. She swung her legs quickly up in front of her, using her toes only on the edge of the brace. It gave slightly under her weight, but she didn't hang long. Her body arched until she'd cleared the edges of the opening, and she rolled to her right, landing on her stomach on the inside of the ceiling.

"Yes!" She pumped her fist. A man's voice suddenly echoed down the hall, and she hurried to replace the open tile. It dropped neatly into its spot as someone walked below her. She heard only one set of footsteps, so who was he talking to?

It took her a moment to realize the man was Bulldozer, and he was singing.

She held her breath, but he crossed below her and went left, not right and the direction of her room. She heard a door open and close, then silence again.

Moving slowly, like a spider, and trying to keep near the rafters where the anchors were strongest, she headed in his direction.

When she heard Bulldozer humming below her again, she silently lifted a tile out just enough to peer into the room below. Her gasp was loud in her ears, but neither Bulldozer nor the other man in the room seemed to hear.

It looked like an examination room in a doctor's office. Bulldozer leaned over a counter, playing with some kind of medical-looking tool, and on the exam table in the center of the room...

Lay Tom.

"THAT'S NOT SPECIAL," Regan told Tyler as they descended into darkness. "Anyone could pull that pipe." *Focus on the silly details, not the churning nausea building with every inch we drop.*

"True." He held on to her even though he didn't have to. The floor was very stable in its movement, very smooth. She didn't pull away. Heat seemed to be the antidote to churning nausea. At least for a few seconds.

"The next step is the special one," he said. The floor glided to a stop with a gap of about four feet between it and the bottom of the wall above. Tyler ducked through, stepping down onto another white-painted concrete floor. Regan followed, and as soon as her weight was off the platform, it rose again, taking her veneer of calm with it. What if they had to get back out that way, fast?

Focus on the... This was more what Regan had expected. Smaller than the one above, this room had six visible cameras, an intercom set into one wall, and a panel beneath a computer monitor. Her muscles tensed against the feeling of being watched, braced for a loudspeaker to shout at them or something, but nothing happened.

"How does your father fund all this?" she asked, not caring but still trying to distract herself. Her free hand clenched. She unclenched it, but it curled right back up of its own accord.

"I have no idea." He dropped her hand and turned his back to stand at the computer. Regan immediately put her hand on his shoulder—he wasn't going to shut her out now!—but he was immovable. She moved up to stand next to him and watched him rapidly type a series of letters and numbers, sending him from one screen to another.

"Don't start lying to me again, Tyler," she warned, the edge in her voice betraying her nerves.

"I'm not."

The lights dimmed. He kept typing. A motor started up with a whining, spinning sound, somewhere behind the wall they faced. Her nerves revved with it until she thought she'd lift off the ground on her own.

"You are."

His lips pressed together. Eyes still fixed on the screen he said, "I think he was still working on some government projects."

Holy crap. No wonder he hadn't wanted to tell her where his father got the money. "The government has sanctioned all this?"

"I don't know."

"They knew all along what he was doing?" Her voice went shrill. "What he planned for my daughter?"

"I doubt it." This time his voice was less tight. His body relaxed an inch, projecting relief that dampened Regan's own tension. The computer screen flashed three times, then a big black box came up saying, "Welcome Home, Son." He grimaced, his eyes flicking sideways at her, then back to the screen. "Told you I'd still be able to get in."

"Good for you." For the moment, she was focused on her anger. "The Harrisons told the Air Force what they thought Archie's plans were. Did they just overlook it?" She didn't need Tyler to answer. Of course they did. There was no reason for them not to, especially if they thought they could control Archie and get what they wanted from the immunity program. The entire fricking government was against her.

"We are so screwed." She spun and gripped the rail surrounding the hydraulic shaft for the platform they'd just descended on. Implications cascaded over her, pummeling her hope that soon this would all be over. "Even if we get her out of there, they'll just keep coming after us."

"No." Tyler's hands closed over her shoulders. "There's no 'if.' We *will* get her out. And then we'll call the police and he'll go to jail for kidnapping and you can both start living a normal life."

Her shoulders dropped under his grip. Her hands released the rail. "I don't know what a normal life is."

"You'll create one."

The computer behind them beeped and a rumble came from their right. She turned. The wall was opening, a thick, steel, reinforced vault-type wall. She waited, expecting more black-clad action figures to come jogging through, ready to spray them with machine-gun fire. But nothing happened.

With a deep breath and a hand on her churning stomach, Regan followed Tyler into the darkness.

KELSEY LAY IN the dark ceiling, incredulous terror paralyzing her. How had they gotten him? Why? What were they doing?

The paralysis was good, because it kept her from slamming through the tiles to the room below, and from screaming at the top of her lungs, which she somehow would have managed despite the lack of air. The screams reverberated in her head, though, until something snapped, and hysteria shut off like flicking a switch.

You're his only help. She slowly sucked in a long, silent breath. Lights danced at the edges of her vision, but she heard her mother's voice: *Never leap until you know where all your nets are.* Okay. She could do this. *Observe, assess, plan.* Her vision sharpened like a camera lens.

Bulldozer was busy at the counter with something she couldn't see, so she watched Tom's chest rising and falling in a very slow rhythm. He'd probably been drugged, which would make it difficult to get him out of here. Which she would. *Don't leave any option but success.* That one was her own.

Confidence seeped back into her, despite the obstacle. Yes, that was good—this was an obstacle. Thinking of it that way made it easier to be analytical. So her original plan—to find the exit, get out, come back with help—totally blown. She couldn't leave without Tom. What if they had Van, too? She thought of crawling around in the ceiling trying to find her friend, trying to get *two* drugged people out of here, and blackness pressed down on her.

Don't leave any option but success. And don't accept "maybe" problems, either. She'd deal with what was in front of her. Tom. She waited, watching, her heart squeezing with love and despair as he lay motionless below her. Impervious to her attempts to mind-meld with him and jolt him awake. If only her mother was here—God, she hoped she was okay.

Kelsey's shoulders screamed from her cramped,

half-supported, half-leaning position as she lay still, trying to plot her next move. The door opened and Archie walked in. She couldn't see him, but recognized his voice right away.

"How is he?"

Bulldozer looked over his shoulder at Tom sprawled on the table. "Still out. Don't know how much they gave him, but he should have been waking up by now."

Kelsey's breath caught. What was wrong?

"Give him a stimulant. I don't want to delay this phase of our project."

What? Tom was part of all this? No, he couldn't be. That was far too coincidental. And…and he'd been sick, she remembered. He'd caught Van's cold and joked he hadn't even had the benefit of making out with her first. So what was this guy talking about?

"Don't you want to make sure the girl's blood will work, first?"

Archie stepped forward into Kelsey's vision, his hands in his lab coat pockets. "That's completely separate. We're running three phases of this program now. The girl's blood can take us down one road, but we've got to analyze the mother's before we proceed with phase one-A, the original plan. Assuming they can bring her in, of course. She's been such trouble." He tsked, sending a new wave of pride and fury through Kelsey. *That's right, asshole.*

"We've already injected Mr. Johnson with the original compound. His system will process it within two days. We can mate them within a week after, and the child, phase three, will be the ultimate achievement."

"I don't think the girl will go along with this."

Stop calling me the girl! Kelsey was so outraged by what she was hearing she wanted to rip off Archie's head. This was so...so...diabolical!

"The girl will go along with anything, once she has her boy toy in residence with her. She won't know what else is happening."

"How can you be sure they'll—you know?" Bulldozer lifted Tom's arm from where it hung down next to the table and injected him with something, probably the stimulant. The men watched him in silence for a minute before he stirred.

"If they don't, we'll do it manually. But it will be considerably easier if they do. Don't worry. They're teenagers. They won't be able to help themselves." Archie jumped back as Tom suddenly rolled to his side and vomited on the floor.

My poor baby. Kelsey wished she were down there, helping him. He was going to be so scared and confused when he realized what was going on. But if she tried, they'd just lock them both up again.

Tom rolled onto his back and opened his eyes. They locked right onto Kelsey's face. She quickly put her finger to her lips. He took in the room, the men, the syringe still in Bulldozer's hand, and shoved himself off the table with a roar.

"Where is she, you bastards?"

Unfortunately, he was still unstable. His wild swing missed both men and he toppled onto the floor.

Bulldozer caught him before his head connected and tossed him back onto the table. Tom retched again, then tears squeezed out from beneath his closed eyelids. Answering tears dripped down Kelsey's cheeks. *I'm sorry, baby, so sorry.*

"I'll kill you," Tom whispered. The men laughed.

"Leave him here until he stabilizes," Archie told Bulldozer. "No sense getting more vomit in Miss Miller's room. It won't be conducive to romance."

"I'll bring him some food. Should help."

"Excellent. Now, with the blood sample you drew…" There was a click of the lock, then Archie's voice faded with both sets of footsteps down the hall.

Tom jumped to his feet on the table and reached for Kelsey. She stuck her hand down through to grab his, but they couldn't reach any farther unless she moved, and there wasn't time.

"They're going to find me gone," she whispered urgently. "I'll find the exit and come back for you."

"No, I'll come with you!"

"You can't, the ceiling won't hold you. I mean it! I'll be back soon." She tugged her hand free and more tears fell at the rip inside her. "Do they have Van?"

"No, she's back home. I talked to her—well, I don't know when, but it was shortly before they took me. Kelsey, what—"

"No time! We'll do all that later." Before she lost her resolve, she pulled back and replaced the tile, then started crawling. *New goal*, she told herself, trying to focus. But she couldn't shake the fear that she was never going to get them out of here.

WHEN THEY ENTERED, the dark corridor lights automatically came on, this time without Tyler's command. Regan spotted motion sensors and assumed they sent a signal back to security or the main office or whatever. Tyler strode confidently down the hallway, apparently not worried about being heard or seen.

Regan couldn't believe they were doing this. Everything told her it was a trap.

There were no doors in this endless hallway. Lights went on ahead of them, off behind them, like in some sci-fi movie. Regan didn't see cameras, but knew they were there. She drew her pistol and readied herself. But it didn't ease her apprehension.

Tyler punched a code into a keypad at the end of the hall. It beeped but stayed red. He hesitated, then punched again, a little slower. The same thing happened.

"Did he change the code?" she asked, looking back over her shoulder.

"Apparently." He frowned and thought, then punched something completely different. This time the light flashed green, and they could hear the hum of the electronic release. He pulled the door open quickly.

Regan stayed behind him. He could catch the first wave of black-clad goons.

But again, there was no one there.

"I don't like this, Tyler." They were now in a small antechamber with more halls branching in three different directions. "Where is everyone?"

"I told you, he sent his entire—"

"But he has no security here? No scientists? Who's working on the project?"

Tyler nodded to the right hallway. "The labs are down there. About two hundred yards, then down a level. They wouldn't be up here. And he never had reason to need much security."

But he couldn't be stupid enough not to know he needed it now, Regan thought. Not when he'd kidnapped her daughter.

"Which way is Kelsey going to be?" she asked.

Tyler hesitated. "I think that way." He pointed left. "It's more medical. Exam rooms and stuff. There's no room to the right where she could be secured."

"Lead on."

They moved through what felt like miles of corridors, all looking the same. Regan memorized their turns, years of planning escape routes making it easy. Tyler stopped at the top of a dead-end hallway. "Down here, I think. There's a room at the end like a bedroom, a kid's room. He wouldn't tell me what it was for."

Regan rolled her eyes. "And you're just putting it together *now*?"

"I only saw it once, on the first tour he gave me," he growled. "I forgot."

Regan ran down the hall toward the door at the end. She zeroed in on the handle, knowing it would be locked, knowing she couldn't get in, but her heart speeding up and her breath coming in a rush nonetheless.

To her shock, the handle turned when she grasped it. The door pushed open…

Into an empty room.

It was a little girl's room, just as Tyler had said. She felt him come up behind her, but couldn't see or say anything through the sudden swelling in her throat and tears blurring her vision.

She wasn't here.

"It's okay." Tyler squeezed her shoulders, tugged her back. "We'll find her."

"Yeah?" Regan rubbed her sleeve vigorously across her face. "How big is this place?"

He didn't answer.

"So where do we freaking look?"

They both froze at the echo of a muffled shout. It was deep and male, not Kelsey, but it could be because of her. They dashed back up the hall and turned right, moving in unison. Regan's feet seemed to beat out her daughter's name. *Kels. Sey. Kels. Sey. Kels. Sey.*

Tyler got to the corner a split second before she did and slammed to a stop, jerking back and pushing her behind him. She could hear footsteps and voices now, something about blood and centrifuges. They were going the other way. She waited, impatiently, until Tyler peeked around the wall and nodded. They hurried, a little slower and more quietly now. Tyler pointed to a door halfway down the hall.

But then Regan heard a scrape above her. She stopped and looked up. Nothing moved, but she heard the scrape again.

"Tyler!" she hissed in a loud whisper. He halted and came back.

"What?"

She pointed upward and mimed him lifting her to the ceiling. He nodded. She stuck her gun back in her waistband, stepped into his hands, and pushed up through the tile. There was nothing in front of her, but as she turned a blur of movement warned her too late. Something slammed into the side of her head. Lights exploded in her vision and she crumpled. Tyler barely caught her, lowering her to the floor with a curse. He leapt up and caught the edge of the ceiling, but his weight pulled it down with a squeal of metal and shower of dust. Regan heard a small scream. She scrambled to her feet as Tyler lunged again, pulling down more of the ceiling, and a body came crashing through to the floor.

"Kelsey!" a voice bellowed from inside the room next to them.

"Oh my God." Regan rushed to the coughing, gasping body and realized it was her daughter, hidden in pieces of acoustical tile and twisted metal. "Kelsey."

"Mo—" *cough* "—Mom?" Kelsey reached up a hand and Regan hauled her to her feet. "What the hell?" She coughed again and squinted at Tyler. "Tyler?"

"Are you okay?" Regan patted her down until Kelsey pushed her away. "Thank God we found you." She leaned against the wall when her noodly legs tried to give out, but kept one hand on Kelsey, not entirely convinced she was here, safe—at least for the moment—and whole. "What did he do to you?"

"I'm fine. Help me get Tom out."

But Tom apparently hadn't been willing to listen impotently to the commotion. More tile came down, and he plummeted to the floor in front of the door. There was more coughing and choking and hugs—and then running.

"We're all going to get lung cancer," Kelsey wheezed.

"If we don't get a bullet in the back first." Regan cringed and reached back to pull her along by the elbow. "Faster." Now that the initial wave of relief had passed, being reunited with Kelsey poured strength into her like concrete, reinforced by rebar of determination.

Tyler in the lead, the group pounded through the maze of hallways back toward the entrance they'd come through, but crashed to a halt as they approached the last doorway. Tyler flung out his arms as if to shield them, but Regan pushed up next to him.

"The prodigal son returns." Archie stood in front of a group of well-armed men. The soldiers Regan had been expecting all along.

Tyler glanced down at her. "Told you."

She shrugged. "Okay, you were right. But I told you, too." She waved her hand at the guns.

"Yeah. Sorry. I guess they recovered a little."

"Ya think?"

"A child's betrayal is the most painful," Archie said. He shoved his hands in his pockets and rocked forward on his toes. He looked like a lecturing pro-fessor, but sadder. Regan saw no signs of madness or fervor, and wondered if that made him more or less dangerous.

"You betrayed me first, Dad." Tyler didn't sound like he was still angsting over it. "You think you can disappear without a word, then drag me back into your pathetic life without regrets?"

"Pathetic?" Archie's eyebrows rose, and Regan could see what Tyler would look like in twenty years. "Hardly pathetic, son. Groundbreaking. The stuff for history books. I'll transform not only the way we live, but the way we protect ourselves. War as we know it will no longer exist."

"You're so delusional," Tyler said. "First off, you think you can get away with kidnapping and detain-ing a couple of kids? Or murdering them, which I'm sure was your plan once you didn't need them any-more."

Archie looked appalled. "I would never kill them!"

"You tried to kill Regan."

"No, she misunderstood. They were supposed to bring her back here. If they could," he added in a mutter.

Regan had had enough. "Look. We don't need to go through the whole Scooby-Doo scene here." She pulled her pistol and aimed it at Archie's head. "Let us out."

There were a couple of chuckles behind Archie, but he didn't look amused. "Don't be foolish, Ms. Miller."

"Oh, I'm not. See, you put yourself in a bottleneck.

You've got four machine guns back there, but only two can shoot without plowing down you and their own men. I can get three shots off before anyone else fires. That kills you."

"But they *will* fire, and you'll be dead, as well."

"Yeah, and so will Kelsey. I'd rather have her dead than part of your program," she lied, her heart clenching at the words of bravado, but her hands steady on the pistol. Cold determination had set in the instant she saw the men, and now it sank down into her, icing out everything else.

"Hey!" Kelsey cried indignantly.

Regan didn't waver. "Let us out."

Tyler pulled his own weapon. "You gonna kill your own son, Dad? Can you watch any of us die right in front of you?" He waited, but there was no response. "I don't think you can. You never liked that part of the business. The reality of death, an inescapable aspect of being in the military. You know what, though?" He took one step forward, then another. The group ahead of them backed up a step. "I was STT. I'm pretty used to death." He yanked on the slide of his pistol, chambering a round, then aimed again at his father's head. "You want to risk it?"

Archie backed up a little more, but having four guys behind him made retreating problematic. He stopped, eyed his son and Regan, then gave a tiny nod. "Hand to hand." Then he stepped aside.

The hallway filled with grunts and thuds as the guards surged forward, meeting Tyler with gloved fists and the butts of rifles. He went down on one knee and was swarmed.

But Regan didn't stand helplessly by, watching her future be destroyed and waiting her turn. She let out a screaming yell, reversed her pistol in her hand, and started slugging away. Her first blow landed on the skull of a guy bent over Tyler and he dropped like the proverbial ton of bricks. Tyler surged to his feet and slammed an elbow into another's solar plexus.

And then the corridor was a haze of black uniforms and flying fists, warlike bellows and grunts of pain. Tom and Kelsey didn't hang back. Regan saw flashes of color among the black. At first she tried to shield her daughter, but that made them both more vulnerable, and as long as the kids remained on their feet, she concentrated on her own fight. Time stretched, and minutes or hours passed with pain sweeping over her in waves, from the glancing blow on her right cheek to the ache in her hand where she clutched the pistol, to a kick she took in the left kidney.

Then, suddenly, it was over. The soldiers were on the floor, she, Kelsey, and Tom were not. Tyler held his father against the wall with a forearm across his throat.

"Get out of here," he shouted at them. "Call the police."

Regan stood in the hall, her chest heaving. She looked from him to Kelsey and Tom, who were already near the door. They could get out easily now. She took a step that way.

But then she looked back. Tyler appeared invincible, even oozing blood, but the men at his feet would not stay there for long. And there could be more. She couldn't leave without him.

"Go," she told Kelsey and Tom. Her heart split in two. But her daughter, her mature, bright, brave daughter, only nodded.

"Be fast," was all Kelsey said. Then she grabbed Tom's hand and ran.

TWENTY-THREE

"ARCHIE'S PLEADING GUILTY to the kidnapping and to misuse of government funds," Ben told Regan on the phone a few weeks later. Tension she hadn't been aware of fell away, and the rush left her light-headed. She sank onto her sofa and lay back, suddenly without the strength to hold her body upright.

"What about all the goons?"

Ben chuckled. "We've gotten them all taken care of, don't worry. I have a lot of connections. There are no strays. And the facility under the park, which was originally supposed to be a Cold War bomb shelter, has been closed up."

"They're going to have the data," she said. Her neck ached. Maybe not all the tension had disappeared. "The government. They'll know about Kelsey, and—"

"Nope." Ben's voice went gruff, the way it always did when he got emotional. "It was all destroyed. I supervised the operation personally. Mine, too. My granddaughter will never be in danger again."

Regan knew that was impossible to promise. There had been too many people, too many years, and today's storage systems allowed easy backups and redundancies. But she couldn't live the rest of her life the way she'd lived the past eighteen years. If Ben said he'd destroyed it all, she'd hope it was true and move on.

"Thank you, Ben."

"How is she, by the way? We talked to her yesterday, but it's so hard to tell."

Regan smiled. "She's great. Back in her routine like nothing ever happened."

Not totally true. Kelsey had insisted on returning to Whetstone immediately, not wanting to derail her education before it even started. Van had taken a little longer to convince her parents, but managed to get back mid-week. Tom's coach was livid at his disappearance and had benched him, and his father had stayed in a hotel for two weeks, shadowing his son and making sure he was truly safe before deciding things would be okay.

Regan thought the transition back was too abrupt, and expected nightmares, jumpiness, and clingy behavior, but she drove down to Whetstone twice, and both girls seemed as close to fine as possible. They talked about Kelsey's father, and except for a lingering sadness, Kelsey seemed far lighter than she ever had in her life, now that the burdens they'd lived under were gone.

"We'd like to have you for Thanksgiving," Ben said now. "House is still a bit shot up, but…that is, if you can handle…my wife tells me I'm being an insensitive prat. I'm sorry."

"Prat?"

"She's reading Harry Potter again. Anyway, we'd like to see you for the holiday."

"Why don't you come here?" she said, and he quickly accepted.

She hung up a few minutes later and returned to her home office, where she'd been juggling the bills that had piled up. It was amazing how wrong the stupid little things that made up a life could go in eleven days. She'd lost her job at the club, who she hadn't bothered to call once, not even right after the attack. They would have been understanding if she had, she was sure, but when she'd "disappeared," they'd cut her off. She'd managed to find a new job, a better one, but she hadn't gotten her first paycheck yet and things were getting dire.

The front door opened and she jerked, adrenaline spiking, before she heard Tyler's voice. Dammit. She rubbed her forehead, suddenly just as exhausted as she had been when she and Tyler emerged from the tunnels into the bright sunlight in the park. Kelsey and Tom had gotten the police there in record time— must have been a slow crime day—and they'd found four trussed guards, a sedated Bulldozer, and a furious and talkative Archie Sloane tied up in the main corridor.

Tyler came into the room and bent to kiss her. "You okay?"

"Ben just called." He sat on the futon and listened as she told him about the conversation. "So you shouldn't have to testify against your father or anything."

"Good." He looked pensive, but didn't say anything more. Regan wondered if he was ever going to let her in. He'd stayed in California for a while to help Ben and Jeanne ferret out the traitor and manage cleanup, and had returned to his house next door just a few days ago. Somehow they'd fallen into a comfortable routine, coming into each other's houses and sharing meals and sleeping arrangements as if they'd been together for years, without sharing the important things.

Like how they felt about each other.

"You scared me when you came in the door," Regan said.

"I'm sorry. Should I knock?"

"No, I need to adjust. It's been very weird not having to…you know." She blew out a breath. "I'm still taking six different routes home from the grocery store."

"You'll get there. It's a lot of training to undo." His mouth turned down and he studied the carpet. "We haven't talked about the last moments—you know, in the tunnel."

"I know."

When he lifted his head, she was shocked to see torment in his eyes. "Did you stay because you thought I was going to kill my father?"

Regan's mouth fell open. "What? No! The thought never crossed my mind!"

"Then why?"

"Oh, man, we should have talked about this sooner." She laughed. "I stayed because you needed me more than Kelsey did. I couldn't leave you with all those guys and risk losing you."

He slumped in relief. "I didn't bring it up because I was afraid of the answer. I know you didn't fully trust me, but…" He shook his head. "If you thought that about me, I was afraid there was no chance for us."

Regan got up from the desk chair and sat next to him on the futon, weaving her arm around his and threading their fingers together. "I've been thinking a lot about this trust thing."

"I understand, Regan, I do." But she could tell by the heaviness with which he said it that understanding wasn't enough.

"The thing is, I did trust you," she admitted, the words coming more easily than they should have. "All along. I convinced myself I couldn't, but every step of the way, no matter how much I questioned you, I gave you far more than I would have if that trust hadn't been real."

But how she felt about Tyler was only one small part of the equation. The rest was so much more difficult.

His hand tightened on hers. "And?"

"And what?" she hedged.

"I'm glad. It means a lot. But it's not enough."

She sighed. "Tyler, I'm a mess."

"You're not the only one."

"Seriously, though." She stood and started pacing, ignoring the déjà vu. She'd had it a lot since she came home. "You're rebuilding. You've opened your security firm and have three clients already. I'm working a desk at an insurance company, which, by the way, is not my life's ambition. I don't know what my life's ambition *is*, now that Kelsey seems like she's going to be okay." She stopped. Her eyes filled with tears. "She and Tom are engaged."

"I know." His voice was right behind her, but he didn't touch her. "But they're not getting married until she graduates."

"Doesn't matter." She pressed her hand to her mouth, hating her weakness. "The worst part is this isn't empty nest. It's—" she choked on the word, "—it's jealousy."

"Ah, babe." Tyler turned her and pulled her into his arms. "It's okay."

"She's getting everything I wanted for her." But it was everything she'd wanted for herself, too. She closed her eyes against the guilt. How could she be jealous of her own child?

"She's getting it because you made it possible for her to have it." Tyler rubbed his hands up and down her back, and the tension ebbed away again. "You just need to figure out what *you* want now. You're so young, Regan, you have as much life ahead of you as she does, even if you don't feel it."

She hadn't thought about it like that. Suddenly, everything looked different. "I could go back to school."

"Yep."

She had no idea what she would study, what she wanted to do, but hell, she had time, didn't she? Something loosened inside her, relief unfurling like a baby fern. She leaned back and smiled up at Tyler. "Thank you."

He returned the smiled, but it looked sad. "You'd have figured it out."

"What?" She touched the corner of his mouth. "What's wrong?"

"I just—I'm afraid—shit." He dropped his arms and moved away.

"What?" she asked again.

"I'm part of the old life. What if there's no place for me in the new one?"

"Are you kidding me?" Regan grabbed the edges of his shirt and pulled him back to her. "Tyler, I've spent nineteen years being afraid. I lost my parents, Scott, my future. As long as I can remember, I was afraid of losing Kelsey, the only thing in my life I loved. So determined to never love anything else I'd have to leave behind. That's over now." She kissed him, trying to tell him physically what she wasn't sure was coming out right verbally. He wrapped himself around her, devouring her mouth, and they poured their love into the kiss, the power of it taking over all her senses so that she actually felt the shift. The transition. The past was over, its hold no longer active.

The fear was gone. She was ready to live.

* * * * *

ReaderService.com

Manage your account online!

- Review your order history
- Manage your payments
- Update your address

> ### *We've designed the Harlequin® Reader Service website just for you.*

Enjoy all the features!

- Reader excerpts from any series
- Respond to mailings and special monthly offers
- Discover new series available to you
- Browse the Bonus Bucks catalog
- Share your feedback

Visit us at:

ReaderService.com